PRAISE FOR *FL...*

Karen Grose has knocked *Flat O...*
tense psychological thriller twi...
ending. Best to read with the lights on!

—LAWRENCE HILL
Award-Winning Author of *The Book of Negroes*

Fast-paced intrigue with provocative characters and high stakes. If you liked *Mr. & Mrs. Smith*, be sure to read *Flat Out Lies* to its shocking end!

—DIANE BATOR
Author of *Written in Stone*

Flat Out Lies is a twisty, gripping tale! A seemingly ideal family, anything but perfect. This riveting psychological thriller will leave you questioning everything you thought you already knew. I was completely captivated beginning to end.

—THE RETIRED BOOK LADY (Book Blog)

Flat Out Lies is a shocking thriller, replete with deadly twists. After *The Dime Box* (which was selected by Amnesty International for its 2021 Book Club, and which received a Silver Medal from Literary Titan in 2020), award-winning author Karen Grose has created yet another expertly crafted story that will keep you on the edge of your seat from cover to cover.

—HAYLEY PAIGE
Founder and CEO of Notebook Group Limited

ALSO BY KAREN GROSE

The Dime Box

FLAT OUT LIES

KAREN GROSE

NOTEBOOK
PUBLISHING

First published in 2024 by Notebook Publishing, an imprint of Notebook Group Limited, Arden House, Deepdale Business Park, Bakewell, Derbyshire, DE45 1GT.

www.onyxpublishing.com
ISBN: 9781913206680

Copyright © Karen Grose 2024

The moral right of Karen Grose to be identified as the author of this work has been asserted by her in accordance with the Copyright, Design and Patents Act, 1998.

All rights reserved. No part of this publication may be reproduced, stored in or introduced into a retrieval system, or transmitted, in any form or by any means (electronic, mechanical, photocopying, recording or otherwise), without the prior written permission of the publisher, aforementioned. Any person who is believed to have carried out any unauthorised act in relation to this publication may consequently be liable to criminal prosecution and civil claims for damages.

A CIP catalogue record for this book is available from the British Library.

Typeset by Notebook Publishing of Notebook Group Limited.

To John, with love

ONE
Ria

A car honked and Ria lurched forward past the last of the shops. Turning on the radio, she shuffled through the stations. Slow songs, happy songs, news. Another brawl between rival gangs downstate. She dreaded the day Liam and Jacob were old enough to drive. Living in a small town kept those kinds of problems at arms-length.

Hands at ten and two, she eased into the driveway careful not to topple the bags in the back seat. Dammit. That letter to her Aunt was still in her purse. Checking her wrist, she swung open the door. The groceries could wait. There was enough time to get to the mailbox at the end of the street and get back home to work.

Up ahead, a man knelt in an empty flowerbed beside the sold sign stuck on his front lawn. Dry grass and mud clung to his jeans. As Ria approached on the sidewalk, he glanced up.

"Demar," he said, flashing a smile.

"Ria, from 124." She stopped and pointed behind her. Though they'd only met briefly, she knew who he was. Pewter hoops hung from his ears; his neck was inked like a rattlesnake. He didn't blend in around here.

He mopped his brow with the back of his hand. "The landscaping around here is unbelievable. I'm trying to catch up."

She smiled back. *Good luck.* A flat of purple and yellow chrysanthemums lay by the sign. The colour would irritate her neighbours more than they cared to admit, and the idea of that pleased her.

"Can you pass me a plant?" he asked.

Ria bent over to pick one up. Dark spots blurred her vision. Bit of dizziness. Great way to impress the new neighbour. Wishing she'd grabbed lunch downtown earlier, she knelt on the grass.

"Put your head down," he said, and placed his hand gently on her shoulder.

She leaned her head toward her lap. Beads of moisture ran down her forehead, stinging her eyes. Demar sat beside her and passed over his bottle of water. Awkward? Kind? She could smell the sweat on his shirt. Flustered, she pointed to his garden.

"You're planting the flowers too close," she blurted.

"What do you mean?" he said.

She gently removed a floret from his left hand, and a trowel from his right. She dug a little hole, with more space than he planned. She planted it, patted the earth, turned and smiled.

"Hey, that looks way better," he said. "Thanks."

That ice cream in the back seat would be turning to soup. As she got up to go, a cat threaded himself around her ankles, hoping for a scratch. Demar pushed it aside and she said goodbye and crossed the road. Less than a block away, she reached the mailbox.

Pop, pop.

She stopped in her tracks. She knew that sound. Gunshots.

She dove behind the red Escalade. Should she move? Stay put? She checked her arms and legs. No blood. No bullet holes.

Crouched on her heels, she peered through the back of the SUV's tinted windows. Where was the shooter? She peeked around the side of the bumper, panic clawing at her chest. Demar was staggering backwards. Blood soaked his t-shirt. He fell to the ground. Half his cheek was missing.

She wretched, then sat. Breathe. Focus. The phone. Where was it? There. In her purse. As she struggled to unzip it, she heard the shriek of brakes, violent honking beside her. A car door flung open.

"What the hell happened?" a neighbour yelled from his driveway.

"I don't know." She could hardly breathe.

Her hand trembled as she held her device. Her boys. Then someone was screaming. Was it her? Stop and get it together. They were safe in school. She wished she could blink and disappear, be with them, hug them, not let them out of her sight. Instead, she punched at the screen.

"9-1-1. What's your emergency?"

"Someone was shot."

"Where are you ma'am?"

"Highland Avenue."

"Ma'am? Stay on the line. Did you see it?"

"I didn't see anyone, please hurry."

Ria disconnected. She peered around the bumper of the SUV again. Demar lay on the sidewalk. She scanned the trees around the house for the shooter. As she crept forward, her adrenaline surged, a wave of fear at what was lurking in front of her.

"Demar," she called out. Twice.

He mumbled, his fingers twitching.

The neighbour shouted, "Get back."

She darted behind the SUV. Soaked in sweat, she pinched the bridge of her nose. A gnawing, familiar feeling rose in her throat. She'd only felt it once, yet it had left a permanent scar living deep into her subconscious. Her phone rang. She put it on silent, lay down on the road and closed her eyes.

Within a minute, sirens wailed in the distance. Breathe, up, move. She gripped the strap of her purse and stumbled along the sidewalk.

The street was mayhem. People streamed from porches, running across lawns, trampling flowers. Two police cars were parked diagonally across the road, their red lights revolving, colour bouncing off the windows around them. Ria looked across the road. Red brick, black front door with a bay window to the left, painted shutters. 142 Highland Avenue. Her own house—only eight doors away—looked identical, except for the basketball net, the bikes and the man bleeding out on the driveway.

Neighbours prattled on the pavement. She pressed two fingers to her neck. Her pulse was going at least a hundred beats a minute. Breathe in. Breathe out. Keep breathing. A uniformed officer unfurled a roll of yellow tape and strung it between two trees on the boulevard.

"All of you," he shouted. "Get back."

Ria took in the scene. In front of her lay Demar, legs bent at an impossible angle, blood pooling on the sidewalk. The hole in the side of his face was deep, uneven. White. She could see a piece of bone. To the right, a firetruck, and the ambulance. To the left, a nondescript car stopped outside the perimeter. Two men in plain clothes hopped out, ducked under the tape, and spoke to the officer stationed in the middle of the street. She pulled her phone from her purse and took a few pictures. Radios cackled. Voices called out. Words. Phrases. She rocked forward slightly and tried to catch them all.

After the stretcher rolled by, paramedics pumping Demar's chest, she pocketed her phone. Behind her, the crowd had thinned. A few neighbours lingered on the lawn deep in conversation. Ria shouldered her purse and headed home.

Clutching a hand to her chest, she collapsed in the soft leather chair behind her desk. Struggling to regain control, she flipped on her playlist from Spotify. The blend of her favourite oldies calmed her. When the tightness in her chest eased, she picked up the phone. It rang twice.

"Catskill Fire Department. How can I help you?"

Jim had voice made for radio. Deep. Smooth. Calming. "Honey, it's me. Our neighbour got shot."

"Sorry, what?"

Ria knew she sounded panicked, so she slowed herself down. "In his driveway, the guy who moved in."

"When?"

She looked at the ceiling. She could see an empty space where Demar's cheek should have been. "This afternoon, just now."

"What?" There was shuffling and then a door slammed. "Listen, we just got back to the station from a townhouse fire. It was a mess. I'm a mess. I don't know what you're talking about."

She took a breath, trying to squash her irritation. "Can you find anything out? Maybe ask someone?"

He sighed. "I'll keep my ears to the ground."

"What time will you be home?"

A pause. "No idea."

She suspected as much yet forced herself to stay focused on the reason for her call. "See you at dinner, then? Call me if you hear anything."

She stayed in the office, frozen to the spot, until the kids burst through the front door. Liam, almost seventeen, threw his backpack on the floor. Four years younger, Jacob trailed behind. He knew two volumes: quiet and over the top.

"Mom," he hollered. "The bus dropped us off wrong."

"Chill out," Liam said.

She held Jacob in her arms. Chill wasn't an option, at least not for Jacob. He thrived on steady routine, but Liam was perpetually annoyed by his younger brother. She couldn't recall a single day in the last year when the boys weren't locking horns.

"There's, like, police cars everywhere," Liam said, stepping back to avoid them. "What's going on?"

She shrugged. "I have no clue."

The last thing she needed was Jacob wound up any further. She straightened the backpacks dumped in the foyer and locked the front door. Until she found out more, she'd keep the boys inside.

From her office window, Ria surveyed the street. A film crew returned to a van, pulled out a couple of black bags, and packed their things. Even now, four hours after she heard the gunshots at the mailbox, she couldn't shake those images stuck in her head. She squeezed her eyes shut. For twenty-five years, all she wanted to do was build a new life. A calm, stable life. In the drawer of her desk, she found the Xanax and popped two pills under her tongue. She was safe. She'd be fine.

She let the sweat rise, cool, then dry on her forehead. Having lost a good part of the afternoon, she stretched out her fingers and got to work. With her mind racing, she couldn't focus enough to do the detailed work the clients of her digital photography business, Pixel-by-Pixel, required, so instead she scanned a string of messages, updated her calendar and responded to emails.

"Mom?"

She looked up to find Jacob standing in the doorway, his hair combed flat, a white dress shirt tucked sharply into chinos. "Hi.....what's up?"

"You told us we'd eat at six," he said. "Aren't you hungry?"

She glanced at the top right corner of her screen and bolted from the chair. She hadn't eaten all day. In the kitchen, the chicken was browning, rice fluffed in a pot, the salad ready. Ria gave him a hug.

In the minute it took to set the table, footsteps thundered overhead, down the stairs and stopped behind her. She glanced over her shoulder. Liam was dressed in black from head to toe, ready for a funeral. Bobbing his head to whatever blasted through his earbuds, he pulled out a carton of milk from the fridge and took a swig.

"What?" he said, registering the displeasure on her face.

She pressed her lips together. She wanted to say something but didn't know what she should mention first. The outfit or his saliva on the milk carton? The snark? Let it be. This shooting was upsetting everyone.

"Get a glass and sit down, please," she said.

"I'm going for pizza with my friends."

"Not tonight, you're not." No one was going out anywhere. She arranged the chicken on a platter, grabbed a serving spoon and turned to face him. "Family dinner."

"Right." Liam shut the fridge. "*Family*. And where's Dad?"

She stiffened. Met his eyes. She wondered, too. She swallowed her discomfort.

Across the kitchen, Jacob was pacing, her phone to his ear. Crimson blotches spread up his neck, across the tops of his cheeks and into his forehead.

"Dad's eating at the station," he told them. "Again."

At the table, she picked at her plate while Jacob nattered, and Liam ate in stony silence. After the dishes were cleared and the kitchen tidy, she returned to her office and opened her laptop. Big red letters flashed across the screen. BREAKING NEWS: CATSKILL MAN SHOT DEAD.

She drew in a breath. No doubt, Jacob would have

questions. How could anyone explain such senseless loss? She learned early life wasn't fair. Some families stuck together, others did not. Hers would always be united. After everything she sacrificed, she'd make sure of it.

TWO
Jim

It was going on seven o'clock when Jim left the restaurant, after making his excuses and cutting out early. SUVs hugged the curbs, fancy food shops, a velvety coolness in the air. He tugged on his baseball cap and walked the distance back to his car at the station. Easing from the parking lot, he glanced in the rear-view mirror at the bruising of fatigue under his eyes.

It'd been a long day. His muscles were aching from attending the fire at the townhouse. Chained to his desk afterward, paperwork ate up the rest of the afternoon. Unable to extract any information about the shooting, he knew there'd be questions waiting when he got home.

A river of traffic moved slowly in each direction, bikes hoofing it uptown. Out the window, Catskill was edging into dusk, the glow of the streetlights turning lawns into dark patches. When he turned into the driveway, there were two police officers standing on the sidewalk in front of the house.

Jackpot.

The timing was perfect. He could get all details straight from the horse's mouth. Maybe giving Ria the information she wanted would help calm her down.

"Hey Jim," the shorter one said, after he exited the car. "Glad we caught you."

Not a mile on their faces, both looked barely out of high school. Auxiliary officers were volunteers stuck with the canvassing. It was a thankless job. No clue of their names, he slapped them on the back.

"Been a long night, guys?" he said, "What have you got?"

"Nothing here," the taller waved at the houses behind him, "But once the vic was collared and boarded, he flatlined in the ambulance-"

"The guy at Mercy now?"

"They tried to resuscitate but he bled out and was pronounced DOA."

Jim swore, scrubbed a hand over his jaw. Despite that he and Ria had never met the guy, any life cut short was awful. "Come on in." He motioned toward the front door. "My wife called about the whole thing earlier."

"You've been at work, then?" The officer shrugged. "No offense."

"No offence taken." He confirmed he had, stating the truth, but leaving out a little part.

He led them inside, joking about their overtime. When he called out for Ria, she popped her head from around the corner in the kitchen. She looked like she'd seen a ghost.

"It's only a couple of questions," the officer assured her, after they were seated around the table. "Nothing to worry about."

Ria didn't look convinced. Her hands were trembling in her lap. The taller opened a notebook but didn't pick up his pen. It wasn't a surprise. Going on eight o'clock, he'd likely heard the same story twenty times in twenty different houses. He asked if she was home at the time of the shooting. Off her nod, he asked her to tell him what had happened.

"Take your time," he reminded her.

She took a breath and described her trip to grocery store, followed by her need to drop by the mailbox. The officer nodded, listening,

"So, after I helped Demar plant-"

"What?" Jim said. "Wait, you were right there? Talking to him?"

"Before I was. On the lawn, in front of the house."

"Did you see a shooter? Anyone running away?"

When she shook her head, the officer suddenly had a realization. "Was it you who called 911?"

Ria looked at her hands, mumbled something. Her face went beet red. When the officer probed, clarifying they were trying to pinpoint one unaccounted hang up, she admitted it was hers, said she'd panicked, put phone on silent.

Jim looked from the officers to Ria to the officers again, waiting for them to spell out the implications. Neither spoke.

"Ria," he sighed. "You can't do that to control."

"Who?"

Leaning forward, he slowly explained dispatch was the hive of activity central. They took 911 calls, dispatched emergency vehicles and when someone hung up, they were obligated to return the call to ensure their safety. "You have no clue what goes through their minds when you don't pick up. It's not only rude," -he paused- "it's dangerous."

The officers' exchanged glances. The shorter cleared his throat and quickly pulled out a sheet, asking for the names and birthdates of everyone living in the house. As he was recoding the information, Jacob appeared at the table.

"What's going on?" he asked.

Jim smiled, "Hey buddy. Mom's helping these guys. How was school?"

"Because of the dead man on the street?"

He nodded. Nothing got past that kid. He was too smart for his own good. Leaning over, he ruffled his son's hair and asked where Liam was.

"Upstairs on the phone with the fellas." Jacob sat beside Ria, took her hand, and laced their fingers together. Then he turned to the officer and added, "Inside joke."

The shorter held his pen mid-air, nodded, and started to fold up his paper.

"Wait," Ria held up her palm. "That's it?"

"For tonight, yes," the officer said. He explained it was simply their job to collect information. If follow up was required, the detectives assigned to the case would be the ones to reach out next. "Things like this, I mean homicides," he corrected himself, "can take weeks, sometimes even months. It's not like on *Law and Order* where everything gets wrapped up in an hour."

Ria's mouth dropped. Jim drew in a breath, unsure how she was going to respond. She was a smart woman. Headstrong. Did not like to be underestimated. When she scraped back her chair and told Jacob to get ready for bed, he slowly released it. Trying to move the conversation along, Jim suggested it was getting late.

"Guess we're done here." He scooted off his seat. Outside, a siren whooped on the street. He waited. Then, "I'd offer you a beer, but there's eyes out everywhere."

After the officers thanked Ria for her time, he brushed by her and whispered, "They'll get to the bottom of it. Come on, we'll walk them out."

Back in the kitchen, Ria looked tense. She was frazzled, vibrating, eyes scanning the room, like she was searching for something.

"Everything okay?" he asked.

"It's-this whole day. The shooting, the questions-"

"-were standard procedure," he reassured her. "Nuts-and-bolts type stuff."

She scowled. "To you, maybe."

"Where's your faith? I told you, they'll deal with it. You look like you don't believe me."

"I don't know." Her voice wobbled. "I don't know what to believe."

Though it seemed like there may be more to it, he didn't press. He'd cut his night short and missed the football game on TV. He was tired, sore. All he wanted was to go upstairs and soak in the tub. He stood beside her as she scooped chicken and brown rice into two plastic tubs. After she snapped the lids shut and passed them over, he opened the fridge to scan the shelves for an empty spot.

"Why were you late?"

"Too many damn reports." Better to cut things short.

When he shut the fridge door, he could feel her search him with his eyes. His throat went dry. It was intimate, unnerving. Should he wait? Should he go? She demanded his gaze, blinked, then turned away. As Ria wiped down the counter, the phone rang.

Grateful to have dodged another bullet, he climbed the stairs, caught up for a few minutes with the boys, then drew a bath. Stripping off his clothes, he replayed the conversation they'd had with the officers. Their manner, their tone, was gentle, polite. While he didn't understand how Ria could be so worked up about someone they didn't know, he supposed it would've been helpful if he'd been a little more attentive. She'd witnessed a man murdered in cold blood. With the endless catalog of horrors he'd experienced during twenty-five years on the service, sometimes he forgot that not everyone was used to death.

He lay back, letting the warmth flow through his body,

until the bathroom door creaked open, cool air flooding the room. Dressed head-to-toe in a checkered flannel nightgown, Ria sat on the edge of the tub.

"That was Mrs. Potts," she said, dipping her fingers in the water, "she asked if you could look at her sink. With everything going on right now, I told her it'd likely have to wait until next week."

"Next weekend," he reminded her, "I have that course."

When she looked down at him, she did not look impressed. "In Seattle this year? Is it mandatory?"

He confirmed it was. The crew's annual training course was one of the best parts of the job. Four hard days of drills, four evenings out. He was looking forward to it. To live a little, let loose.

"Before you go, can you do me a favour?" she reached for the rack on the wall, "Can you find out what happened today?"

"I get it's upsetting. Yeah, I'll try."

"Something, anything. The boys and I need to feel comfortable. Safe. We can talk about it when you get home tomorrow after work." Doubt clouded her face. "You'll remember, right?"

He nodded his agreement, promised to do it. In the bedroom, he put on sweats and a t-shirt, half-listening as Ria went on about work, the garden, Saturday night's dinner at his parents' house. He could hear the nerves jangling in her voice.

The bed creaked under his weight. Patience wasn't her strongpoint. It had been less than twelve hours since the shooting. What the hell was he supposed to find out?

With everything going on right now, there was enough on his plate. If he wanted Ria off his back, he'd have to dig up something. The last thing he needed was her on edge.

THREE
Jim

Jim lowered the window to let the cool night air blow on his face as he pulled away from his parents' place. The smell of puke wafted from the back seat. He tried to block out the *click, click, click* sound Ria made chewing her fingernails as he passed the yellow crime scene tape roping off their neighbour's front yard.

As soon as he pulled into the driveway, Ria wriggled out of her seatbelt and left him alone in the car. He watched her through the steady fall of summer rain on the windshield as she scurried up the pathway with the boys and slammed the front door of the house.

Thank you, dear god. Peace.

He exited the car. The street was still, quiet. In the garage, he searched for a utility bucket and jerked on the tap. His phone buzzed and when he saw who it was, he picked up.

"What?" he said. "You can't get enough of me?"

His brother laughed. "How's the happy little house?"

"Who knows? I'm in the garage."

"Maybe you should sleep out there. Give Ria a chance to cool off. Poor Liam is going to be hearing about this for years," Frank said. "It sounds like that stiff on your street got her going. What's the deal with that?"

"I have no clue. I don't get women," he snapped off the tap, "and I have an ex-wife to prove it."

But he knew what Ria had done. He had to give it to her. Because he'd forgot to ask his colleagues about the shooting and didn't come home Friday night at her command to dissect it, she brought it up to his parents. Put him on the spot. Riled them up, too. Hell-bent on finding out what happened, Ria insisted he share every little detail he knew. They were all too busy to notice the kids, and dinner came to a crashing halt after Liam disappeared, and they'd found him belly-up to the bar in the basement.

Frank said, "And what was Liam thinking sneaking off into the liquor cabinet?"

"He's seventeen. He doesn't-" he looked around the garage "-God knows what else he's up to."

"We know about the weed. And the unexplained absences. That was last year, right? The suspension?"

"I was blamed for that, too." He spotted the soap and dumped some in.

"Relax," Frank said. "Mom and Dad were laughing about it when I left."

"They won't be when they see their driveway."

After Ria gave Liam an earful out there, his turn came next. *How could you lose track of your son? I can't be the only one keeping an eye on the kids.* The whole goddamn street must've heard her.

"Listen," Frank said, "They're asleep, like Liam is now. Deal with him tomorrow. Talk to Ria then."

He dreaded the conversation. "When's that supposed to happen-" he stirred the water with a stick "-Before I drop Jacob at the library? After I grocery shop? While I do the errands on the stupid yellow lists she sticks to the fridge? Our entire life is scheduled around what she wants. The house, her work. Not everything revolves-"

"Calm down,' Frank said. "You're wound up. Are you okay?"

"I'm fine." It was his stock answer whether he was fine or not.

"It doesn't sound like it."

Jim threw the stick aside. His brother sounded worried. He tried to ignore the growing knot in his stomach.

Over the past six months, he'd screwed up at the station. Came in late, ghosted the tail end of a shift. Almost got caught. There was no reason to suspect him of anything, so he covered it up, acted normal and did his job. Since then, he'd lied to Ria, his captain, and the crew so often, he found it difficult to keep his story straight.

Frank said, "I'm pulling in the driveway. If you need anything, you know where I am."

"Yep, give my best to Rachel," he said. "Sorry she couldn't come tonight."

Jim hung up. When he turned to pick up the bucket, two black-soled shoes stood directly in front of him. He reeled backward. Water soaked the hem of his next-door neighbour's nightgown; he could see it under her red raincoat. There was no leash in her hand.

"Your car door is open." Mrs. Potts pointed a crooked finger to the driveway. "I saw it from my window."

"Yes, thank you. One of the boys isn't feeling well."

She nodded. "It happens, you know. It happened to mine, too."

"Where's Pebbles?"

"At this hour?" She smiled. "Long past her bedtime."

"Smart dog. It's a nasty night to be out anyway."

"Seems so, Jim. Lots on your mind?"

He sucked in a cheek. How long had she been standing there? How much of his conversation with Frank had she heard?

He remembered she'd asked him to drop by and look at her sink. With all the shooting business, he'd forgotten. He agreed to come over next weekend.

"That'll be fine. And Jim?" She raised an eyebrow. "Since my Artie woke up dead, I have no one to talk at. Sleep on that. Good night."

After Mrs. Potts disappeared into the darkness, he walked around the garage to give himself time to calm down. Talk *at*? Was that how Artie died? Was that how he'd die? 'We'd like the fish, please' at the restaurant, when he would've ordered steak. 'It'd be quicker to ask for directions', when they got lost driving. Ria chewed his ears off and over time, he realized it was safer not to express an opinion at all.

As he pocketed his phone, he thought of Frank. Tight growing up, still close today, Frank had always had his back. Did his brother suspect he was hiding something? He'd never been able to conceal anything from his brother. Frank knew him too well. When they were kids, he slipped a twenty from his mother's purse and though he denied it, Frank made him put it back. He was always there, picking up after him, ensuring he stayed on the straight and narrow. If Frank asked him if he was alright again, he'd need to answer carefully. Downplay. Blow it off. Sound causal. Frank was the sort of person who would not give up easily.

In the shadows of the lights of the garage, he shivered at the storm about to rip through his life. If anyone asked outright, he'd be forced to tell the truth. He couldn't wait to get out of town, away from the ringing phone, away from Ria's constant nagging about the murder. She wanted certainty, and all of a sudden, he knew he wasn't able to give it to her. He needed space to figure out his next move.

FLAT OUT LIES

*

Late Sunday afternoon, Jim unscrewed the top from a beer, took a long pull and sank into the living room couch.

"Jim," Ria called out from her office. "Did you pick up paint? Are the boys home?"

He tried to hide his irritation. "I did, and yes, they're upstairs."

He waited for her to acknowledge all the running around he did today. No response came. As James Taylor's deep voice filled the air, he shuffled through the newspaper. The Yankees had secured a spot in the playoffs, the Giants and Jets wouldn't have a prayer.

"What time's your flight tomorrow?"

"Ten-thirty."

Though he'd miss the boys, he wished it were sooner. This year's course was on rope rescue and confined spaces. The irony he'd be replacing the space he was trapped in now with Ria for space restricted with his crew wasn't lost on him. When she asked if he'd dealt with Liam yet, he folded up the newspaper, swore. Repeatedly. Hadn't she been home all day?

He went upstairs and pushed open Liam's bedroom door. The room smelled like a backed-up toilet. He flicked on the light. Dirty socks. A garbage can overflowed. Crushed cans on the windowsill.

"Anything you have to say for yourself?" he asked the bump in the bed.

Crickets. The bump didn't stir.

"Fine. You're grounded the rest of the month."

Liam lifted himself onto his elbows, the remnants of last night's supper smeared to the side of his head. "It's September. The first month of school. Are you crazy?"

"No. I'm your father. No phone. No laptop. No driving. If you want to be treated like an adult, act like one."

Liam rolled his eyes. "You're pathetic. But-"

"Not negotiable." He didn't care if three weeks with no internet was, as Liam would say, *like forever*. Nor would he agree lack of access to a smart phone was an issue of human rights. His stomach tightened as his son ran his hand through his hair and dried chunks fell onto the sheets. He should've worn a hazmat suit.

"What about my homework?" Liam asked.

"Use paper."

"Think that's funny?"

He nodded.

Liam rolled his eyes. "It's not."

When Liam pulled the covers over his head, Jim picked up Liam's laptop and phone and slammed the door behind him. Down the hall, he dropped to the chair in his bedroom. Frank was right. He was wound up. Not his best moment.

With a shooter still loose in the neighbourhood, he wondered if taking Liam's phone was a mistake. What if there was an emergency? Save for school, Liam was grounded now, stuck at home, so hopefully wouldn't need it anyway.

When he picked up Liam's laptop, a photo of his friends appeared on the screen. He knew they drank at parties. Played cards. Probably talked about how to get laid, too. He guessed they talked about it a lot because no girl in her right mind would sleep with any of them. They weren't part of the in-crowd like he'd been in high school, but they were good kids. Tight. Loyal. Imaginary gangstas, they coined their friendship #TheFellas. He laughed the day they'd told him, but the name stuck.

Ria called from downstairs. "I'm swamped with work right now. Would you mind getting a start on dinner?"

He winced. At least dinner with the boys would mute Ria's ongoing inquisition. He'd already shared what he knew, but it still wasn't adequate. He was sick of the questions, the gossip, the drama posted on Facebook. It was fake news. Parse fact from rumour.

He closed the lid of the laptop and shoved it in his dresser drawer, then took a quick look at the trail on Liam's phone.

LIAM: hey #TheFellas. Got lit last night

CHUCK: Weren't u @ grammas?

LIAM: YOLO

RUDY: parents?

LIAM: nothing yet

ZIMMER: in for the buy tmw? $1000?

LIAM: yep

NICK: gotta dip cya

He had no clue what Liam was up to, but he had bigger things to deal with. The mess he was in could come at a much higher price.

FOUR
Ria

Ria swung her legs off the bed. She'd been exhausted all weekend and hadn't appreciated Jim calling her dramatic. But there was something to be said for a good night's sleep. Here she was, energetic again. New day, new week.

She dressed quickly, humming to the song on the radio. The house was quiet, the boys' bedroom doors closed. There was no car in the driveway, the suitcase by the front door gone. Save for the running shoes left in the hall, she hoped Jim hadn't forgotten anything else. In the kitchen, she peeled off the yellow sticky note she'd tacked to the fridge itemizing what he needed to take. Too late now.

While the coffee dripped through, she buttered four pieces of bread and slathered them with tuna fish. She licked her fingers. Salty and cold, the taste of their holidays in Florida, the blue ocean, sunburns, white beaches. In the daytime, the boys swam for hours, while she and Jim lounged on oversized towels, eating fresh crab cakes, laughing at the parade of college kids strutting across the sand, screeching each time the waves rolled in. Now the only travelling Jim did was alone.

She cut the sandwiches in half. When the boys stumbled downstairs, she handed them their backpacks and trailed them out to the front porch. Cloudless sky, beautiful sunshine. A woman walked a dog, sprinklers adorned lawns, a family piled into a minivan. She couldn't believe it. Three days after a shooting, the block looked like a small-town postcard. After she waved the boys off to school, she locked the front door. Life may have returned to normal for some people. Not for her. Not now that Jim had left her alone in the house with a murderer on the loose.

His reaction the night of the shooting was baffling. After he'd come home late, all she heard was raucous laughter. She looked down the hall and nearly had a heart attack. The ten minutes they'd spent with the police felt like an hour. Then all weekend she couldn't focus. She reminded herself for the second time in three days the shooting wasn't about her. The notion anyone would reappear from the shadows to uncover her identity or threaten her family was ridiculous.

In her office, she pulled her laptop forward and clicked on the News10 broadcast. Half listening, she rifled through her desk for her reading glasses.

"-older section of Catskill, where a forty-eight-year-old man was shot and killed outside his home at approximately twelve-thirty Friday afternoon."

She glanced out the window. Yesterday, she'd tried to relay what she read on Facebook with Jim again, but he refused to talk about it. So, she didn't tell him Demar's last name was Robinson. Didn't tell him he was recently divorced or that he owned the night club in Manhattan. Out of town at his training course, Jim would get all the details from the fire-fighting crew.

"First-hand," he'd remind her, "Not gossip."

Nor did she tell him she took photos to add to the collection of images she stored in a password-protected file on her laptop. After what she'd been through, she took comfort in ways that other people didn't understand. It was something she'd always done. Something she'd always do. Images to capture the moment. Images to study later.

She didn't feel guilty for not telling him. Wired that way, she withheld pieces of herself, buried the secrets of her past. She'd fought hard to have a normal life. Jim saw her as she was now. While the shooting on the street was hitting too close to home, threatening to unleash memories she'd avoided for years, she'd prevail.

The broadcast droned on. "Police continue to investigate and are asking anyone who may have been in the area at the time to....."

Hours behind what she needed to get done, Ria clicked the radio off. She opened a spreadsheet and ran a finger down the narrow columns of type. The numbers confirmed what she expected. Month after month, *Pixel-by-Pixel* was tracking toward another banner year.

Outside, a police car rolled down the street. *Focus.* She poked around for a while, but nothing held her interest. Who would shoot someone in broad daylight? It was unsettling. Brazen. Disturbing. She could not stop thinking about it. The gunshots. The blown-out face. Surely someone noticed the shooter running away. Did the shooter come from the ravine? Escape through the trees? No one passed her at the mailbox. She scrolled through the Highland Avenue Facebook page, increasingly restless. Nothing from the police. Nothing new from the neighbours.

She drummed her fingers on the desk. Someone must know something. Friday, people were in shock, palpable panic, today could be different. To move past it, she needed to find out what happened. It was the only way to put it to rest.

She scrambled to her feet. In the bathroom, she smoothed her hair, her blouse, her skirt. She pulled out the Xanax from the vanity and took two pills. Then she found a red tube, ran it around her lips and pressed them together to set the colour.

Hello, beautiful. She snapped the sheath shut.

Outside, she surveyed the street. No one on the sidewalk, nobody gardening. Vacant porches. As she passed 142 Highland, she slowed. The house was still, the curtains drawn, a ring of yellow plastic tents on the driveway. Inside was a circle of blood, dried to a rusty stain. She sucked in a breath. There Demar was, alone, lifeless.

A chill crept over her skin at the thought. Her brain would not shut off. It kept running through everything like a movie in a loop.

The police will deal with it, Jim had said.

How? Although it was their job, she didn't have any faith. The cruiser was gone. No detective followed up. They weren't doing anything.

Swiveling her neck, she swung her arms across her chest, back and forth. The breeze picked up, cooling the heat on her cheeks. She recalled the reason she was outside in this spot last week. Though Jim may disagree, there was something about a hand-written note. The plump envelope, the folds and curls of the paper, slow thoughts scratched in ink. Part of her wanted to look back to see if she could find it, but she didn't.

At home, she kicked off her shoes. The stress was getting to her. She made half a dozen calls but came up empty. Despite a last-ditch effort for intel, she hoped the updates through the media in the next week would provide answers about the murder and put her fears and doubts to bed.

In the kitchen, she rummaged through the freezer to determine what to make for supper. At least she could slow life down for the kids. Lasagna would do, a deep-dish apple cobbler. Comfort food.

In the office, the day flew by. Clients. Zoom Meetings. A quick dinner with the boys. In the living room afterward, she righted blankets crumpled on the couch, furniture squished together. She picked the pillows off the floor, placed them on the couch and folded the blankets. Better. The house was a big step up from the rental she grew up in, with its dirt backyard, streaked windows, moldy yellow siding, and fetid bathroom. But Jim had forgotten this place was supposed to be their starter home. He was happy here, comfortable. Marriage was a compromise.

A glass of wine at her elbow, Ria caught the news. Save for an announcement about an upcoming press conference, there was no update, nothing current reported. She refilled her glass, then scrolled through the photos on her phone. When the pictures of their family dinner appeared, she drew a finger along the line to determine which ones to send to her aunt.

She picked six on the roll depicting a normal, happy family. She sent them off, locked the front door and went upstairs. The sun was going down, casting a pinkish glow over the street. She was relieved Jim was away. It gave her room to breathe. She curled up in bed with the book she'd been trying to read the past few months. Written to cure relationships, she hoped it could rekindle theirs. Maybe, she could finish it.

A few chapters in, Ria dropped the book in her lap. It was slow going. Outside the wind picked up, rattled the window frame. Her eyes locked on the pane. Beyond it, a flicker of light. Her arms prickled. Was someone out there? Or had she imagined it? The doctor warned her more than once about drinking while taking medication.

Across the room, she peered into the shadowy dusk. A shiver ran down her spine. A bulky shadow and a tiny red ember glowed in front of the giant cedars surrounding the house across the street. She moved away from the frame. She didn't want to be illuminated if someone was watching the house.

Back to the wall, she tried to centre herself and slow her breathing. She needed to stay calm. Panic would only make things worse.

Downstairs with the lights out, the hallway was inky black. She grabbed the carving knife from the kitchen drawer. Jim would jump down her throat. Who cares? She wasn't taking any chances. What type of mother would she be if she couldn't even protect her own kids?

As she unlocked the front door, a car backfired off in the distance. She stared down the length of the tree-lined street. Dark but for brake lights at a stop sign, turning left. The car disappeared around the corner.

She cursed Jim. Not the best time for him to be away. Ready to run out the door and save lives, he was not here to save her now. She turned on every light in the house, checked the windows were all firmly locked, and double bolted the front door. In the bedroom, she flopped on the duvet and pressed her face to the pillow.

Like the psychologist showed her years before, she soothed herself by recalling happier moments. The songs in her head. Her childhood dog Lexie with her soft muzzle of fur. Camping trips. She pictured her room at her aunt's house. The double bed, the powder blue walls, the light radiating through the curtains. The glass of warm milk. Her aunt's gentle hand on her back, the circles she made between her shoulder blades. Ria closed her eyes as she listened to the sound of her aunt's voice in her head: "Not your fault, dear, not your fault."

FIVE
Ria

"What's all this?" Jacob asked, "Is Dad coming home early or did you invite the army over?"

Ria forced a smile, "Don't you want to start your day sunny-side up?"

When Jacob laughed, she did too. She sounded like a high school teacher. She glanced at the table. Eggs. Bacon. Fresh fruit. Pancakes. She tossed one on her plate and smothered it with maple syrup. When Liam strolled in half-asleep, she passed him a plate.

"Dig in," she said, "Your stomach is a bottomless pit."

When Liam scowled, Jacob said, "It's a metaphor, dufus."

"Stop your chirping, asshole." Liam punched him on the shoulder.

"Boys," she said sternly, then to Liam, "Somebody better teach you to control that mouth of yours."

He grinned. "Many have and many have failed."

Her temperature rose. Cooking usually gave her comfort, energized her. It was a good thing, a soothing thing. Not today. She was running on fumes, ragged.

Last night, she'd laid in bed tossing and turning. All she heard was the wind and the clank of ancient pipes and the pitter-patter of rain on the window. Lost in her thoughts, trapped in her worry, she'd pinched the skin on her thighs, a little pain to ease the fear. It was past two a.m. when she finally drifted off to sleep.

As the sibling quarrel continued, Ria bit the inside of her lip so hard it bled. If the boys didn't get out of the house soon, she was going lose it. Part of her wished Jim was back. They managed them better together. She did not sign up to be a single parent.

When her phone rang, she picked it up, grateful for the distraction. In the living room, she chatted with a client, stretching out the conversation. She caught the sound of running water and the dishwasher banging shut. After the front door slammed, she dragged herself up and went out to the front porch to relax.

Mrs. Potts sauntered along her front path with her little white dog, crossed the road and stopped to talk to a neighbour. Mrs. Potts was always at her front window, eyes on the street. She must have seen the man outside last night. Was that what they were talking about? She leaned forward, trying to capture their conversation. *Speak up.* Should she change to go over there? Screw caring what people thought at a time like this. Fat lot of good it did yesterday. She slipped on a pair of old crocs and tore across the road.

"Did you see anything strange last night?" They looked at her, their faces blank. "Someone was right there on the sidewalk where you're standing."

"No," Mrs Potts said. "And hello to you, too."

Ria gave Pebbles a little cuddle, then turned to the other woman. "He was there," -she pointed- "smoking right in front of your house."

The woman shook her head. When Ria stepped forward to show them the cigarette butts on the sidewalk, there was nothing there but pavement.

Back on the porch, she slumped in the rocking chair. From

the moment she'd heard those gunshots at the mailbox, she was losing control of everything, even the places in her head. She knew what she saw. Someone had been smoking. Hadn't they? Maybe the last few days had finally caught up with her.

A walking club strolled by. Yoga pants, bright tank tops, white running shoes, swinging ponytails. She'd never seen the in-group up close. They owned the larger houses six or seven blocks down the road, the ones with double driveways, wrap around porches and smart manicured gardens. High cheek bones, heads thrown back laughing, not a hoot what anyone thought, not a care in the world.

They reminded her of Paris, a lifetime ago, the person she was there. Overseas, the fallout from the fire was no longer an albatross around her neck. Freedom gave her the chance to shelve her medication, throw caution to the wind. Living in a city seeped in culture, she explored the sites, slept with who she wanted, dressed the part.

Paris felt like fifty-years ago, and yesterday. When it surfaced, it brought up powerful emotions. She longed for the idea of it, the dream of it, the buzz of energy, the rush. Afterwards, slipping into another skin was easy. The point was to disappear. Start fresh, move into another life. If she was honest about it, there were feelings of loss, old selves left behind. Months, years felt longer here, boredom settling in.

This was Jim's hometown. The boys' too. But the truth was she never truly belonged. It was hard to fit in here---a claustrophobia at odds with the wide-open porches and the unlocked doors, where everyone had dated everyone, where everyone knew everyone's business.

In her office, she flopped down in the chair. "Alright," she whispered after she fired up her laptop. "Where to start?"

She glanced at her wrist. Past ten, already. She replayed her messages to find out if Jim had called. Nothing. There were two hang ups, which was unusual. Plunged into silence, unease lodged in her throat.

Right now, she was uncomfortable in the house alone. A firefighter, Jim was a solid protector. Why hadn't he called back? Staring at the phone, the shift that occurred in their relationship became more apparent.

She recalled her past boyfriends in Paris. Of them all, Marco was the one who made her feel most safe. It was important to be honest, no matter how difficult it was to swallow. Had she made the right choice? Out of the blue, he'd called two years ago to find out how her life had turned out. Should she check back in? It'd be reassuring to hear his deep familiar voice. Why not? She picked up the phone. Chasing potential business contacts was part of the job.

"Good morning," she said, trying to sound upbeat. She was embarrassed by the enthusiasm in her voice. Too much, perhaps?

"The surprises never cease." Marco blew out a long breath. "You're doing well, yes?"

"I don't even know where to start." Better tone.

As they glossed over acquaintances long scattered across the world, Marco said, "Do you ever miss those days? Think about it?"

Neither of them answered this.

"Before my next client, quick, tell me what's up."

She got the message. He was busy. She told him about the boys, her growing business. Jim. "All in all," she said when she was finished. "It's going okay."

"This work, you do it all from home?"

"In my office." The last thing she desired was to share her private space, but if she wanted her business to grow, she needed to be diplomatic. Not much, a simple room set off from the front hall, the space was hers alone and she loved it. Frames hung on the walls, photos she was most proud of. A Finger Lakes sunset. Hunter Mountain. Images which started her career.

"How'd that happen then?" he asked. "The transition, I mean."

"Simple things, really. People wanting photos slimmed down for-"

"Dating websites?" He laughed. Loud and confident.

She didn't respond. In a world where first impressions counted, she understood why her skills were in demand. When he made a disparaging remark about cougars, she informed him she ran an equal opportunity service.

"Beauty and the beasts?" he said. "Doesn't it creep you out?"

Did it? Was she startled the first time a CEO wanted his ex-wife faded out of a family portrait? No. She empathized. Out of sight, out of mind, made good sense. She was taken aback, though, when he asked for the blank space to be filled with a picture of his new wife. Since then, she'd seen it all.

After the selfie culture exploded on social media, she'd returned to college to upgrade her digital skills and built a reputation for helping clients facing awkward situations. Some required a light dusting to help them out of a pinch, others a heavier editing. A few required their online presence deleted. Nothing fazed her.

"It's impressive," Marco said, before he hung up. "Let me check the website and I may have something for you."

Ria couldn't believe it. She told him about the shooting at her doorstep, which he knew nothing about. Yet in one short call, Marco grasped the value of her work. Despite explaining it a hundred times to Jim, his perception of what she did hadn't changed from the day she launched.

"What are you up to?" he'd asked, coming around the side of her desk and handing her a coffee.

"Retouching rips and removing scratches on photos."

He'd looked at her strangely. "That makes money?"

Money was a sore topic. Before they married, Jim hadn't been honest about his debt. Or that he transferred his ex-wife cash every month after their divorce. Once Ria found out, she kept most of what she earned locked away. Rarely was it discussed. One year she made two times Jim's salary and made sure he saw her tax return.

Instead of responding to his question, she pointed to the screen of her laptop. "Not as much as restorations. These wedding pictures were ruined by bad lighting. And these images destroyed by house fires? They're difficult."

He'd laughed. "How hard can it be sitting at a desk? Try fighting real fires."

Save for anything to do with the kids, she didn't speak to him for a month.

A full day ahead, she dragged her mind to the tasks at hand. Through the morning, she worked on a grainy image of a ship sunk two hundred years ago in the Arctic's Northwest Passage. As she lightened pieces of the stern, the letters read HMS, but the others remained unclear. *Bus?* In the afternoon, she met with a foundation requesting a series of First World War images colourized for a travelling exhibition.

When she left the meeting, two young men stared at her from across the street. They gave her the creeps. Between the man smoking outside the house last night and the hang ups, it made her feel like someone was following her. Monitoring her movements.

A few doors down, she dropped by the bank. She transferred fifteen-thousand dollars from her business account into a safety deposit box she'd set up before she was married. *'Ensure men treat you well, yet always keep money for yourself,'* her aunt once told her. She'd followed her advice. Every woman needed a buffer in case things went south. Or, to quickly disappear.

She'd read somewhere marriage was a trade-off. Couples needed one another for all sorts of reasons. In exchange for his easy-going nature, she took care of the cooking and housework. Two boys to wrangle, he did groceries and yard work. But as solid and loyal as Jim was, he simply wasn't that exciting. It was like living without colour. Or eating lukewarm oatmeal.

It was hard to believe sixteen years had flown by. Days she missed the past, she locked her office door and revisited the old photos on her laptop. Boyfriends, the Eiffel Tower, the underground bars. Marco.

There were other images, pre-Paris, buried deeper in the file. Some washed over her like a wave. Others felt more like a dream. The odd day, dormant memories surfaced to suffocate her. Trapped in darkness, she felt nothing. Nothing at all.

She stopped her mind from wandering, tugging at memories best left alone. Save for her relationship with her aunt, she'd buried that place twenty-five years ago.

SIX
Jim

Jim sailed through the front door. He threw his keys on the table and picked up the mail, rifling through the flyers and envelopes.

"Hey," Ria called out. "You're home early."

He put the pile down. Someone sounded more relaxed. And not in her office? He strode down the hall and brushed her cheek with a kiss as she sliced and diced vegetables on the counter. Around her the kitchen looked like a tornado swept through; there were pots and pans everywhere. He asked her what was going on.

"It's for your Mom and Dad, remember? They're coming for supper tonight."

"Why?" He groaned. "We saw them last weekend."

She pointed a knife to the stove. "I made a pork roast. Can you go grab the mint jelly?"

He stomped off to the basement. The root cellar, sandwiched between the laundry room and the furnace room, was long, narrow, and windowless. He slid between the metal shelves stacked with mason jars of jams and chutneys and chili sauce. Head to the frame, he stood motionless, trying to recall the reason they chose to live so close to his parents.

It'd been Ria's idea. Family was important to her. With only an aunt left, she suggested they live there. At first, he'd been hesitant, but as the sting of his first failed marriage hadn't dissipated, he kept his reservations to himself to keep the peace. Years later, he'd wondered if they'd have been better off living in Skaneateles. Or Dering Harbor. Or any other small town where the drive to Walmart or to visit family was a daytrip.

Upstairs, he dropped the jar on the counter, grabbed a beer and plopped into an Adirondack chair out on the back deck. He took a deep swallow and belched. The four-day course had killed him. He closed his eyes, the sun warm on his face. Mrs. Pott's ten-pound ball of white fluff ran back and forth on the other side of the fence. He loved that dog. Its high-pitched bark had the strength of a Doberman.

Suddenly, the back door flung open, and Ria said, "Your parents are on the way. Quick, get ready." He glanced at his shirt and pants. Before he could protest, she said, "For once, please, don't argue."

As she stepped inside, Ria suggested they catch up after his parents left. Her request brought him up short. That was impossible. In Seattle, he'd overheard the captain mention something about an investigation into a breach of station policy. This job was his life. One choice, one mistake, had multiplied.

After a quick change into something Ria would find more suitable, Jim poked his head in Jacob's room. Standing in front of the mirror, a red tie in one hand, a blue in the other, he left Jacob alone. He knew how seriously Jacob considered what clothes he wore. His decision would take forever.

At the end of the hall, Liam's bedroom door was ajar. He peered through the crack. Slumped on the side of the bed, Liam peeled off his socks and threw them in a corner. Then he flipped over, stretching his six-foot frame across the bed, and shoved his arm down between the box spring and mattress. When he found what he was looking for, he pulled it out, flicked a button on the side and tapped out a message.

Jim's jaw dropped. So much for being grounded. He leaned in closer. It wasn't long before Liam got a response; he was already typing back. He flung the door open and hollered, "What are you doing?"

Liam dropped a burner phone into the tangled mess of sheets. Jim marched into the room and extended his hand. Liam's face sunk as he passed it over.

Back in his bedroom, Jim sat on the edge of the bed. His rubbed his temples and relaxed his jaw. Where the hell did Liam get a burner phone? More importantly, why was he using one? Only one yellow icon on the screen. Snapchat. He swore. Self-destructing messages. When Ria called his name, he shoved the burner phone in his dresser with the other devices.

Downstairs, his parents were standing in the front hall. His mother said, "Why isn't your front door locked?" She glared at him. "A week after a shooting? You'd think people would be at their windows, keeping an eye. Does this street have Neighbourhood Watch?"

He sighed. Why would they need one? Ria had the job. She'd called him Monday night hysterical, talking about hang ups, certain she saw someone outside scoping the house. He could barely hear her over the din of the bar where he was drinking with the crew. Hungover when he called the next day, he'd left a voice mail, but never heard back.

"Are you just going to stand there?" she asked.

He took their jackets. As she marched down the hall, his father cupped a hand to his mouth and said, "With everything going on the last week, it's like she was vaccinated with a gramophone needle."

Only three hours since he landed, he could feel his back and shoulders stiffen. He should've taken the later flight. He didn't want a repeat of last weekend. To dissect every new piece of gossip. To be forced to discuss the murder. If they'd asked him, he could've told them what was going to be reported. Let the police do their job.

Too late to stop it, he settled his parents in the living room, and busied himself, bringing in drinks, the serviettes, the salt and pepper shakers, the cutlery. Might as well get this over with. He called the boys and then he and Ria carried in supper from the kitchen.

"Look at this." His mother surveyed the dishes. "Ria. You're an angel, darling."

The salad bowl slipped from Ria's hands and crashed to the floor. Her mouth opened, then closed, and she dropped to the carpet. Jacob surveyed the mess and ran out of the room. Jim squatted and pressed a serviette to the chunks of tomato and cucumber and red onion scattered across the floor as Liam grabbed a roll of cutlery.

"Oh my god, Mom," he said, waving a knife in the air. "That would've been awesome on TikTok."

His father snatched it from his hand. "Jesus, Liam. We don't need anyone else dying on this street."

"That man, you mean?" Liam laughed. "I bet his ex-wife did it."

Jacob scowled. "It was a gun, Grampa, not a knife."

"Dad," Jim said in a warning tone.

His father raised his palms in the air. "I didn't say it, but if this street's going to pot, how about moving?"

When Ria looked up, he knew what she was going to say before she opened her mouth.

"We've talked about it," she said.

Jim balled the serviette in his hand. They hadn't. Texting was not talking. In the early days, when she lived well beyond their means, the extra shifts he picked up bailed out their perpetual leaky budget. Since then, despite the bundle they'd sunk into the place, she still found it too cramped. He'd seen the links she sent of spacious floor plans in new developments popping up in the region. They weren't moving. With two kids and on his salary plus even what Ria made, they couldn't afford it. *Thank God*, she didn't know about his other expenditures.

"Are you friends with the victim's family?" his mother asked.

"No," Jim said. They had a hard time being friends with anyone on the block. Ria drove them away with the constant Facebook posts she thought were funny and by sticking her nose in everyone's business.

"Shame." His mother frowned. "Back in our day, we knew all our neighbours."

He fell into a chair. He couldn't take much more of this. When his phone vibrated, he pulled it out of his pocket. The blood drained from his head. One of the crew sent a text informing him the captain wanted to see him. No, she did not know what it was about. Yes, in his office tomorrow and the matter was urgent. He inched down the back of the seat, working hard to calm the tremble lodged in his chest. Was this it? Had someone found out what he'd done?

He looked around the room. As the kids ate, his mother droned on. Hunched in a chair, his father scooped shrimp from an avocado with a spoon, stuffing them in his mouth. Drawn and pale, Ria rested her head on her hand, and balanced an empty plate on her lap. Wasn't she hungry? The knots in his shoulders that had formed before dinner tightened. He took a slow, deep breath and blocked them all out.

"Jim."

He blinked. No idea how much time had passed, he pushed his plate aside, trying his best to focus.

"Flip on the TV." His father called out. "It's nearly seven."

Once they were seated in the den, Jim picked up the remote and the picture blinked to life. It showed a large empty room, a cluster of microphones at the front, and people coming in and out of the shot. A large man with black hair and a sharp nose stepped up to the microphone.

"Good evening," he said. "I'm Detective Surinder Singh and this is my partner Detective Ming Li." The camera pulled back and a tall, Asian woman with a bob and green-framed glasses appeared by his side. "We're working to determine exactly what happened at one-thirty on Thursday September 4 when forty-eight-year-old Demar Robinson was shot and killed outside his residence at 142 Highland Avenue in Catskill."

Detective Li adjusted the microphone. "At the moment, we have no witnesses and no suspects so we're asking for your help. If anyone has any information pertinent to the investigation, please reach out and contact us at our offices on Main Street." Detective Li took off her glasses and looked directly into the camera. "This is an unusual occurrence, and we understand the community's concern. We'll be doing everything we can in the coming days to bring whoever committed this brazen act to justice." She looked down at her notes. "We'll have another press conference next week to share any additional information we have at that point." The date and time flashed across the bottom of the screen.

"Again, we're asking for your help," Detective Singh continued. "No detail is too small. You can reach us at 518-222-"

"What if you know something before that?" a reporter asked.

When the camera panned across the room, the reporter repeated the question.

"If we have updates, you'll be the first to know. But tonight, folks, we won't be taking any more questions." Detective Singh raised his hand. "Thanks everyone."

The screen went blank. His mother spoke first, complaining about the lack of information. His father agreed.

"Who is this guy?" he said. "Maybe those rumours it was a hit are true. Bad blood from the nightclub? His divorce? Maybe he's a nickel bag drug dealer?"

An image of Liam's burner phone stuffed beneath his socks upstairs flashed in Jim's mind. Then the trail on his cell phone confirming Liam was in for a thousand dollars. Was that money for pot? Was their neighbour dealing drugs? The shooting was almost a block away, and the victim more than twice Liam's age. The idea his son would be mixed up in the shooting was ridiculous.

"This whole thing gives me a bad feeling," his father said. "Something's not right. Trust me."

Jim's supper rose up the back of his throat. *Trust me?* Right now, he couldn't trust himself.

SEVEN
Ria

Ria wandered downstairs after another night she'd lain awake for hours, finally dropping off too close to dawn. In the kitchen, remnants of breadcrumbs littered the counter, the discarded knife slick with butter. When she picked it up, it slipped from her hands and hit her cup, spilling coffee all over the floor.

"Crap."

Her hands were unsteady last night too.

Angel darling.

She hadn't heard those words in decades. They were what her mother called out every day after school once she'd weaved through the junk decorating the back yard and came through the screened door of the house. Fragments, broken pieces of her past, crept from cloudy corners. She squeezed her eyes shut. She couldn't deal with it. Not now. She tugged a piece of paper towel from the roll to mop up the mess. The caffeine didn't help her nerves.

She slipped out to the back deck. The ravine, usually teeming with plants and wildlife, was dark and silent. A thin coat of dew left tickled her toes. She lifted a foot and shivered. As dawn broke, the wind picked up and she pulled her robe tightly around her. The branches moaned as the sky tinged violet, and then turned the dull yellow of a week-old bruise.

The sound of birds chirping caught her attention. She

looked around the backyard and noticed a trail of footprints in the mud. They started near the back fence leading to the ravine and continued straight up to where she was standing. She hadn't noticed them yesterday. Had someone been back there last night?

"Can you lock up?" Jacob said, through the screen door. "We're leaving for school."

"Where's Dad?"

"Mom, it's Friday. He has coffee club," Jacob said. "It's on the calendar."

Right. She rushed inside and opened the fridge, passing brown paper bags to the boys. Down the hall, she locked the front door behind them, then snapped open the blind in her office. Stretched on the chair, she picked up the phone. When Jim answered, he sounded worn out. She wondered how it was possible. He wasn't the one who'd been stuck home alone. Who'd taken care of the kids. Who hadn't slept last night. She got straight to the point, asking him about the footsteps in the backyard.

"I didn't see any," he said.

Which meant they were invisible? Silence on the other end. She picked at a nail. God, he was irritating. "They go from the fence by the ravine up to our deck. Were you walking around outside yesterday? Are they yours?"

"Mine?" he said. "How could they be? I was sitting in a chair."

"That's weird."

"How's it weird? You saw me sitting there."

She heard the clacking of computer keys and listened to him breathe. More silence. "So, they aren't yours?"

"No." He sighed. "And you asked if I was walking around yesterday. Maybe they're still there from last weekend when I was cleaning up outside."

She felt a spike of irritation. Why not say that in the first place? When he hung up, she slammed her fists on the desk.

Last night, he hadn't commented on the avocado stuffed with shrimp. Or the roast. Or her hair, piled up loose in a knot, the way he liked it. Or the red shift she picked out for him. A bit of a squeeze now, the last time she wore it was the night Jacob was conceived. They'd gone to a restaurant and held hands across the table. With no sense of time, they'd watched the candles flicker and closed the place down. On the way home, they'd parked under the stars along the edge of Catskill Creek and did it like teenagers in the back seat. She'd hoped the dress would've reminded him he hadn't touched her in months.

In the kitchen, she found the bottle of merlot left over from the night before and filled a glass to the rim. Although it wasn't the champagne she and Marco used to have over breakfast, it was the next best thing. Smooth and fruity, the first sip warmed her. Happy hour somewhere in the world, she knocked it back and poured another. She picked up a magazine in the living room. Comforted by the messy lives of actors and politicians and the skinny, botoxed beauties in *People*, she returned to her office a half hour later, ready to work.

Settled in her seat, she reviewed the yellow sticky note tacked to the side of her laptop. She needed to keep her mind busy, keep her focus. Her clients, often in a jam under tight timelines, were short on patience.

She sifted through pictures and double-checked estimates. As she sent out quotes, her mind wandered to her conversation with Marco last week. Though it was quick, it felt good, easy. Would he call her back? Pass along business?

On the corner of her desk, a photo of her aunt stared back at her. *Tell me how this is a good idea. After everything we've been through? You don't know this man, anymore.*

"Come on, Aunt Beth." Yet she understood the concern.

The night her mother had died, her aunt's face buckled. She'd never seen her cry before. That house fire became national news, a collective awakening about the importance of working smoke detectors. There were downsides to being a living example. Her aunt was forced to move, she to change her name. Nothing fancy, nothing traceable. Her aunt could've blamed her. Maybe she should have, but she didn't. People protect their own.

As she worked through her emails, she couldn't get her aunt's voice out of her head. *All I'm saying is don't poke the bear. Promise me you'll stay in your lane...*

She leaned back in the chair. Was that what this was about? More a generational thing. There was no danger in talking to another man. An expert in invisible, she wasn't dead. Given the chance, she'd never act on it.

Yet whose fault was that? She replayed her conversation with her aunt when she described how she and Jim were going through a bit of a rough patch. It was exhausting being angry, his stubbornness, the endless arguments. At six-three, Jim punched well above his weight. It could be intimidating, too. She never should have mentioned it.

A half hour later, her inbox empty, she returned to her screen and switched gears. The morning picked up speed and within hours, her ship had a name. *HMS Erebus.* Mid afternoon, her phone lit up. Blocked number.

"Nice website." A deep voice.

She stopped what she was doing. "Marco?"

"Galante, himself. Glad I caught you." A click of a lighter. "I checked out your client list. There's some big names there, yes?"

"I've been fortunate," she said.

"Gen Z, huh. Those kids spend more time documenting

their lives than living it." He let out a long breath. "Are you into professional sports, too?"

She snorted. "I'm more of an armchair athlete."

It was a lie. She hated sports. But after those first jobs with the first agency, she became a fan of the *business* of sport really fast. Contracts paid well, and the agents appreciated her work. She asked him what he did, and he said he dabbled in product.

"Mainly imports and exports," he explained. "Toys, clothes, and electronics on Amazon and eBay. Anyway, now I have a better sense of your digital chops, I have a problem I think you may be able to solve."

Her past provided plenty of practice circumventing trouble, but until she knew what Marco wanted, it was best to stay silent. She listened to his voice. Rich. Strong. Mellifluous.

"You're someone of few words," he noted. "A bit of a vault."

She pressed the phone tight to her ear. "It keeps business afloat. What can I do for you? The basics are fine."

"I have a photo that requires adjusting."

"That's a little bare bones. Adjusting how? Do you have a timeline?"

"I'm more concerned with the details. Give me your email and I'll send it and call you back."

Ria recited the address and when Marco disconnected, she yawned and gazed across the street. The sun was low, casting long shadows across the lawn. The sound of children's after-school voices filtered through the screen.

Ping

She scanned her inbox.

Access on your smartphone. Encrypted and double-protected. First password is bella. Second is the last six numbers you used to call earlier. You have thirty minutes.

She clicked on the link and within seconds, an image

appeared. Sitting on the ground with his back against a large boulder, the man in the photo let his arms hang loose at his sides. His head hung awkwardly to the left. There was no expression on his face, but he was staring straight into the camera. Mid-forties. Dark slicked back hair. Sharply edged sideburns. Clean shaven. Dressed in fitted jeans and a soft black leather jacket, he looked like a Navy Seal.

The image was not how she remembered him. Flip flops and board shorts and colourful shirts. Tanned, trimmed brows. Beard as thick as a carpet. She leaned in and squinted at the photo. Was that what Marco looked like now? Those eyes. The ice, blue eyes. He'd aged well.

Where was he? She pinched at the screen. To his right, a forest of pine trees. To the left, a cabin by a lake, red and yellow leaves scattered across the ground. She wondered who took the picture. When it went black, she tapped the red button on the screen.

"Is that you?" she said.

Marco laughed. "No, it's a paesan."

Ria didn't believe him, but there were times it was best not to try to untangle fact from fiction. She knew what her mother would've said. As a child, she'd heard it a million times. *Mouths lie. Eyes tell the truth.*

For the next ten minutes, Marco went into greater detail. That the job was to be done with the utmost discretion. That the work was to be meticulous. That when both eyes were replaced with what would appear to be bullet holes, she could guarantee they'd look realistic.

"You want to look dead?" she said.

Marco went on to explain she could alter the background, crop the image or create a close up if she needed to. "The blood splatter will be key," he said when he was finished. "Can you do it?"

She couldn't speak. She couldn't even breathe.

"Ria. It's a picture, yes? What's the damage?"

"You said gunshot wounds."

"The cost, bella, the cost."

She thought back to her previous work. She had no frame of reference for a modification like this. There had to be something comparable among the thousands of images buried in the personal file on her laptop. She studied the Navy Seal's clear, ice blue eyes. She'd need to do a little research.

"Right now," she paused to buy herself some time, "I'm guessing somewhere in the ballpark of-"

When he suggested a price, she nearly dropped the phone. It was a lot more than she would've proposed. More than double she'd ever been paid before.

"Half to start. Half when you finish. Cash. We use Cyberghost and Torbrowser. Do you have them?"

We? The dark web? She abhorred the idea of passing over such a lucrative job, but she wasn't stupid. She glanced at the screen. The image would dissolve in three minutes.

Should she back out now? Wash her hands of it? In Paris, rumours had swirled around he and his family were connected. At the time, she'd laughed them off: *organized crime, police raid, charges dropped.* Her adrenaline surged. Now *that* she understood.

Flattered he reached out to her; she missed the highs of the past. The tingling limbs, the fluttery heart, the meticulous planning that heightened her senses. Brighter colours, the warm sensation through her veins, mind-blowing sex. Back then, it energized her. Now she did without.

Her thoughts were spinning in fifty different directions, curated memories, chipping away at the life she'd worked so hard to achieve. She'd lost touch with who she once was. Invincible. Untouchable. Was this the opportunity? Was Marco the connection? She wanted to move on, to leave that old rush, the past behind. She'd tried. She couldn't.

"I'll take the job."

EIGHT
Ria

Ria dumped an overflowing basket of dirty clothes in the laundry room Monday morning. She had no idea how they'd made it through another weekend. Liam was so sullen shopping she was unsure which of the two of them felt most punished. Something about Jacob was off, yet she couldn't put a finger on what was causing his anxiety. Then there was Jim. All weekend he'd kept to himself, and she didn't know whether she wanted to burst into tears or confront him. Last night she'd envisioned dropping a curling iron into the bathtub as he was stretched out in the water, eyes closed, relaxing.

Not that they had a curling iron anymore. After the unfortunate mishap years ago, she was so upset, she'd marched downstairs, flung open the back door and jammed it in the garbage. She had no idea how many times she told him clutter on the side of the sink was an accident waiting to happen, but he'd stubbornly refused to fix the bathroom shelf. When she asked one last time and he promised to do it after Sunday football, she'd waited patiently, no prompts, mindful not to mention it again.

That night, while he was soaking in the tub, the curling iron slipped off the counter and fell into the water. After the paramedics assured them he was fine and the ambulance pulled away, she recalled screaming, *'Who's too busy for safety now?'*

After all the shock wore off, they'd had a good laugh about

it. The next week, with the shelf back in place and the toiletries where they should've been, everything returned to normal. Everything was forgiven.

She sorted the lights from the darks, thinking about how they'd got from that point to where they were now. Back when they were happy, they skated in the winter and booked summer wine tours. On weekend road trips, they slept in, ate brunch on patios and then attended afternoon theatre or roamed the shops. They snuggled up when they watched Netflix in the evening, instead of sitting apart. She missed those times, the fun they had together, the way Jim made her feel.

There was a lot to discuss with her therapist this afternoon. Though she'd skipped the last two appointments, if the therapist could stay focused on Jim today, maybe they'd get somewhere. Figure out how to get this relationship back on track. There was no reason those early years couldn't be rekindled. Frustrated, she was doing her part. Why couldn't he? Was it too much to ask?

After she threw a load in the machine, she headed to her office. To distract her from the mess her family was in, she looked at the old photos of Marco she'd dug up from an old file. From twenty years ago, the images were faded. She thought about him all morning, wondering what he was doing, where he was, whether working with him would give her what Jim could not.

Past noon, she grabbed her purse, and headed downtown to a small brownstone building for her one o'clock appointment. The receptionist drew a pencil down a typed list of names, scratched a checkmark on the page, then flicked a hand in the direction of the waiting area.

"Have a seat."

Ria folded herself into a chair at the end of a row. She

knotted her hands, her leg bouncing in sync with her nerves. Walls painted winter white, an orderly line of pictures, music played softly in the background. None had their intended effect.

On the table beside her, a face stared out from the cover of a magazine. Heart shaped, lips in a pout, eyes rimmed with the colour of charcoal. She leafed through it, scanning images, skimming articles. Five minutes passed, then ten.

"Excuse me," she called out.

The receptionist came around from behind her desk and shuffled to a door. She knocked twice. It remained shut.

Ria tossed the magazine on the table. After she had gone to her family doctor six months ago to discuss her growing stress, he doubled her medication and referred her to the clinic. At her first appointment weeks ago, the therapist looked so young. Not more than thirty, and with no ring on her finger, she doubted the woman could help her. Surely one of the senior therapists could've taken her on. Someone with more experience. Someone on time. Should she pack it in and leave? Suddenly, the door swung open.

"Ria?" the therapist said, a bright smile on her face. "Good to see you back."

She stood and entered the room the therapist indicated. It was small, fifteen by fifteen feet, with an antique table, nothing on it but an open black laptop. Behind it, a bookshelf. To the side, a window. The therapist closed the door behind her.

"My apologies." The therapist offered a dead fish handshake. "How were the last few weeks?"

"Fine." They weren't. Between the murder on the street, Liam's attitude, and Jim's indifference, she was at the end of her rope.

"Please." The therapist waved at a chair. "A little more than that would be helpful. Let's start with the yoga. Did you pick up pants and a mat?"

Ria smiled back. This again. Yoga, herbal teas, journaling. Why did these therapists think these insipid ideas would cure any real problems? In that moment, Ria made up her mind.

"This isn't working," she said. "You and me, I mean."

She should've known it wouldn't. Last time she'd been in therapy was part of a court order, but she'd been so much younger then. In her early twenties, she couldn't stand the man the court assigned. His beaky nose, his beady eyes, his sweat-stained shirts. His endless stream of questions. His pencil, scratch, scratch, scratching on the yellow pad. She forced those thoughts aside.

The therapist's mouth tightened, and she put the pen on the desk. "It's only been a few sessions."

Ria closed her eyes. She knew what the therapist would say next. Counseling starts with trust. Trust takes time. Time builds confidence in the process. The last therapist had lied to her too. When she opened them, she felt herself caught in the fire of the therapist's gaze.

"Am I boring you?" the therapist asked.

"No." But she was.

"You're a million miles away, Ria."

"I told you." Had she? "I'm exhausted."

The therapist nodded thoughtfully. "Is it the new dosage your family doctor prescribed? I noticed you've been on the same thing since your early twenties, but then he doubled it."

"The pills are fine." They were unopened in bag at home. Since the night the man was smoking outside the house, she stopped taking them. She needed to be more alert. "Can we move on, please?"

The therapist rubbed the base of her neck. "Fair enough, but you haven't given me much to work with."

She pointed to her laptop. "What else do you need?" Right now, what she needed was coffee.

The therapist tucked her hair behind her ears and cleared her throat. "Let's go over what we have, then." She read each line aloud.

"Client, female, 49 years old, married sixteen years, experiencing communication challenges with husband-"

"No," Ria clarified. "He's driving me nuts." Some days talking to Jim was like talking to a wall.

"Alright," the therapist said. "I'll add that." She tapped at the keys, then continued. "Client refers to the root of the problem as a behaviour she calls turtling."

Ria interrupted. "And he's never home. When he is? He shuts down." She could tell the therapist wanted more. "Last week? I was trying to talk to him about the baseball game he has tickets for Saturday, and he sat there staring into a bowl. Eating slowly, bite after bite. It was like that soggy brown mess of All Bran was the most fascinating thing in the world to him. Didn't look up. Didn't say a word. Didn't acknowledge me." It was like being bunkmates in a prison cell.

The therapist went on. "Client manages conflict by giving her husband space."

"What?" Ria said, when the therapist paused.

"I know we've discussed this, but if your husband-"

"Jim," she sighed. "His name is Jim." After three sessions, how could she not remember?

"Yes," the woman said. "If he were here, it'd be helpful. It's impossible to repair a relationship if you aren't both present."

Ria gripped the arms of the chair. When she suggested they attend couples therapy in the summer, Jim flat out refused. Maybe because two boys drained her, maybe because he always blasted the game from the living room, maybe because she had plenty of practice making problems go away by herself and it wasn't worth the fight, she hadn't bothered to mention it again. Instead, she found her own therapist, but this one wasn't going to be the one to help.

"Listen, Ria. You're obviously unhappy. I can provide a referral and send along my notes."

She nodded. "Thank you."

After a stream of paper shot out from the printer, the therapist passed it over. Ria stood and sighed. Like a cat with nine lives, she'd had three. Childhood, wildhood, now. In each one of them, she'd been a fixer. She'd take care of Jim herself.

After she returned home, Ria separated the lights and darks in the laundry basket. When she came across the bright red top Aunt Beth had given her, she held it in her hands. It'd been a week since she sent her aunt the photos. She missed the days she could simply jump in the car to visit her, but now she'd moved into a long-term care home, the four-hour drive back was prohibitive. Her aunt's absence ached in her chest, and she was desperate for her comforting arms. She threw a load into the machine, then retrieved her phone from her desk and pulled up the contacts.

As her Aunt's voicemail greeting started to play, the sound of her voice took Ria straight back to when her mother died, the rawness of her grief. Her eyes stung as she remembered her mother's funeral. Afterwards, friends and neighbours streamed through her aunt's front door, all unwanted save for the casseroles and butter tarts they held in front of them. Never around so much food in her life, she'd piled a plate high and skulked off to the guest room. Hushed voices and the dull thud of the door opening and closing floated up from downstairs. Eighteen years old then, she polished off the plate, a moment of bliss in the chaos.

"Listen," her aunt said. "We've gone over this for years, you and me. How many times do I have to tell you? It was an accident."

Ria nodded. She knew. She didn't need to be told. She pulled a lighter from her purse, snapped the wheel with her thumb and ran a finger through the flame. An old habit she'd picked up as a child, she'd found herself coming back to it since the shooting. *Angel.* The day her mother died, she'd buried that person too. Her breathing slowed, and her anxiety eased for a moment. Engraved with two letters and a dove, it was all she had left to remind her of her mother.

"It's done, Ria. It wasn't your fault. Let it go."

Her aunt--the only one who'd ever loved her, who'd protected her, the only person who truly knew her. She had helped her through that time, and she would help her through this, again.

NINE
Jim

Sounds came from the other side of the bedroom. Six-thirty Sunday morning. Ria was puttering around in the dark. Her humming was annoying. Forever Young. The Titanic song? Sometimes Jim had no idea of the tune at all. Did she make them up? How anyone could be so happy at this hour was beyond him. He shoved the pillow over his head.

When she finally left the room, he stretched across the bed. Heat radiated from under the duvet, a flimsy sapped warmth compared to yesterday.

It had been a delicious fall afternoon. The small clearing in the woods at Catskill Park blended so well into the cedars on the side of the escarpment, it was impossible to see the hikers who snaked their way through the trails below. Slick with sweat, he smiled at the woman on the blanket beside him. As he eyed the flat of her stomach, she raised her body towards his and he ran his finger down her abdomen, along the inside of her hipbone, to below. Her body tensed as she closed her eyes and waited. Afterward, he lifted himself onto an elbow and wiped the beads of moisture that had formed on the bridge of her nose.

"Missing the ballpark?" she'd said, smiling.

"If the Red Sox were playing, we'd be there," he told her.

"A park is a park."

"As a matter of fact, it's not. Remember Fenway?"

She held a finger to her lips. "Hear that?"

A waterfall cascaded down the cliffs beside them. He reached into the picnic basket nestled at the edge of the blanket and popped a frozen green grape in his mouth.

"Didn't bring my swimmers."

"Aren't those optional?"

He grinned. Having finally told his brother about Jaylyn, he didn't feel the need to go through the charade of taking her to the baseball game; his alibi for the day and asked her instead to go hiking for the afternoon. At the entrance, he'd stopped beside a dented metal can, dug into the pocket of his jeans, pulled out the Yankees tickets and tossed them in the garbage.

Telling Frank hadn't been so bad. Except for the initial look of shock on his face. He'd told them how they'd met. What she was like. About her twin brother, Jaxon. Afterwards, he didn't feel as guilty. About the relationship. Where they were. Or the wasted baseball tickets.

He'd passed Jaylyn a wine glass. She was tall and long-legged and full of life. An adventure seeker. Everything Ria was not. He gazed up at the cloudless blue sky, relaxed for the first time in months. He could count the number of times he'd been stressed out in his life on one hand. His divorce. When Ria was picking at him over something. Last week.

When he'd showed up for the meeting with the captain, he came prepared to tell the truth. That he was in a relationship with someone junior who reported to him. That his home life was rocky, and he didn't know where the relationship was headed. After months of being paranoid, his emotions running wild, he was ready to face the consequences.

But when the captain strode into the office, rather than being fired like he thought since he got the text, he was asked to investigate a ship fire training course in New York City. The crew who normally roamed the halls vanished; the gossip usually wild when the captain called one of the crew to a sudden meeting died down. No one said a thing.

"Earth to Jim." She'd nudged his shoulder. "Have I lost you?"

Jaylyn's face was angled to the sun. She dragged her fingers through her hair and smoothed it to a loose knot on the top of her head. Dark strands slipped between her nails and tumbled past her shoulders. Although he needed to make some big decisions soon, lost was the last thing he was right then.

Sunday morning and reality returned. It'd been a long week of early starts. Work was nuts, he still had to talk to Liam, and after the media grilled Detectives Singh and Li who yielded nothing new about the shooting, Ria asked him to dig for dirt again. When he couldn't find any, she'd refused to talk to him for three days. It was like being on a rollercoaster. Up and down, round and round. Jaylyn had showed him being in a relationship didn't have to be this way.

He got up and went for a run. After he raked the back yard to clear his mind, he took Liam's laptop and phone out of his dresser and went to his son's room.

"Get moving." He passed them over. "We need to discuss this burner phone."

Once Liam threw on some clothes, Jim steered him out the front door. As he fired up the engine and backed out of the driveway, Liam pulled his hoodie up over his head.

"Start talking," Jim said to his son.

"Forget it."

"That's not going to happen. What's wrong?"

"Nothing."

It didn't sound like it. A series of disasters ran though his head. A failed course? Was he about to be kicked out of school? Girl problems? He tried to reconcile the idea of Liam as a father and prayed he wasn't going to be a grandfather next spring. When he glanced across the front seat, Liam was typing on his phone.

"Dad." He didn't look up. "No one's pregnant."

"Come on, bud. Then what?"

Liam paused. "You know how you always say it's a short trip between-"

"The penthouse and the outhouse?" Jim was surprised to find he could laugh.

"This isn't funny. Like you never did something stupid?"

He stared at the road. The comment hit a little too close to home. But Liam was seventeen; how bad could it be?

Liam took a shaky breath. "Want a coffee?"

He wasn't following the logic. "Because...?"

"It's #TheFellas. We need to meet up at McDonalds."

He yanked the steering wheel to the right and stopped at the side of the road. "I'm sitting right here. Tell me what's going on."

"I don't have all the details. In case you forgot, you grounded me."

Right. The thousand dollars. His heart sunk. He should have followed up sooner but there was so much else going on.

Twenty minutes later, Jim followed Liam's black jeans, black jacket and black toque through the food court. The laminate popped and buckled under his feet and the smell of grease mixed with a faint odor of cigarettes made him nauseous. Ahead, #TheFellas were huddled in a back corner. Chuck, whose parents called him big-boned, was stuffing French fries in his mouth. Nick, who they called Rudolph, had a face so cratered and swollen, if they ever got lost at night, his nose would be the red light to guide them home. Zimmer held the group's attention, the arms of his bright green jacket waving, hands a flurry.

"Yo," Liam said, as he slid into a chair. "What ya got?"

Zimmer smiled. "Yesterday."

"Snatched." Liam gave him a fist bump.

Jim had no idea what they were talking about until Zimmer grinned. Looking at him full on, Jim could tell he had his braces removed. His dark hair cut short, his smile now bright, he was a good-looking kid.

"Congratulations," he said.

"Thanks, Mr. S. Metal-free has privileges. Want some?"

Zimmer held out a bag of sticky toffee. Jim declined, left the boys at the table, and picked up a coffee. When he got back, Chuck had brown liquid mess oozing down his chin. He looked away disgusted.

Chuck laughed and wiped his face. "We are the people our parents warned us about."

Nick rolled his eyes. "Sorry, Mr. S. Zero class."

"Right," he said. "What's up?"

Nick, Zimmer, and Chuck glanced at each other. Liam chewed on the bottom of his cracked lip, then turned to his friends.

"I told him," he said.

"Wanksta."

"Don't throw shade at me. I wasn't there when it happened."

Zimmer scoffed. "Should I remind you why?"

"All I said was we needed help."

Jim took a seat. "Would someone tell me what the hell is going on?"

"We're in a situation our parents don't know about," Nick said. "You won't say anything, right?"

"I can't promise that." He knew their parents from the

neighbourhood. Friendly with them all, he chatted with them at the school or when he picked up Liam after parties.

"It's not a situation," Liam said. "I'll start. We wanted to make money, so we've been playing cards at school."

Jim took a sip of his coffee. So what? Didn't every kid? He had.

"To chillax," Zimmer added. "And we won-"

"Eight hundred dollars." Chuck smiled.

"Then at home, we took it online," Zimmer continued.

Jim frowned. "Don't you have to be nineteen to gamble online?"

"Point." Liam's face darkened. "It was while I was grounded."

Chuck wouldn't meet his eye. "It doesn't matter 'cause we lost-"

Liam cut him off. "Four hundred dollars on matched betting. How does anyone do that?"

"Long story," Zimmer mumbled. "It's supposed to be no risk."

When Chuck reached under the table, the smell of dirty socks wafted across the space. He held out a bag of Cheetos as an offering. Jim declined, but Liam took one.

"So, you need to make it up?" Jim did the math in his head. The boys needed four hundred dollars. Minimum wage was fourteen dollars an hour. They'd need to work thirty hours to recoup what they lost.

"We do," Nick said.

He shared what he worked out. "One of you must be employable."

"Dad. Shut up. They're not done."

"We switched to blackjack," Chuck said. "We were doing good. Seriously moving up. Then, out of the blue, we hit." Chuck and Zimmer looked at each other and beamed. "Two thousand bucks."

Jim planted his elbows on the table and held his breath. He already knew what was coming: there was no sure thing in gambling.

"We bet it all. Everyone agreed." Nick looked at Liam. "Except him."

"Thank you, Captain Obvious. You fuckin' losers."

When Liam threw his arms in the air, Jim gripped the cup. He'd never seen his son so furious. Zimmer, Nick and Chuck sat dead still.

Finally, Zimmer spoke up. "We tried to fix it." He took his phone from his pocket and tapped it furiously and passed it over. "See?"

Jim peered at the screen. "DirectLend Express?"

"It gives you money."

"For free," Chuck added.

Liam glared. "Nothing's free, dickhead."

Jim looked at his son. Of #TheFellas, he appeared to be the only one of the four with any common sense. But that wasn't saying much.

Zimmer snatched his phone back. "That's not what it said." He scanned the contents of the website. "Here. Loans with protection for the unexpected." He raised his eyebrows at Liam and Chuck, to bring the point home. "Complete the application online and submit for a lending decision that comes back in sixty minutes."

"Wait," Chuck paused. "That's the same as an hour."

"Terms for your needs," Zimmer read on. "The next part is complicated. A line of credit. Something about default? I'm not sure what that is. Hang on." He scrolled down. "Here's the form."

"Stop for a sec." Jim cleared his throat. "I don't get it. The personal information?"

"About that." Nick sighed.

"Nick has the same name as his Dad." Chuck's face brightened. "Same name. Same spelling. But we call Nick's dad Mr. Strombos."

Jim's stomach dropped. "You used his?"

Then everything tumbled out in warp speed.

"My parents were away that week and left a credit card for emergencies."

"We didn't use it again though. We used a pay stub and some bill we found stuck on the fridge-"

"Our house taxes."

"Not his bank card though. We used Nick's."

"One form. Round the clock service," Zimmer told him, impressed.

"It was kinda like going to a drive through," Chuck tried to explain. "Except slower. And instead of fries, we asked for 5K. We didn't expect to get it. Maybe half?"

Jim opened his mouth, then closed it. He had no idea what to say. How much had they been drinking?

"Here's the kicker," Chuck on, proudly. "If you don't repay the loan, all you gotta do is tell them and you don't have to. Our Grade Eleven Business teacher has it all wrong. Maybe we should tell him too. Anyway, Nick passed out and like, when we fired up his laptop, there it was. Five thousand bucks in his account. I know what you're thinking, Mr. S. but it's not illegal because #TheFellas? We all use the same password."

"Eat your Cheetos and shut up," he snapped.

Jim thought he was going to explode. They had no idea what he was thinking. Drunk and stupid were the least of their problems. They'd committed fraud. This could involve the police. He sat still and took everything in.

"Where's the money now?" he asked, trying to keep his voice even.

"We played it," Nick said.

"How much of it?"

Zimmer's voice went quiet. "Five."

"Hundred?"

Chuck offered a smile. "All of it."

He shook his head in disbelief.

"They told me the next day at school, Dad. I freaked out." Liam's voice was getting higher and faster. "Nick's parents were coming home in two days. We had to get it back. I have this friend with an older brother who knows someone who lent me the money."

"We cleaned it up," Nick said. "My Dad has no idea."

Jim tried to keep his voice monotone. "You owe your friend's brother-"

"More like someone he *kinda* knows," Liam corrected.

"Five thousand dollars?" When Jim grabbed Liam's arm, he wrenched it away. "Goddammit. How could you be so stupid?"

"Dirk." Liam looked at the table. "Dirk's his name."

Jim could hear fear creeping into Liam's voice. "Dirk who?"

"I don't know, but he said if I don't pay him back with interest," Liam voice broke. "He'll put a bullet in my head at the end of October."

Sour coffee filled the back of his throat. His son had looks, charm, and smarts, which he got from him. The problems he had this morning paled in comparison. He didn't have five thousand bucks lying around. He couldn't earn that much taking extra shifts the next thirty days. If he went to the police, the four boys could be charged, their future jeopardized. Ria would go ballistic.

He tented his fingers in front of him. What was he

supposed to do? Last weekend when he'd confided in Frank about Jaylyn, his brother offered to help. While this situation wasn't what he anticipated, he'd have to ask him for the money. For Rachel and Frank, who invested in Bitcoin years ago, five thousand dollars was couch change.

"We'll fix it." He looked up at the boys. Hell, what was one more secret. He hesitated, then said it quickly before he changed his mind. "This starts and ends here. You cannot say a word of this to your parents. Liam, not a word to your mother. She's too stressed out. This could push her over the edge."

TEN
Ria

An uninterrupted day ahead, Ria flicked through the notes on her desk, pried open her laptop and went online to do some research for her project with Marco. She didn't know much about Torbrowser and Cyberghost, but by the time she clicked off, she knew more than she had last week. Before the boys arrived home from school, she made a quick call to Rachel.

"How are you feeling?" she asked.

"Better. I'm in Tokyo, a glorious thirteen-hour flight away. If I spent one more day with Frank, hovering, making tea, straightening the damn blankets, it's not the flu that would've killed me."

Ria laughed. An executive in the field of crypto currency, Rachel travelled to exotic places, staying at swanky hotels, sampling local delicacies. Nicer places than anywhere she'd been, no kids to hold her back, no mundane household responsibilities. Ria did her best to listen, but everyone had limits. She cleared her throat, then explained what she needed.

"Tor's good to browse anonymously," Rachel said. "It's a single layer to keep your IP address and location invisible."

"For the dark web too?"

"No. Use it with Cyberghost. The VPN adds extra protection. It reroutes your traffic, then encrypts your connection clears the cookies and your browsing history.

"Automatically?"

"Yes. Buy it with a credit card or Bitcoin."

Hearing the word Bitcoin made her flinch. Years ago, she and Jim had missed their opportunity. Before Bitcoin went mainstream, Rachel tried to convince them to buy in. While she was willing, Jim's wariness had been their downfall. Had they taken a small loan from the bank and invested in it like Frank and Rachel did, they'd have the same lifestyle. A mansion across from the golf course in Hyde Park. Landscaped gardens, a staircase curling up to the second floor, walls of windows. The living room was as large as their whole first floor.

Years later, the only thing she insisted Jim read was one simple article to drill the point home. The New York Times reported that anyone with the insight to buy a thousand dollars of Bitcoin in 2010 would've have made over one hundred and seventy million dollars. To this day, he knew she couldn't let it go. She'd never forgiven him. Righteous bastard. What a waste.

"Once you get it," Rachel said, "you can check out all the blocked websites."

"Is the bandwidth unlimited?"

"Yes, and you'll have uninterrupted downloads too."

"Don't tell Jim," Ria said. "He'll want to stream football."

Rachel groaned. "We're sport widows-"

"Amen to that." For years, they'd had to endure games blaring from the den. Waited for Jim and Frank to break into their usual emotionally stunted, fart-filled banter only they found hilarious. It was annoying. With two kids, she didn't need a third.

"Who's your new client?" Rachel probed. "Someone from the media? An unrestricted inquiry? Law enforcement?"

Law enforcement? She took a sip of water from the glass on her desk. No. Her client was the criminal. She knew he was because last week, she'd read through the fine details of every article she'd printed. Marco was living somewhere upstate. Her sister-in-law was the closest thing she had to a best friend. While she trusted Rachel, he'd been crystal clear about his expectation regarding confidentiality.

"Whoever it is," Rachel said, "Don't get caught seeding and leeching copyright material. That falls under reproducing and distributing. Nobody's worth it."

She laughed. "You saying you won't visit me in jail?"

"I'm happy to load your commissary card, but I'm not a fan of those sticky plastic seats. I won't be available the next week or so. Good luck with it."

Ria spent the next three days poking around the dark web. At first, she stumbled over the lack of organization. Most of the websites had the suffix '.onion', and there were a host of different search engines. Didn't the place index? She stopped at a site called Hidden Answers, found a book club, and checked out some crypto prices. Her eyes widened at the price of Bitcoin. She felt her face grow hot. As she moved along, a link for kid videos appeared and an image flashed across the screen. Her stomach lurched. She clicked off immediately.

Back in Hidden Answers, she scrolled through the forum. Stretched out on the living room couch, she sipped a glass of wine, searching, reading, posting. Better equipped to navigate the abyss, she located an online shopping market, scanning the message boards, combing through the threads. Money could buy anything. Stolen credit card numbers, fake documents, social security numbers, college degrees. She found a site for phony coupons. She laughed; Jim would go crazy here.

He was obsessed. There was always a fat wad amongst the plastic forks and the packages of ketchup in the kitchen drawer.

Fifty cents off a loaf of bread. Two-for-one cereal. Forty per cent off toothpaste. They weren't organized by brand or product or expiry date. It drove her nuts. If he insisted on acting like an old maid, the least he could do was store them in a coupon binder. Better yet, download an app and go digital.

She discovered hacked accounts for Uber, PayPal, Netflix, and Spotify for sale. Rugs. Cars. Luxury counterfeits. New passports? She recalled what she went through twenty years ago. Filled out a form, submitted to a police record check and mailed the package with a money order. Three months later, she'd received a birth certificate confirming her new name. How times had changed. It was so much easier now.

By the end of the week balanced with normal family demands, she had one last site she wanted to explore. When she opened her laptop and typed, a message appeared on the screen.

Invalid password.

She wiped a sleeve to her forehead, glanced at the caps lock and tried again.

Invalid password.

She tapped a finger on the mouse and stared at the words, trying to think it though. Heat rose in her face, suffocating her thoughts, making her unsure of herself. She tried again. Nothing.

A film of sweat covered every inch of her skin. It was like she was living in a rainforest, one moment sweating to the point of dehydration, the next she was wracked with the chills. The swings in her thermostat between hypothermia and the raging fires of hell were becoming dangerously close to unbearable. She kicked off her shoes, then ripped off her cardigan and threw it in a corner.

She couldn't concentrate. Across the room, she cracked open the window. A door banged from somewhere inside the house.

"Hello?" she called out.

She listened for a second for footsteps. Words. Breathing. Her chest tightened. Fear. Sharp and hard and sudden. Something wasn't right. Then she grabbed Liam's baseball bat hidden in the corner behind her office door. Barefoot, she crept to the bottom of the stairs. The house was eerily still.

"Who's there?"

Ria climbed the stairs slowly. Crap. She forgot her phone. Move or stay put? Another step, scanning, straining to hear. Halfway down the hall, Jacob's bedroom door had swung shut. She held her breath, then she turned the doorhandle and opened it. The room was empty.

She collapsed on the landing and swallowed a laugh. Between work and the mid-day press conference about the shooting which revealed no progress in the police investigation, she was paranoid.

Should she be?

Now she knew more about Marco, she needed to be cautious. Stay guarded. Take it slowly. But if she wanted a taste of that old rush, she'd need to loosen up. Feel the energy. Impossible while taking her pills. They stifled her creativity and made her feel dull and sluggish. She was glad she'd stopped taking them since the shooting. It helped her feel she was on top things, alert to the possibilities.

In her new life, the medication kept her ordered and contained. But over the course of her marriage, she'd forgotten herself entirely. Her wants. Her needs. She was sick of trying to be happy through the happiness of others. She wanted to be herself again. Indecision wouldn't get her any close to the type of person she wanted to be. Somehow the two lives had to coexist.

Her legs had numbed from how long she'd had them folded under her. She struggled to her feet. Downstairs, she flung open the back door. China blue skies capped the deep green treetops of the ravine. On the deck, she fell into a chair. The gentle breeze calmed her; the cool air soothed the heat on her skin.

As the wind picked up, the gate leading to the ravine hung wide open, swinging softly back and forth. She strode down the steps and slammed it. On the other side, she spotted cigarette butts. She stared into the depths of the ravine. Then she opened the gate and passed through, tiptoeing through the mud and the leaves. She counted. There were six. A sour taste filled the back of her mouth. Someone had been back there. Watching.

ELEVEN
Ria

"Where's Dad?" Jacob asked.

"At the station," Ria said. "Where else would he be?"

She pushed on the gas pedal. After Jim stormed out, she'd gone to bed, but when she woke up in the middle of the night, he wasn't beside her. Out of bed in a shot, she searched the house, then checked the garage. The car was still gone. She filled a tumbler with vodka, then sat on the living room couch, knees drawn up, arms wrapped around them, and waited. She hadn't expected he would do what she'd said.

Not only was their argument loud last night, it got ugly. *Where was he, again? Why wouldn't he talk to her? What had he found out about the murder? Money. Moving.* Not one clear answer. When she'd pressed, Jim shut down. Refused to discuss it.

It was like the futile press conference and the cigarette butts she told him about, too. She'd tried to reason with him. A man was out there, walking around, and Jim was not prepared to believe the man existed. As he'd grabbed his jacket, anger got the best of her.

If you walk out of here, don't bother coming back.

"Mom," Jacob yelled from the back seat. "You passed the coffee shop."

"Shit." She flushed. The word slipped out. She hit the brakes, jerked the car to the left and made a quick U-turn into the line at the drive through.

"I'll have a whole wheat bagel, cut in half, toasted, no butter," he said. "But we can't eat in the car. Dad doesn't like it."

"Dad's not here, is he?" she said. "And Dad can't always get what he wants."

She pulled the car to the window. Though Liam was at home in bed, one of the two boys might as well learn the truth about their father.

After she paid, she passed the bag into the back seat. Back on the road, traffic was light. Five minutes later, she stopped in front of the library. Pressed to the edge of the door, Jacob was taking short breaths. The seatbelt tight around his waist. An anxiety attack? She wasn't the one who stormed out last night. That was on him. Not her.

After she gently coaxed Jacob out of the back door and up the library steps, she parked at the far side of the lot. She pressed the button on the side of the steering wheel. Her husband's voice reverberated through the car.

Can't take your message right now. Leave me yours.

"Jim, give me a call please."

She tugged at the sun visor and slid open the compact mirror. She scraped her fingers through the length of her hair, a few weeks past a cut. Reclined on the front seat, she listened to the radio. So many sad songs. When the commercials broke the streak, she punched in his number again. Straight to voice mail.

"Where are you?" Aware she sounded panicked; she changed her tone. "About last night. I'm sorry. You know I didn't mean what I said, so please either come home or call me back."

A woman with auburn hair highlighted with bold streaks of copper passed by the front of the car. It was like being mesmerized by logs burning in a fire. She had an overwhelming desire to reach out and touch it.

FLAT OUT LIES

It reminded her of the boy she met once on a summer vacation with her parents at Long Point State Park. Lighters in hand, they'd spent their days burning bugs, slivers of driftwood and the junk washed up on the beach. No one paid them the least bit of attention until the night flames licked up the sides of the wooden outhouse. They'd dropped the lighters in the stink hole and circled back through the dark woods. She could still feel the bubble of excitement, running barefoot alongside the people who came rushing with buckets and bottles of water in their hands. Andrew? Alex? Bucktoothed, red hair cut close to the scalp, a husky frame. Aaron. Yes. She wondered what became of him.

She glanced at her watch and picked up the phone again. "I've been awake half the night, Jim. With everything going on in the neighbourhood, I'm worried. How do I know you're safe?"

She hung up and cringed. She sounded like her mother. Smothering. Frenzied. Desperate. Like the time she and her friends said they were all sleeping over at each the other's houses and snuck off for the weekend to Syracuse. She got busted the moment she stepped off the Greyhound at the terminal Sunday afternoon and was forced to watch her mother go apeshit in front of her friends. Since then, she vowed to never be anything like her. Yet here she was.

"This isn't funny anymore," she said, after she pressed redial again. "I said sorry. What else do you want? Call me back now."

The phone remained dark and silent. She unfurled her hands to examine her fingers. Rough skin, swollen red cuticles and pudgy digits. With everything on her mind, it wasn't a surprise. Not even the thick woolen mittens her mother duct taped to her wrists each night when she was nine had stopped her from biting her fingers. She chewed the skin around her thumbnail, ripped it off with her teeth and spat it on the floor. She chewed the tops of her fingernails to even them out, then hit redial.

"Jim? Are you dead? Pick up the goddamn phone."

She cursed. Didn't every marriage have cracks and blemishes? Her parents had. Raised voices behind doors, muttered statements in the car, simmering tension. Her mother, a struggling actor, smoked like a chimney. Her father, an underemployed engineer drank heavily. 'Bordering on a problem,' her aunt later corrected. Either way, her clothes were threadbare, her stomach empty. Each year her parents ripped off school photos stapled to the front of the envelope, yet never bought them. When her father went to dry out, her mother cried for weeks, cocooned in her bed until he returned. She was eleven the day he left the final time, and her mother spent three years barricaded alone in her room.

The damage was done. Ria learned to cook. To do laundry. To sign school notes. At the age of thirteen, she taught herself to drive. Each week she went to Aurora to pick up groceries and the odds and ends her mother insisted she needed at the second-hand store. It wasn't all bad. Once the car was packed, she'd stroll to the drugstore and thumb through the magazines, studying pictures of places she'd never been. Europe. Sydney. Japan. Aruba. After she slipped the magazine beneath her shirt and walked out, all she thought about on the way home, sunlight bouncing off the windshield, an arm resting against the open window, and warm air blowing though her hair along the winding country roads, was how one day, someday, she would see them all.

Wanting to know where the dog was, she'd knocked on her door only once.

"What about Lexie?" she asked.

"Your pup?" Her mother waved a hand from her bed. "Gone. Olive, his new family calls her."

She waited for her father to call, running every time the phone rang. It was never him, and one day she hung up and smacked the receiver against the wall so hard it left a dent. She missed his smell. His smile. Missed searching through his pockets for loose change. But the first years without him, she'd missed her dog the most.

"It was a different era," her aunt said when she brought it up years later. "Parents didn't talk about stuff like they do now."

"Did they think I wouldn't notice? We lived in the same house."

"The ugliness? I'm sure you did."

"And my Dad's shit. Wherever he is."

"I haven't got a card in years, Angel. He's probably still shacked up in Wisconsin. A troubled soul, my brother was. Both were."

A spider scurried across the dashboard. She trapped it in her hand, pulled off a leg, watched it twist and turn, then crushed it under her palm. In the glove box, she found a tissue and wiped away its mangled body. She tried Jim once more but got no answer. She lowered her phone and typed.

Where the hell are you?

Three dots appeared as he wrote. *With Frank.*

She drew in a sharp breath. *Hope you're having fun.* She changed *fun* to *a nice time* and hit send. When he didn't respond, she gave herself a swift, mental kick. What else would she expect? What would make him reply? Food.

Want to order in tonight? Greek? Pizza?

His answer came back quickly: *Eating here.*

When can we expect you home?

She stared at the phone and waited for a response. None

came.

In her purse, she found her mother's lighter and clicked the wheel. Reds and yellows and blues bobbed and danced in front of her eyes. She held her palm over the flame and counted, trying to quell the anger rising in her chest. High school students spilled out the doors of the library with backpacks and books. When Jacob stopped on the steps to survey the parking lot, she dropped the lighter in her purse and waved.

At her desk midafternoon, Ria pulled out a file. Elbow deep in a monthly profit report, the phone rang. Blocked number. Marco? She hoped so. With everything going on, she could use the lift.

"Ria, honey? It's Tracy down the street." The woman's voice sounded like an earful of melted caramel. "Do you have a minute? We were hoping to talk to you."

We? Honey? She held her tongue. Unsure how they got her number, it was the language of the in-group. All rail-thin, book club hostesses with glossy lips, she didn't even know which one of the women was talking.

"Those two detectives are useless," Caramel Voice lamented there were no updates about the murder on the street and how the police weren't returning their calls. "Have you heard anything?"

Ria pressed her fingers to her forehead. Her neighbour was asking because of Jim. One of the downsides to his job was the mistaken belief he had confidential insight into every crime, accident, or fire in the community. People were always asking questions, prying for information, and then were disappointed when he didn't share. Gossip was currency on the street. No thanks to him, she never had any to give.

"No," she said, disappointed. "I haven't."

"The communication is pathetic. We don't feel safe. We're

getting doorcams and demanding a community meeting so the police can answer our questions."

Ria rolled her eyes. While they were blowhards who loved the sound of their own voice, she agreed the street deserved some answers.

"They took the patrols away, you know." Caramel's voice rose. "They didn't even tell us about it. Did you get to chance to talk to them before they left?"

No. Why would she? The last time she had spoken to the police had been a nightmare. Nineteen then, she'd been unaware of her rights. It'd never happen again.

"Anyway, this may sound petty but..." Nails tapped the other end of the phone. Ria held her breath. The real point of the call? "That yellow police tape? When do you think it'll come down?"

She wasn't born yesterday. Her neighbours wanted the tape gone because it drew attention. Cars drove by more slowly. People got out and gawked. Plus, the longer it was up, the more likely it would impact their property values.

"That's a good question to ask at the community meeting," she said. "Anyway, if I hear anything, I'll post it on Facebook."

"Can you call me first?" the woman asked.

"Sure." She wouldn't.

Click.

The numbers on the profit report blurred. She clenched and unclenched her fists. She wasn't stupid. That phone call was painful. All those women wanted was her to talk to Jim and pass them on information. Liam hadn't come out of his room yet, and she could hear Jacob pacing upstairs, back and forth, from his room to their front bedroom window, waiting for Jim's car to pull into the driveway.

Head in her hands, she sat quietly for a moment, then she

picked up her chair and slammed it against the wall. For a second, she stood there, staring at the overturned chair and the dent in the drywall, unable to grasp what she'd done. She needed to figure out how to dig herself out of this mess, but this wasn't the way to do it. Inhale. Exhale. She grabbed the chair leg, whipped it around and turned it upright.

Her laptop open, she breathed in through her nose and out through her mouth. Slow steady breaths. Then she pulled up her file and clicked through her collection of images. Years of dedicated work, her research. Images that soothed her, images that calmed her. Car wrecks. Bloated bodies on beaches and waterways. Shark attacks.

As her mind cleared, she dug a little deeper. A hyperextended knee. A piece of ear hanging by a thread. A mangled foot, blood pooling around it. The jagged edges of bone sticking out of a forearm. Tissues, splinters, sinew. Close range shots, devastating damage. There was only one image in the file she couldn't bring herself to look at. Shadows. Footsteps. The creaking door. A hand, pulling her back to that fateful night. The feelings were still too raw.

TWELVE
Jim

After spending a peaceful night at Frank's house, returning home felt like preparing for battle. Before Jim went inside, he stood on the front steps of the house next door. It was grey and close to dusk. Chimes echoed through the foyer. An outside light came on and a shadow appeared through the frosted glass shuffling toward him. Mrs. Potts peered out through a one-inch crack in the door.

"Come in," she said, smiling. "How's Liam feeling?"

"Liam? He was sick weeks ago." Mrs. Potts nodded. Message received. She'd asked him to come look at the sink ages ago. He apologized.

When she backed up, he followed her down the hallway. Mrs. Pott's house was a mirror image of their own: two small rooms to the right, one with overstuffed brown corduroy furniture, the other a dining room. The dark and dreary kitchen had its original laminate floor and cupboards. Mrs. Potts stopped in front of them, a book tucked under the folds of the flowing green fabric wrapped around her. It was the size of a tent.

"What are you reading?" he asked.

"Fifty Shades of Grey." His eyebrows lifted before he could stop them. "I saw two ladies talking about it on TV and I said to myself, Lucinda, you're never too old to stop learning."

She cackled and smoothed down what was left of her

thinning hair. When Pebbles appeared in the doorway, Jim held out his hand. The dog crossed the kitchen and inched his front paws forward until he was lying in his basket in the corner, eyes watching their every move.

"Don't mind Pebbles," Mrs. Potts said, looking up at him. "He doesn't answer to anything but food." She cocked her head. "You look tired."

He nodded. He was unable to sleep at night because Ria tossed and turned in bed, then got up and prowled at all hours, walking to her office only to pivot and walk back upstairs again. Last night at Frank's was the first time he slept soundly in ages. Then how many calls? He'd ignored them, hadn't bothered to play back the swearing and hissing and shouting of her messages. He didn't have the energy to deal with all the drama. He put his tool belt on the counter beside a bottle of drain cleaner. Water pooled in the sink.

"What's the problem here?" he asked.

Mrs. Potts showed him her hands. "Artie's ring fell down the drain. It fit him fine, but it's too big for me. How tall are you?"

"Six-three."

"Artie was five seven." She pointed to the cupboard. "Can you fit under there?"

Flat on his back, he wriggled into the depth of the dark space, unscrewed the drain trap, and held a bowl underneath. As the water dripped through, his phone vibrated on the counter.

"All these technological gizmos," Mrs. Potts said. "The ping, ping. The videos. The pressure to do the World Wide Web. Why don't you people talk to each other?"

He laughed. "The people are under here fixing your sink."

"Three pink hearts." She paused. "And someone will meet

you next week for lunch. Anyway, if you ask me, I think these gizmos make people unhappy."

Heat rose in his cheeks. She had a point. With the number of calls Ria made earlier, his phone was making him unhappy. One text from Jaylyn was so much easier.

"Has something happened, Jim?"

"No." He held the ring out in his hand. "Here it is."

"To you, I mean."

Her fingers grasped the ring in his palm. When he slid out from under the counter, Mrs. Pott's clear blue eyes stared back at him.

"It's none of my business, I know, but you can talk to me. Artie always said I was a good listener."

He took a breath and blew it out slowly. Artie passed away five years ago, but she still missed him. How was it possible? With their blowout last night, he couldn't imagine missing Ria after ten years.

Glancing at Mrs. Potts, he wondered what to say. How could he explain what he couldn't explain himself? Mrs. Potts had a soft spot for him and no time for Ria. Until he decided about what to do with his marriage, he couldn't say a thing. He didn't want her advice. He didn't deserve her sympathy. He collected his tools and when she handed him money at the front door, he said, "You keep that. That's why we have neighbours."

"Then take this." She held out a box of chocolates. "Which reminds me, before winter comes, I need a shovel and a bag of salt for the front walkway."

After he promised to pick them up for her, the door swung shut.

The sun had set over the neighbourhood. As Jim walked home, his legs felt heavy. Barely able to move, he cursed himself for his waffling. His wavering. His indecision. The lights on the path guided his way to the porch. Outside the front door, he paused, then pushed it open.

"Dad." Jacob stumbled downstairs and ran into his arms.

After Jim gave him a big hug, Jacob led him down the hall. Empty Popeyes containers lay scattered on the kitchen table, the smell of chicken and grease in the air.

"Well, well." Ria smiled. "Look what the cat dragged in."

"Sorry," he glanced at the boys. He could hear the irritation in her voice. It was easier to apologize and hope she moved on. They didn't need to be part of this.

"How was dinner?" he asked.

"I got fish sticks," Jacob said. "Without the breading."

Liam glanced over. "It looked like snot on fries."

Jim laughed. Ria didn't.

"Actually," Jacob told him. "There are fish that look like mucous. They're called hagfish. They're eels and they're eaten in Korea as a delicacy."

"Good to know, idiot." Liam scoffed. "Why don't you go live there?"

As Jacob's face reddened then fell, Ria raised her eyebrows. "Please," she warned, silencing his and Liam's laughter. "That's enough."

The room stilled. Across the table, Jacob had a book in his hands. Liam was slouched on a chair, his face buried in his phone. He knew his oldest was likely texting with #TheFellas, discussing their current predicament, praying he'd get out of it alive. On the way home from the food court last weekend, he'd promised Liam he would help, but also said he wanted to poke around a bit before they handed over five thousand bucks at the end of the month.

Ria said, "One of the girls on the street called today. They're asking the police to hold a meeting to provide the community with an update."

"About the shooting?" he said, picking up the containers.

"What do you think? I told you people don't feel safe."

When she asked if he would be around to go and he confirmed he would, the tension between them eased. He wasn't fooled. After the boys went upstairs to finish their homework, he braced himself.

"Jim." Her voice was firm. "Have a seat."

He didn't move. Five feet between them, he couldn't take another order. He couldn't stand much more of the brittleness, the tension, the flinging of insults, the chipping away at each other.

"I'm sorry about last night,' she said, thin-lipped. "But do you have any idea why I'm angry?"

He opened his mouth to say something. Reconsidered and closed it.

"You're not present."

"I'm right here in front of you." He waved. "See me?"

"Don't be dramatic," she hissed. "I meant emotionally. It's not enough."

His chest tightened. Obviously. He wasn't enough and what he could give her had never been enough. When her phone rang, he added, "How can I be? You're glued to your laptop working. You're obsessed."

She put the device down. "It's called ambition, something you might consider."

Her comment rattled him. "Low blow, Ria." He was enough for Jaylyn. She would never say something like that.

"Is it?" She waved her hand in the air. "Look around. We live in a mess."

"Is this about repainting the living room?" They'd had this conversation before. He'd get to it.

"No, this house is too small."

"So, it's about moving?" They'd had that conversation too. He didn't want to have it again. He thought she'd accepted that he and the boys were happy. When she rolled her eyes, he threw his arms in the air. "What now? It's like Whack-a-mole. I can't keep up."

"Whack-a what?" she said.

"Forget it. Stop harping. We don't have the money to move anyway."

Ria looked as if she was about to through a barb at him, then unexpectedly bit her lip. "I have to call a client," she said tersely, as she left the kitchen.

Jim went to the living room. It smelled like a funeral. No idea why she insisted on having so many pillows lined in neat rows on the couch; he threw them all on the floor. He nudged the vase of flowers on the coffee table aside with his foot. Water spilled over the rim, soaking the magazines and the books. He ignored the river snaking across the glass and the sound of the trickle, drip, drip, dripping, steadily onto the carpet.

The pain in his chest softened. What would happen if he left? Frames filled with birthday parties, soccer games and holidays stared back at him, smiling pictures she'd made them take to depict happier times. There wasn't a photo of Ria's parents anywhere. He'd seen pictures of her parents in backyard BBQs and camping trips, but they divorced when she was young, and he guessed she didn't want to be reminded. Would his photo, their photos, end up the same way if they split?

If he filed for full custody, she could work as much as she wanted. He was relieved Ria would have her aunt for support. She was the only person who could put up with her. He wondered how the situation would play out, a wall he didn't feel ready to climb. Could he start again with Jaylyn without guilt?

Jim eased himself from the couch. Down the hall, the double doors to her office were closed. Suddenly there she was back in the kitchen, rifling through her purse.

He stared at her. "I thought you were making a call."

"I did. Now, I'm going to bed."

"Are you serious?" He needed a drink. "Looking for these?" He held up a small plastic bottle.

She turned. "No, I stopped taking them."

"Have you talked to anyone about it?"

"I will. My doctor."

"And me?"

"My aunt too. I'll call her later."

The idea of the impending roller coaster made him feel sick. "You're agitated. You're yelling. Could this be why you saw footprints in the back yard? Or the pile of cigarette butts?"

Her face lit up. "Six of them. You saw them too?"

"I did, but they could be anybody's. People walk along that path every day. Ria, you need to take your pills. We don't need you falling apart." There was no point in telling her he thought she already was.

Her face reddened. "Wanting an explanation isn't losing it-"

"That's not what I'm saying."

"Then what? I trust what I saw, but you still don't believe me."

She slammed her fist on the table. The conversation was going nowhere. He could really use that drink. As he grabbed his jacket on the chair, she flailed her arms in the air, like she'd walked into a spider web.

"You think leaving will solve this?" she shouted.

"I'm going for a walk," he said, calmly.

"Why? So, you can talk to Frank about me, again?"

He raked his hands through his hair. She *was* losing it. He could talk to his brother if he damn well wanted. Maybe he'd go see Jaylyn. As he picked up his coat, she lunged forward and grabbed hold of his wrist. He jerked his arm away, then hustled out the front door, Ria shouting as he went.

THIRTEEN
Jim

After a sleepless night at Frank's, Jim arrived at work Monday morning. His pulse was racing, air stuck in his lungs, sweat covered his upper lip. If he had a heart attack, he couldn't blame Ria. While he didn't know how to deal with her mood swings, she wasn't the one sneaking around, keeping secrets.

At his desk, he held his pounding head in his hands. He didn't understand how they got there. While the first years of their marriage were magical, by the end of the fifth, he discovered two things. Happy wife, happy life, wasn't possible. For years, he did everything she asked. House chores, extra shifts at the station, a second child to rekindle their marriage, but she always wanted more. Even with all her attention focused on the kids, he'd tried hard and failed miserably. Quick to demand what she wanted, quicker to point out his flaws, how much was he supposed to sacrifice?

It hadn't always been that way. The night they'd met, she'd breezed through the front door of the bar. Velvet slip dress, kitten heels and an impossibly small handbag. All remnants of her life in Europe. Sloppy drunk, she shyly asked for his number and called the next day. Destiny was the word she used. Wiser now, he would've said 'doomed.' Six months later, a freak early November snow squall on their wedding day should've been an omen. But with Liam on the way, what was he supposed to have done? So naïve. So stupid. They'd had a few good years in the beginning. Until they didn't.

"Jim?"

He looked up. The captain stood in front of him.

"Morning," he said.

"I called your name five times."

"Yeah, sorry, I was a little lost in thought. How can I help you?"

When the captain asked for an update on the ship fire training course in New York City, Jim wiggled his mouse. He pecked at the keys of his computer, printed a document, and passed it over. After a quick look, a couple questions, the captain nodded.

"Looks good, unlike the expression on your face," he said. "Want to tell me what's going on?" Jim declined and the captain shrugged. "I respect that. If you need a regional counselor, or someone at IEP," -he pointed to the wall- "The number's there on the bottom."

Jim waved him out. Disclosing his affair with a work counselor was too much of a risk. After their big blowout in the summer, Ria had suggested the same. *Communication is important, she'd said, a two-way street.* How? Everything she did was an attack against him. For sixteen years, he listened. Non-stop. On-and-on. He shuddered at the thought of the issues, her anger. Was it because he didn't want to move? Was it because he was living and breathing?

He closed his eyes to stop the chaos in his mind. In the last few days, he'd had enough talking for a lifetime. Frank was his counselor, a voice of reason, provided perspective. What he needed now was peace, time to figure out what to do next.

Dragging himself up from behind his desk, he went down the hall to the gym to blow off steam. Hit the treadmill, skipped, lifted weights. Pushing himself to the limit, his mind swung like a pendulum. He couldn't take any more. It was exhausting lying, hiding what he did, took so much energy. There was good in her. He'd seen it. He loved her.

Last night wasn't all bad. When Liam told Jacob to move to Korea to eat hagfish, he'd laughed out loud. Jim couldn't imagine living anywhere other than New York. Hot summers, fall leaves, the holiday lights. Save for the crew's training courses and family vacations to Florida, he'd never stepped foot out of the state.

The hardest part was avoiding her questions about the footsteps and cigarette butts. After she asked him to be home more, she'd held his gaze, eyes cold, and refused to look away. She wanted an answer. She demanded it. Although he'd assured her he'd try, the words rang hollow. But she was so uptight, paranoid about what happened on the street, he didn't want her to worry, pile another thing on her plate. Sometimes the wrong thing was the right thing. Wasn't it?

Hot and sweaty when he finished, he returned to the changeroom. In the darkness, he leaned his butt against the wall. His breathe came out so loud he could hear it.

When his phone rang, he stared at the smile pasted on the screen. Hand to his chest, a sickening wave washed over him. Only a few days ago, he wasn't sure what he wanted to do. Now the answer was in front of him.

Jim was looking forward to a quiet lunch.

"Hello, beautiful," he said, as he slid into a booth.

Tanned, Jaylyn smiled back at him. Her shiny dark hair cascaded past her shoulders and the necklace he'd given her sparkled brightly on the neck of her t-shirt.

"Two beers," he said after the server approached the table.

Jaylyn held up a hand. "Water for me. I got up an hour ago."

He shrugged and asked her about her weekend. Unsure of the best time to reveal what he wanted to say, he played with the coaster, tapping each corner on the lines etched into the top of the wood. When the server returned, he took a long pull of his beer and they ordered.

"No Pad Thai?" he asked.

"I'm on a seven-day detox. Keeping the temple clean. You should try it."

"And give up meat? No."

"Everyone's doing it." She lifted a finger. "Excuse me."

After Jaylyn sauntered across the restaurant to the washroom, his phone buzzed. He pulled it out of his pocket. *Miss me?* He thought of answering her, but by the time he typed out half a message, she was standing in front of him. She laughed and squeezed his hand. When he lifted hers to his lips, it smelled like lavender. It felt so smooth. As she described the benefits of her detox, a foot travelled up and down the side of his calf. He swallowed slowly. He knew Jaylyn wanted to travel. After he told Ria he was leaving, they'd take a trip together. Perhaps somewhere warm? A couple weeks on a beach.

Unable to wait any longer, he said, "Can we talk seriously?" When she cocked her head, he leaned in. "I love you."

"That's sweet." She looked to her right. After the server dropped their plates and left, she said, "Um-"

"Please." He picked up a fork. "I'm not good at this, so let me finish. I've been thinking a lot. I know we've only been together six months, but-" He tapped his chest. "You and I? It feels right. I want to start a life with you."

She stared from across the table, eyebrows knitted. "You want to move in?"

"Only as a first step. Once the boys adjust-"

"The boys?" She muttered under her breath. "I can't do that. Have you live with me, I mean."

"Is it too soon?" Her salad sat untouched.

"No. I don't need judgment at work. Besides, Jaxon's out of jail."

What? How had he missed that? It must have happened during the time he'd pulled back in early September, worried about the office gossip. He'd seen photos of Jaxon in Jaylyn's apartment and knew about her brother's B & E's. The carjacking. The extortion and drug offences. From everything she'd told him, it was only a matter of time before he'd be back in.

"Have you seen him?" he asked.

"He's my twin." She frowned. "Because my family disowned him, doesn't mean I did."

"And he's doing-"

"Fine. He's in a rooming house in Albany. His parole officer got him some construction job he hates."

"It's good for him," he said. "The long hours will keep his nose clean and away from the gang stuff."

Jaylyn's face darkened. "God, you sound like my parents. Anyway, about us? That's not how this works."

"How do you mean?"

"It's a thing." She sat back. "You know what that is, right?"

He put his fork down. The way she said it so casually unnerved him. He didn't but he nodded anyway. He picked up a glass of water and sucked on an ice cube.

Her face fell. "Oh my god, you don't. This is awkward." She leaned in and lowered her voice. "A thing is when two people are exclusive, but not completely." She looked past him, up over his shoulder. "You know? Together, but casual."

His temperature dropped back to normal. After all, he reminded himself, he was still married.

"Maybe more than that," she said. Their eyes met. "Like not all in."

The ice cube stuck in his throat. He couldn't swallow, let alone speak. What was she saying they'd spent six months together and she didn't feel the same way? There was someone else? More than one someone? He gripped the serviette in his lap.

"Are you seeing other people?" he asked.

She stared at him in disbelief. "What do you think I'm doing when you're with your wife?" His ears burned. "With your kids?" He hadn't thought much about that either. "Sitting around waiting for you? Jim. This is just for fun. It was great, but there's no future here."

"Come on, there has to be." Nerves shot, he motioned for the server. "Let's go to your place. I'll drive. We'll take the afternoon off and work this through."

"Forget it." She tapped her phone. "Jaxon's on the way."

Heavy silence hung between them as he picked at his plate. After the bill came, he trailed Jaylyn out the front door. On the sidewalk, he pulled her into a bear hug.

"Stop," she said. "Don't make this hard."

He pulled back, and let his arms drop to his sides. She tapped at the screen of her phone, then paced the sidewalk.

"Do you want your stuff back?" she asked. "There's a couple t-shirts at my place."

"After you dumped me?" he said. "Forget it."

"God, I'm sorry." A single slow blink. "Can I make it up to you?"

"How?" Was she having a change of heart? She was giving him the same kind of smile she gave him when he leaned in for a first kiss.

"Maybe we could be-"

"Friends?" He snorted. That wouldn't be happening.

"We could try..."

Her voice trailed away to nothing, and she turned her attention to the street. A blue sedan pulled up. As she stepped off the curb, the passenger's front window descended. Jaxon leaned across the front seat and glared at him, then flexed his tattooed fingers on the steering wheel. The car door opened and slammed shut and Jaylyn gave a little wave from the window.

After the taillights disappeared, Jim stalked off down the sidewalk. A lady and her dog scrambled out of his path as he turned the corner to the station. For a long time, he sat at his desk, the hum of voices in the background. He tried to collect himself. How could he have been so wrong? He'd risked his marriage, maybe even his job, for nothing, not that there was anything left to risk. Too upset to work, he packed his things and told the crew he was ill.

Later that night, after Ria was asleep, he sat out on the back deck in the dark with his phone. The texts had stopped. The calls had ended. He fired up his iPad to scroll through the pictures of the spam account he and Jaylyn secretly set up together, but the account had been deleted. Their relationship had evaporated into the ether. There was no fade out. It was over. It was as if they never happened at all.

FOURTEEN
Jim

Wednesday evening, Jim was still processing what had happened. The last twenty-four hours had turned his life upside down. The chance to escape his marriage was gone. He needed to face what was in front of him. Liam's gambling debt couldn't wait any longer. He'd have to make a decision about his marriage on his own. On the living room couch, he took a deep breath and tried to settle his thoughts. The sound of the front door slamming woke him.

He stared blankly at Ria as she entered, bags surrounding her feet. "I picked up a couple bottles of wine." When he sighed, she added, "It's my money. I earned it. I can spend it on whatever I want." She collected the bag from the floor and dropped it on the kitchen table. "We're leaving here at six forty-five."

"For what?" he asked.

"The community meeting about the shooting." She pointed to the fridge. "It's on the calendar. I have work to do."

He'd forgotten about it. Maybe they'd finally get some answers that would wrap up this shooting and get Ria back on track.

He heated a quick supper of leftovers for the boys and himself. Afterward, he knocked on Ria's office door, a signal it was time to go. They grabbed their jackets and followed the growing crowd along the sidewalk. Jim glanced at his wife as they passed through the main doors of the secondary school's gymnasium. He pointed to a row.

"This good?" He managed to sound calm as he asked. Their walk over to the community meeting was silent and tense.

Ria shook her head. "Too far back."

They moved closer to the front. The school principal walked across the stage. He had thin hair, a thick paunch, and his gray skin matched his open collared shirt. It wasn't how Jim remembered him. The last time he'd seen him was during Liam's pot smoking incident the year before. He guessed dealing with a thousand teenagers a day could age anyone. Hopefully he could help clean up the gambling debt for the boys, so he wouldn't be called back there.

The principal stooped over the microphone. *Tap, tap.* He cleared his throat. "Good evening. If everyone can find a seat, we'll get started shortly."

After Ria slipped to the washroom, he looked around his former high school. It was all too familiar. Baseball and basketball pennants hung from the ceiling. On the wall, clocks were caged inside wire mesh. He remembered it all. The colour of the paint. The doors of the change room. The adjacent cafeteria. He used to like the smells wafting out at lunch. But after two decades of Ria's meals, he knew what they'd called Salisbury steak was greasy meatloaf. Cooking was the one part of their marriage she did well. He was yawning as she reappeared in the chair beside him.

"You've been sleeping all day," she said.

"I guess I needed it." He hadn't. He was hiding from her.

She raised a finger to her lips. Detective Li tread onto the stage, a file tucked under her arm. Taller than he looked on TV, Detective Singh followed behind. He gave the audience a half smile and stepped up to the microphone.

"Good evening," he said. "Thanks for coming out. I'm

Detective Singh. I believe you already know my partner here, Detective Li, from our press conferences."

Ria whispered in his ear. "Fat waste of time, they were. If they want to get out of here alive tonight, they'd better have something more to tell us."

Jim kept his eyes on the stage. Detective Singh put on his glasses and held a tablet in front of him.

"I want to assure you our investigation regarding the occurrence on Highland Avenue in September remains active. Unfortunately, the media reported last week

Mr. Robinson's death was a case of mistaken identity. I want to be clear that's speculation. At this point, we're still following up on leads we've received. Phone calls, emails and the like."

Jim's cell phone vibrated. As he slipped it out of his pocket, Ria glared at him.

"Put that goddamn thing down."

He took a fast look. His heart sunk. "It's work wondering if I'll be in tomorrow." He was hoping it would have been Jaylyn.

"Of course, you will. Answer, shut it off and give it to me."

He tapped out a message and handed her the device. She shoved it in her purse. She was treating him like a child.

On the stage, Detective Singh said, "We're combing through other cases to see if there are any similarities or parallel activity."

Ria muttered in his ear again. "How hard could that be? It should only take a couple weeks."

Jim didn't agree with her perception of the time it took to conduct a thorough investigation but bit his tongue. He wove his fingers together and held them in his lap.

"-also posting what we can on Facebook," Detective Singh said. "Of course, if you see anything or have something to tell us, no matter how small you think it is, you can always call or email."

Voices in the gymnasium rose.

"That would mean you have to respond, wouldn't it?"

"How many leads have you got?"

"Two? Four? Ten? It's been weeks. Has anything panned out?"

Detective Singh shifted from one foot to the other and glanced at his partner. "I'm not at liberty to say."

A man with a goatee at the back shouted. "People. Would we be sitting here if they knew what happened? Think about it. They got nothing."

A hum passed through the crowd and several people nodded in agreement. Someone asked when there would be another update, then a woman shouted, "We want the patrols back on the street until you can tell us what happened. What's it going to take? Does someone else have to be killed?"

Questions rang out for another few minutes. It was a hostile audience. Jim felt for the detectives. After they left the stage, he followed Ria out of the gymnasium. She stopped to edge her way into a group lingering in the foyer. He used to think she was the most interesting person in any room, but now he could see how they shrunk away from her. They didn't want to be part of her attitude or incessant nagging either.

He wandered past the school office to a dimly lit corridor. It stank of stale sweat and gym socks. In front of a glass case, he examined the trophies. He picked out his name etched on the sides. Good memories, good times.

High school felt like a dream to him now. Had that been where his self-sabotaging started? It wasn't the first time he'd gone astray. Captain Chill was what they called him then. A title well-suited for the court, he was given ample opportunity to play the field beyond it. Years later, he'd married his high school sweetheart. But he'd carried the lifestyle forward. The first one-night stand was a mistake. The next, a simple release. By the third, he could no longer blame it on isolated errors in judgment. Though he'd been discreet, what he hadn't anticipated was the impact. His marriage disintegrated. His bad. The buck stopped with no one other than him.

Not long after, he met Ria. As they got to know each other, talking for hours on the phone, sharing their lives, it didn't take him long to realize she'd never put up with adultery. Womanizing became a thing of his past. Until he met Jaylyn.

"Jim." Ria's voice echoed down the hallway. "Let's go."

He stole one last look at the trophies. He'd miss the adrenaline rush. The spontaneous meetings. All the sneaking around. But he needed to get over Jaylyn and try to figure out how to make it work with Ria. He needed to grow up. Move on. Work at it. Put in the effort. Take responsibility.

Once he joined Ria in the front hall, they filed out through the front doors and made their way down the street. Ria spoke first, describing her dismay regarding how the detectives stood on the stage, mumbling and bumbling, making fake promises, like they were running for public office.

"They answered a couple of questions," he said.

She looked at him incredulous. "They have no leads, no suspects, no arrests."

"They know what they're doing. It'll come." He hoped it would.

"They won't find the guy," she said. "How much do you want to bet?"

"Not a betting man, Ria. Let them do it." Quickly. The last thing their street needed was a cold case.

Her voice rose. "Can't you get some inside scoop at the

station? From your EMT buddies? For god's sake, Jim, use your contacts. Network. This is our kids' safety were talking about. I mean-"

A full moon slipped out from behind the clouds as she prattled on. He stared at families in their living rooms, squinting at their smart phones or eyes glued to the flat screens. As they passed the park, he heard a clicking sound. Cicadas? Bats? He glanced over his shoulder.

"What?" Ria said.

"Nothing. Go on." Her paranoia was getting to him.

As she continued, there was a faint snap. Leaves crunched. Then a louder snap. A branch? He turned around. The hair on the back of his neck stood up. Someone, or something, was following them. After all her complaints, had Ria been right?

"Are you even listening to me?" she asked.

He raised a finger to his lips.

She threw her arms in the air. "Don't shush me."

After she stormed off down the sidewalk, he retraced his steps to the edge of the park. The air was still, the street silent. He peered into the darkness. Hundred-year-old trees lined the sides. A dark figure clung to a clump of overgrown bushes. All he could see was a mop of dark hair and an oversized t-shirt. His heart leapt into his throat. As he stepped off the sidewalk onto the grass, a man darted from behind the bush and ran into the park.

FIFTEEN
Ria

On Thursday morning Ria stood at the window in her office as Jim walked to the car. Between his storming out on the weekend and the way he'd shushed her on the route home from the community meeting, she wanted to wring his neck. She knew he was hiding something. She was determined to find out what.

After he backed out of the driveway, she sighed with relief. She surveyed the street. It was quiet, empty. It had rained the night before, but now the sun was shining. With the kids already at school, she was happy to have the house to herself. She stretched her legs under the desk. She had a busy day of work ahead. A flurry of post-it notes covered the side of her laptop.

She mulled over the options Marco described for her the day before. The details she required to adjust the image were a little foggy. A brief conversation would clear it up.

"Quick question." Her voice came off a little higher than usual. She cleared her throat. "About the gun, I mean. What type do you want me to use?"

"It doesn't matter," Marco said.

"It matters to the bullets."

"How would I know? A Ruger. A Beretta. A Glock. Use whatever's best for the art. I don't see it as my problem. Trust your judgment."

After she hung up, she tapped her foot on the carpet. *How*

would I know? Please. She didn't buy it for a second.

When she was a child, her father kept a Smith and Wesson in a drawer of the bureau in the living room. She was six years old the night he brought it home.

"That's your last hunting trip," her mother shouted.

"I didn't see her."

"You expect me to believe that?" she spat. "I'm warning you, Wisconsin is done. And that goddamn thing?" Her mother pointed to the gun. "Get it out of the house."

"Relax," her father said. "It's secured. It's not like it's going to kill someone."

During her father's first stint in rehab, she'd snuck downstairs in the middle of the night and pulled the case from the drawer. In the beam of the moonlight, she set it on the table and inserted the tip of a kitchen knife into the lock. She held her breath and wiggled it back and forth. When the lock popped, a shiver ran up her spine. She opened the lid and examined the gun, tracing her fingers along the faint ridges of metal. Lighter than she thought it'd be, the six-inch nickel barrel felt smooth in her hands. She held it in front of her, arms straight out like the men on TV. *Pow, pow,* she mouthed. Then she lifted it to her lips and blew on the top of the barrel. After she returned the case to the drawer, she took the gun upstairs and stuffed it deep in a hole in her mattress.

No one noticed. Only once that year had circumstances forced her to use it. After her mother cut her bangs with fabric shears, she'd waved it under the noses of the kids at school to shut up them up. That evening, the phone rang steadily. Her mother, buried in bed, wallowing, waiting for her father to return, didn't answer. She recalled the feeling in the pit of her stomach when the teacher pulled her out of class the next day to confront her. With her back pressed to the cool tile in the hallway, she'd looked straight into her eyes and denied it. What did the teacher expect? The truth? Ria had kids of her own now. They all lied through their teeth to save their own hides, didn't they?

Ria stacked the post-it notes in a pile. With two other jobs due by the end of the day, the research she'd need to do would have to wait. After she worked through lunch to finish them, two wet lines ran down the sides of her face. She cursed Jim for quashing the idea of installing air conditioning when she'd brought it up in the summer. Of course, he wouldn't consider it. There was no coupon for that.

To stem the midday heat, she went for a walk. On the street, a pair of monarch butterflies floated and dipped over the early fall blooms. So warm so late in the season, she wondered what they were thinking. Fanning her shirt as she passed cars parked along the curb, she slowed at each one and peered inside. Soda cans. Water bottles. Coffee cups, rims stained with lipstick. A cup holder stuffed with coins and bills. A watch? She recalled her trips to Aurora as a teenager, the ability to discreetly pop a lock on a car door. Did she still have the skill? A gray-haired couple, jackets flapping around their waists, pants pulled to their chests, shuffled towards her. Damn. She'd come back later.

In her office, Jim had left a voice mail on her phone. She ignored him. Almost three weeks off her medication, she could feel her insides stirring, new emotions brewing. Dulled the past two decades, the tingling felt unfamiliar, the outbursts eerie. Now those long-forgotten feelings were rushing over her in waves. She wasn't sure what to do with them.

She shifted in her seat. To release them as a child, she'd bit her nails until they bled. As a young teen, she turned to shoplifting. Not long after, she'd given into them. The thought of what she did then made her smile. Across the room, she examined the family picture hanging on the wall, trying to find this different version of herself in the photo. It wasn't in her face. In her eyes. Nor in the way she was standing. What was deep inside her was writhing and twisting, clawing its way out. She was becoming herself again, hidden in the perfect world she constructed. Two lives co-existing. *Welcome back.*

For the next two days, Ria researched online to find everything she could about bullet trajectory to finish the first stage of Marco's job. Bullets don't rise after leaving the barrel. They slow in flight. Made sense. Something about Coriolis drift? She didn't understand it. The link surprised her. The Guinness Book of Records confirmed the longest sniper kill in combat was from nearly twenty-five hundred meters away and the bullet took a hair over six seconds to reach its target.

As she clicked on, she learned no matter the type, velocity, or mass of a bullet, if the target was flesh, the skin collapsed inwards. She thought back to her high school science classes. Pure physics. Had the courses included some of the content she was reading now, maybe she wouldn't have dropped them all. She laid out the stacks of paper she printed and called Marco back.

"What's your preferred directionality?" she asked.

He was quiet at first. "High velocity impact," then he added, "from straight on."

"And the cast of spray?" she said.

More quiet. Ria rapped the phone for attention.

"Small sparse," he said.

She didn't bother to ask about the shape. She already decided on small dots tapered into a teardrop. She ended the call and examined the papers in front of her.

That Marco was something. What had been two days of

research for her, he rattled off the top of his head. She had so many questions. Had he looked down the barrel of a gun? Aimed it at someone's head? Had he pulled the trigger and killed someone? No stranger to organized crime, he'd know how to get it done.

She leaned into the light falling across her desk. After she brought up Marco's photo, she reviewed the palette of colour and compared it to the light in the photo. Long shadows reclined across the grass making it, what? Mid-afternoon? Late-afternoon? She jotted the colorization possibilities on a note pad to double-check the colour image algorithm later. Lost in a train of thought, she heard her phone ring. She didn't recognize the number, but she picked it up anyway. Nothing but air. A few minutes later, the phone rang again. She let it go to voice mail and listened. A pause. More stale air. Whoever it was had not given up. For god's sake, say something. Ten minutes later, it rang again. She twisted in her seat.

"Pixel by Pixel," she said.

Nothing.

"Hello?"

The line went dead. Sweat broke out across her forehead. She scrambled out from behind her desk. In the kitchen, she poured a glass of wine and gulped it down. After she filled it a second time, she sat, sipping. Thinking. Worrying. Who was behind the hang ups? It wasn't the first time she received them. She blocked the numbers as soon as the calls started coming a month ago. But here they were again. Was her past catching up with her?

When the boys burst through the front door, her thoughts turned to what to prepare for supper, which notes required signing and who had what to do for homework. After a quick meal, where the boys talked over each other and she and Jim sat in silence, she returned to her office. He was home now, so he could take care of them.

Outside it was dark save for the streetlamps and the headlights from the cars as they passed. She looked at the time. Nearly eight p.m., and she had another two hours of work ahead of her. It was time for a trial run.

She brought up Marco's right eye. Captivated by its piercing blue brilliance, she magnified it. It was breathtaking. Striking. Something from deep within her stirred. A first glance across the edge of the pillow, his face cast in golden light of the morning sun. She'd heard somewhere eyes were the windows to the soul. They showed feelings. Emotions. Hidden personalities. Secrets. Small signs beyond people's control. Eyes couldn't lie. In a flurry, she marked what she wanted to adjust. She brushed on seven or eight colours from her palette. Merging. Layering. Blending. Gone. Redacted, like her past life. She zoomed out to capture both eyes, studying them one at a time. Eerie alone, together they made perfect sense.

Moonlight poured through the window. Slumped at the computer, she stole another look at the clock. Midnight? Limbs heavy, it was all she could do to keep from passing out on the keyboard. She pinched her cheeks to stay awake. From the corner of her eye, she saw movement. Lurking like an evil shadow. Hairs prickled on the back of her neck. Someone was standing outside the window. There was a glint of metal in his hand. In a jolt, she jumped from her desk. The blurry figure ran across the front lawn to the street. A car started. Circles of light slid across the wall. She ran upstairs and shook Jim awake.

"There's a man outside my office window," she said. "I think he had a knife."

"Is he still there?" He ripped the covers back.

She shook her head. "No, he took off in a car."

"Did you get the license plate?" he asked.

Dammit. She hadn't thought about that. When she didn't respond, Jim flopped back down on the bed.

"That's it?" She couldn't believe it. "You going to lie there?"

He turned to her. "It's one a.m., Ria. He's gone. What do you want me to do?"

"Something! Anything."

He lifted his head off the pillow. "Is the front door locked? Do you want me to come down and double check it?"

She stormed out of the room. What the hell was wrong with him. Of course, he'd imply she hadn't locked up properly. They were both on edge, but she wasn't the crazy one.

SIXTEEN
Ria

Friday morning, Ria's mind was racing, her skin prickling, her stomach rumbling.

She picked up packages, shaking them. One Oreo cookie left in the row. Less than a dozen almond halves slid around the bottom of a tin. Four wrapped candies sat beside a crumpled bag, a handful of crushed ketchup chips lining the bottom. She tipped it to her lips and crumbs tumbled down the front of her sweatshirt. While Jim's job kept him in good shape, over the years she'd slipped a little, put on a few pounds. What had Jacob called her? Puffy. She had no desire to join a gym. Puffy was fine.

In the freezer, the fudgsicles were gone and there was less than a mouthful of ice cream left in the tub. Why did Jim and the boys do this? She'd asked them a million times not to. Enough was enough.

She shrugged on her yellow rain jacket, went to the driveway, and roared down the street. As she rounded a corner, she eased off the gas and fell in line with the other cars. Forty felt like a crawl as she approached the stop light in front of her.

The afternoon had clouded over, and a chilly wind whipped off Catskill Creek. To her left, couples strolled hand in hand along the waterfront trail bordering the shoreline, heads down to avoid the gusts. Dogs darted in and out of the bushes while their owners hung back, leashes, and toys and treats in hand, a careful eye upon them.

Rain fell as the light turned green. She flicked on the wipers, passing through the arch into the downtown core. On the corner was a new restaurant. A quick scan of The Bonehouse revealed all clean lines, shiny surfaces. Close to opening, it'd be a great place for a family meal. In the mall parking lot, she wedged into a tiny spot halfway between the bank and the dry cleaners.

She travelled through the grocery store, loading the cart to the brim, and then shoved the bags in the trunk. In front of her car a man, stooped and bent, stood on the pavement. Eyes rimmed red; his outstretched hand unsteady. He was rumpled like her mother was and had the same tobacco smell. Opening her purse, she passed over a ten-dollar bill. The world could be a tough place. Some days, it was difficult to be human.

She stepped around him and two stores over, she pushed open the door at the dry cleaners. Inside, the lady smiled.

"Ria," she said. "What'cha got?"

She placed a bundle of assorted clothes on the counter. When her phone rang, the lady waved her off. She answered the call, listening carefully as a client gave additional instructions for the restoration of his great-grandfather's portrait. Back at the counter, she collected the hangers of their pressed and cleaned clothes for pick up. Attached was a small Ziploc bag.

"That came from the pocket in Jim's pants," the lady told her.

She peered through the plastic. Then she opened the bag and took out a small colourful chip. It was marked Resort World Casino.

"Did you hit the jackpot?" the lady asked.

When did Jim go to the casino? Too tight, he'd never loosen his wallet to gamble. She recalled the recent nights he'd spent with Frank. Had they gone to blow off steam? Her skin crawled.

It was like she didn't know him. His secrecy was driving her nuts. She looked at the amount on the chip. "It's for twenty dollars." No jackpot.

The lady laughed, pointing to Jim shirt. "No one ever wins. It's a good thing there are other ways to get lucky. Your red lipstick? I couldn't get it all out."

The hair on her arms rose. It was like she heard the words in slow motion through a wind tunnel. She stared at the collar. It wasn't a red smudge. It was pink. And there were more than one. Pink smudges. With names like Deep Fuchsia. Bright Rose. Hot Berry. All shades of a younger generation. Her stomach lurched. Dizzy. With a sharp breath, she grabbed the edge of the counter.

"Whoa," the woman said. "Do you want some water?"

"Water?" What she wanted was a bottle of vodka.

With the hangers clutched in her hand, she turned on her heel and walked out. Outside, the rain was steady. She wove through the newly formed puddles on the sidewalk and fumbled with the keys of the car. She threw the dry cleaning on the passenger's side floor and dropped to the seat. Inhale. Exhale.

"Fuck," she yelled.

A wife always knows, her mother once told her.

She slammed her hands on the steering wheel. Her mother was wrong. She had no idea. Not a glimpse. Not an inkling. Not a fucking clue. His lies. She believed every single word.

Shame tingled all over her skin. Her heart felt like a stone. There was a time Jim only wanted her. Not anymore. Ria racked her brain for the signs. Had she known? Maybe she knew something. Or at least suspected it.

Two years ago, Jim joined a gym. She was the one to notice his paunch was a little rounder. They'd dealt with it together, he, begrudgingly once a week with a workout, she, happily controlling his portion size. A year later and twenty pounds lighter, he could wear the same size clothes as the day they'd got married. He'd also upped his visits to the gym to three times a week.

There was another thing. He'd always hated shopping. They used to laugh about the fact he'd rather have a root canal than take a stroll through a mall. Yet recently he'd bought a new jacket and a golf shirt. And those Calvin Klein underwear? "More comfy than tighty whities," he'd told her the first time she found them mixed up in the laundry basket. But who didn't like soft fabrics around their middle? She slammed her palms on the steering wheel again. How stupid was she? She never thought it would happen to her.

She pulled her mother's lighter from her purse, clicked the wheel, and thrust her fingers in the flame. As the skin shriveled and bubbled, the smell of fatty pork on a charcoal grill filled the car. She leaned back on the headrest. The smell was part of the compulsion. It calmed her. After she choked out the glow with her palm, she ripped the skin off with her teeth. Digging out the hand sanitizer, she squeezed it over the backs of her hands and along the length of her fingers. She blew out a slow breath, pausing to revel in the sting. Then she quickly snapped a picture with her phone to add to the file on her laptop.

After she jabbed the key into the ignition, she picked the shirt up off the floor. She stuffed it in a plastic bag she found squished in the glove compartment and tucked the evidence between the seats. Then she pulled the car forward. The wipers slapped hard on the windshield. People scurried along the sidewalk in front of her, shoulders hunched, umbrellas up.

"Out of the way, you frickin' assholes," she shouted.

She edged into the traffic. The main street was a parking lot and she wanted to smash the car in front of her. Instead, she leaned on the horn. Nobody moved. Trapped in a sea of brake lights, her head throbbed, her mouth felt like sandpaper.

When the light turned green, she pushed down on the gas. The car lurched forward, almost rear-ending the sedan in front of her. Red taillights stretched solid as the lines of cars crawled out towards the suburbs. She eased up and followed behind more slowly. A succession of bikes sailed past the car. She cursed the cyclists weaving, bobbing, and wobbling along beside her. Bloody inconveniences. They were lucky she didn't yank the steering wheel to the right, jam her foot on the gas and run them all over. Several cars honked. Twisting the wheel to the left, she veered away from the bike lane.

Leafy streets and cul-de-sacs appeared by the time she turned onto Highland Avenue. She cut to the right, parked, stumbled up to the porch and stabbed the key in the lock.

Inside, the house was dark and empty. Upstairs in the bathroom, she splashed cold water on her face, then she dipped her head directly under the faucet and drank. When she looked in the mirror, her stomach clenched. She clamped a hand over her mouth. Jim's shirt. The lipstick. Pink smears of colour. She hesitated, wanting to ask questions. Wanting to understand. Where else had those lips been? The spit dried in her mouth. She startled, then blinked.

All the pieces snapped together like a jigsaw. She'd been too busy to see it, despite the obvious signs. The emails dashed off before he went to work. The text messages in the middle of the night. The silence. Had Jim even gone to Seattle? Had he been with pink lips instead? Wanting to scratch her fingernails across his face, she was seeing things she didn't want to see, hearing things she didn't want to hear. She shook her head, willing the images and sounds to disappear. They didn't. Don't look, don't look. Her mind a wreck, she squeezed her eyes shut.

Stop. She turned to the toilet and retched.

As she steadied one hand against the wall and grabbed a tissue, she looked closer at her reflection. The pale, blanched face staring back looked ten years older. She winced, rocking lightly on her feet. Leaning in to touch it, her hand trembled. Snot ran from her nose. Concealer collected in the little lines around her bloodless lips, and she saw a looseness to the skin at her jaw. She picked up the pink hand soap on the lip of the sink and hurled it at the mirror. The bottle fell, bounced twice, and slid across the tile before it came to a stop. The walls swum around her and the scream rising in the back of her throat broke free. He had no right to love her one minute and fuck around the next. It wasn't part of the plan.

She ripped the shower curtain open, cranked on the taps and tore off her all clothes. *Fucking bastard*. She wasn't the type of woman who could afford to love, she had too many secrets. But now she'd uncovered his, he'd pay for it. She stood in the shower thinking of revenge until the water ran cold.

SEVENTEEN
Jim

The faint beep of an alarm clock echoed in the hallway. Jim rolled over, folded the pillow in half and stuffed it under his neck. It was seven thirty.

Jacob's routines were etched in stone. His son would have stretched already and now, was likely folding his pajamas in a neat pile to place on the top of his dresser. They were never to be mixed with the clothes in the laundry basket. The weight of the fabric varied by season. They were washed daily because it was the only way to bring back the velvety softness, without which a good night's sleep was impossible. Next, he'd choose pants and a dress shirt from the line hung colour-coded by shade, perfectly spaced, in his closet. Then he'd make the bed with military precision. By the age of five, Jacob had perfected hospital corners and could bounce a quarter off the tightly tucked sheets.

When the hardwood on the stairs creaked, Jim glanced across the pillow. Ria was sound asleep with her bandaged hand resting lightly on her chest. He'd felt awful last night when she explained how a woman accidentally slammed the freezer door on her hand in the grocery store. She'd looked knackered. Her voice had sounded ragged. It was usually his job to do the weekly groceries.

Across the room, the shower curtain lay in a crumpled pile on the side of the tub. The rod was ripped from the wall. After

Ria got home to tend to her hand, she'd slipped on a pool of water he'd left on the bathroom floor after his shower Friday morning. He had no idea what awaited him today, but it was no wonder Ria was out of sorts. He'd fix them both this afternoon. He'd try to be more careful.

Doing his best not to disturb her, he swung his legs off the bed. Along the hallway, the pajamas folded on Jacob's dresser told him all he needed to know. He didn't bother to stop at the top of the stairs. He knew Liam's room would be a scene of chaos behind the closed door. Thick curtains pulled tight. Clothes hanging from open drawers. Damp towels and smelly junk everywhere. For the first time in weeks, Liam would be sleeping soundly. After he'd gone back to work last Wednesday, he'd discreetly touched base with a contact in the Guns and Gangs Unit to ask for information about Dirk. The name was a mystery. It didn't appear in any data base. When he told Liam the guy he'd borrowed money from was all bark and no bite, his son looked so relieved he thought he was going to cry.

Downstairs, Jim poked his head in the kitchen. Jacob was at the counter with a green bowl in front of him. He moved it three inches to the left. Then he moved it an inch to the right, examined it, and moved it back again. Then he stretched out his arms as far as he could each way, leaned forward and stuck his nose to the flat surface. With one hand, he grasped the bowl and placed it on top a smudge. Jim's heart pinched. He wanted to help him line up the items he knew he'd put in the bowl next. Cereal. Milk. Sugar. But Jacob had a system and if part of his ritual was disturbed, he'd insist on starting again.

So what? What kid didn't have quirks? Not long after Jacob could talk, he went up and down the stairs, counting out loud. Food groups on the plate were never to be mixed. He ate fish fingers, chicken fingers, and pizza with utensils. He'd even passed through a short phase obsessed with chairs. He sat in each one he found, anywhere he could find them, to determine two things. Was it padded or hard? Deep or shallow?

"Am I weird, Dad?" Jacob asked him one day.

"No, bud." He ruffled his hair. "You make the world a more interesting place."

Jacob had looked up, smiled the biggest smile. Unfazed, he continued testing chairs. The methodical tally in his notebook spilled on for pages.

"Youth Assist Line. Can I help you?" a sweet voice rang out.

A help line? Jim stepped back from the doorway. Jacob's cell phone was on the table. When the voice asked for his name, Jacob told her.

"I'm Liv," she said. "How are you?"

"Alright, I guess," he said. "Can you hang on one minute?"

Jacob went to the pantry. He plucked out the box of Cheerios and placed it to the left side of the bowl. After he filled the bowl halfway, his body tensed. He looked at the box in his hand. In the pantry, he replaced the Cheerios snug between the container of oatmeal and a box of All Bran. He retrieved the milk from the fridge and put the carton in the same two-inch space on the counter where the cereal box had been a moment before. His shoulders dropped.

"Are you still there?" Liv asked. "Is everything okay?"

"I don't feel right."

"I'm sorry to hear that. Do you want to talk about it?"

Jacob nodded. "I do, but I'm not sure how."

He picked up the milk and poured it slowly around the inside perimeter of the bowl. Careful. Meticulous. No margin for error. There was no chance the prime real estate in the centre could get soggy. If it did, the critical wet to dry crunch ratio would be ruined. Jim held his breath as his son stared into the bowl.

"How about telling what you feel?" Liv asked.

"Give me a moment to think about it."

Jim smiled. Staff on the Youth Assist Line was calm and patient. They'd obviously been well trained. After Jacob returned the carton to the fridge, he carried the bowl in two hands and sat down.

He picked up the spoon. "I wake up the same time each day."

"Most people's bodies get into sort of a sleep routine," Liv said. "It's a natural rhythm, and it's pretty normal."

"I wear soft clothes. I don't like anything with tags."

Liv agreed. "They can be a pain in the ass, huh? They're itchy."

Jacob took a mouthful of cereal. When he followed it with two in quick succession, Jim guessed the wet to dry crunch ratio was perfect.

"Are you having breakfast?" Liv said.

"I'm having cereal," he said. "It's what I always have on Saturday. I eat it in spoonfuls of three."

Jim frowned. Three? This was new. From the time Jacob was small, he said two or four felt right for him. Had he outgrown that? When Liv asked what Jacob's favourite food was and he told her pizza, she confirmed it was one of her favourites, too.

Jacob paused. "I don't eat it for the taste."

"How do you mean?"

"I'm not sure if you know, but-" he took a breath, "it's triangles packed into a circle in a square." There was a longer pause. "The box? Liv, the box is the square."

"You're right," she said. "I hadn't thought about pizza that way before."

Jacob put his spoon down. "Now you know why I'm calling."

"That's okay," she said. "Have you had these feelings for a while?"

"Some of them," Jacob said. "But I have others that are new."

"Do they bother you?" Liv asked.

Jim knew they did because Jacob had told him they did. He was twelve years old. Repulsed by germs. Washed his hands twenty times a day. Only one scoop of ice cream in a bowl, eaten quickly, so it couldn't get soupy. Though he did his homework correctly, his urge to redo it over and over was torture. 'You're a freak,' Liam told him one day, as he straightened the picture frames in the living room. When Liam teased him about what he did, Jacob downplayed it. Tried to keep it secret. But Jim knew the reason Jacob hid them was because he didn't want Liam to be right. Heat rose in his face as he recognized how laughing along with Liam's antics contributed to Jacob's difficulties.

"They don't make sense," he told Liv.

"If they make sense to you, they're fine."

When Jacob sat straight up, Jim gathered he hadn't expected that as an answer. Though he told him the same thing over and over, sometimes hearing it from someone else made it sound more acceptable.

"Do you have anyone you can talk to at school about it?" Liv asked.

"No," Jacob said quickly. "I usually talk to my Mom, but I don't want to worry her. Right now, she's a bit high strung."

Jim sighed. Wasn't that the truth. Once, he'd said the same thing to her when the boys were younger. She'd nearly ripped his head off. While she likened his behaviour to a turtle, she equated hers to a horse. *What did you expect? You didn't marry a fucking circus pony Jim; you married a thoroughbred.*

"It's tough being a parent, so I can understand that," Liv said. "I'm sure your mom is there for you in her own way."

"Usually she is," Jacob said, his voice wobbling. "But since a man on our street was shot, she's way more stressed out than usual. She's locking doors, and looking out the windows, like she thinks someone is after her. Now my parents are fighting a lot, and she's starting to act even weirder."

His stomach tightened. Jacob's anxiety was off the charts. And he was right. Since the shooting, Ria's paranoia was growing. He could see it etched in her face. In the way she held herself, by what she said and how fast she talked. After Liv told Jacob she was there for him and could call or text anytime, Jacob thanked her.

"You can leave now, Dad," he said, without turning around.

Jim's ears burned. What had he done to help? Nothing. He was such an asshole. Too caught up in the affair, he'd missed all of it. He needed to be a better father.

Without a word, he drifted to the living room, wondering whether he should go for a run. He looked out the window. Five days after getting dumped, he still couldn't get Jaylyn out of his mind. It'd be easy to focus on her rather than his imploding house. Familiar with every trail within a five-kilometer radius of the house, it'd do him some good. The sky was dark, the clouds low, so he lay on the couch instead. Fuck, he loved that kid. He loved Liam too, even if he did pull him into some crazy scam. A toilet flushed upstairs. A truck went by outside. Pebbles barked next door. The cushions beside him shifted an inch.

"You okay, bud?" he asked Jacob.

"I was until last night." His voice dropped. "While you were helping Mom rebandage her hand, Liam put on scary movies."

"What? You don't even like them." Either did he.

"He made me watch Nightmare on Elm Street and then halfway, he switched it to Jaws."

Jim shook his head to get rid of the image of Freddy Krueger. "I was sixteen and I couldn't sleep in the dark for months."

"And Jaws?" Jacob grinned. "Is that why you only go up to your ankles in the ocean?"

"Yes. Why'd you watch them?" Jim felt relieved he hadn't seen them, but he was irritated. He needed to talk to Liam again.

"I don't know." Jacob's eyebrows rose. "Liam said if I didn't, he'd tell everyone I'm a wuss."

Jim sighed. Liam was relentless. He'd explained *ad nauseam* how what he found funny, others didn't. The day he emptied the ice cube trays and refilled them with vinegar. The times he barged into the bathroom to rub Jacob's towel on the toilet seat or throw cold water over the shower curtain. Worst was the time he ripped the labels off all the canned goods in the pantry. What was wrong with him? Save for the fender benders he and Frank had as teens, the meanest thing they did was smear Vaseline on the door handles or rearranged the bookshelves. If their parents noticed, they hadn't said so.

"It's not funny." Jacob's voice grew low and somber. "Will you tell him, Dad?"

He promised he would. They went to the kitchen, and he dropped four slices in the toaster. He asked Jacob to pass him the raspberry jam.

"Liam finished it last night."

He swore. It never ended with Liam. In the root cellar, he plucked a jar from the shelf and at the foot of the stairs, he stopped. A crack of light glowed from the far end of the basement. He squinted through the dim. Two legs stuck out of the top of the freezer. The jar slipped from his hand and smashed on the floor. He sprinted across the room and ripped the lid open. Ria turned to him. Her eyes were bulging. Her lips were blue. Her hair was matted to the sides of her head. She appeared unbalanced.

"What the hell are you doing?" he hollered.

She huffed. "What does it look like?"

He stood, frozen to the spot. She was dressed in gray sweatpants, an old t-shirt, no socks. From the dark and distant look in her eyes, what it looked like was she was having a relapse. He was about to say something when she moaned.

"I'm so hot my sweat is sweating," she said.

He put a hand on the wall to steady himself. What a mess. Everything was falling apart. Everything was broken. Jacob's anxiety. Liam's gambling debt, which he needed to deal with. Their marriage. Ria's health. How was he supposed to cope with all this? He turned away before it blossomed into self-pity. He'd have to. It wasn't like he had a choice. At least if Jaylyn hadn't dumped him, he wouldn't have to deal with it alone.

EIGHTEEN
Ria

"Do you need any help?" Jim asked tentatively as he came into the kitchen.

Ria touched a finger to her lips and professed to think. She could hear the worry in his voice. Since he found her headfirst in the freezer earlier, he'd been dancing around her all day. Checking up on her, in her face every moment. Couldn't someone be hot? He was cramping her space. She wanted to be left alone.

He took a step forward. "I thought with your hand-"

She pounded the walnuts on the chopping board with a mallet. He backed off.

"What about the table?" He hesitated. "Can I do that?"

"It's set."

"The front hall bathroom?" he pressed.

"I've cleaned it."

She stepped aside to avoid him. The serving dishes were stacked in a pile. Shoes were lined up on the backdoor mat. All the school bags were tucked into cupboards. The vegetables chopped, the cheese grated, she glanced at the apple pie cooling on the wire rack. Golden brown and flaky, the upper crust lattice was perfect and the juices still bubbling. A bouquet of fresh flowers sat on the table beside it. She pretended not to notice.

When Jim announced his parents and Frank and Rachel would be arriving in less than an hour, she swallowed the acid built up in her throat. How was she going to make it through the evening? She sucked back a glass of merlot, anything to take the edge off when what she wanted was to drink herself into a stupor. It wouldn't take much. She'd been off her medication almost a month. It wasn't like it would clash with the alcohol. She picked up the bottle, a fast-practiced pour.

"Ria." Jim's face darkened. "Don't you think one's enough?"

She put her hand on her hip. The comment was like nails on a chalkboard. Apparently not for him. Should she confront him now? Ask him about the affair? She felt like she was going to explode. Who the hell did he think he was? She picked up the glass and drained it.

She puttered around the kitchen. Behind her, Jim filled a mug of water.

Drip, drip, drip.

Ria glared at the bottom of the sink. After Jim tightened the taps, she pointed to the cast iron pan. When he passed it over, his fingers brushed against hers, burning her skin. She gave him a twisted smile. Red faced, he slunk out of the kitchen.

Finally. She dropped to a chair at table. Her head was spinning. Inhale. Exhale. She sat quietly to rest her mind, then she finished making dinner. When the Stiles family took their seats in the dining room for two hours later, Ria couldn't wait for them to eat and all go home.

"Ria," Grampa said, "You've outdone yourself."

She popped an olive in her mouth and half-smiled. After three glasses of merlot, it was the politest response she could muster. Her mother-in-law commented on Jacob's tie.

"Thank you," he said. "I have six." He picked up, examined, and placed the cutlery back on the table.

"Whadda ya doing?" Liam said as he jammed a roll in his mouth.

"Looking to see if there's something on them."

When Liam started to mumble, Gramma gave him a sharp look. "If we'd known Jacob was dressing up, Grampa and I would've joined him."

Ria's eyes flitted between her in-laws. Both wore velour tracksuits and looked like twins. She shoved her fork in her mouth to stifle a laugh. As Frank sloshed gravy over the tufts of his potatoes, her father-in-law scooped stuffing from his plate.

"What the Sam scratch is this?" he asked.

"Delicious," Frank said.

Rachel agreed. "This alone was worth coming back for. What's in it?"

"Pork, sage, apples and walnuts," Ria responded. She squeezed her sister-in-law's forearm. "So, Rach, how was your trip?"

Rachel drew her arm back. "Once I left Tokyo? Europe was fabulous."

Ria could see she'd had a good time. Rachel's face was glowing. The silk scarf draped around her shoulders looked chic and elegant.

"Is the oven off?" Jacob asked.

She tried to smile. "It is."

For the next fifteen minutes, Ria drifted in and out of the conversation. The unusual warm fall weather, the upcoming election, the condo development going up to the south. As the dining room rotated around her, she nodded and murmured and topped up her glass. Nobody appeared to notice.

Ping.

She stiffened. To her right, the empty serving dishes rested on the sideboard adjacent to a pile of phones. Was it a message for Jim? She felt her face grow hot. If it was, she wondered what it said. *How's family dinner? Wanna meet up after for sex?* A film of sweat collected at the base of her neck. To sit still was to think. She stood up so fast her chair fell back and landed with a thud on the floor.

"The vegetables," she said. "Anyone for seconds?"

She ran out of the room and refilled the dishes in the kitchen. Inhale. Exhale. Who had texted Jim? She wondered what sound it would make if she pulled one of the saucepans from the wrought iron rack above the stove and smacked him. A thud? A crack? Would he yell? She needed to know who texted. It was like an itch she could not stop scratching. It infuriated her. She'd have to confront him. When she returned to the dining room, Rachel was talking about Blockchain. Jim was listening, blowing on his broccoli gratin. He had a string of cheese dangling from the side of his cheek.

"So, it's like PayPal?" he asked.

"It's a digital payment platform," she told him. "But it's faster and more secure."

"It's cheaper to transfer funds," Frank added. "You can make transactions all over the world."

Frank's voice was low and calm. The last time she'd thought of him was at the dry cleaners. With his access to unlimited funds, had he and Jim gone to the casino? She hated her thoughts, her nasty suspicions. Things were not always as they seem. It was possible. As she ate, she let herself feel a little sliver of hope.

"Is Blockchain illegal?" Jim said.

"It's all transparent." Rachel laughed. "There's nothing criminal about it."

"The deep web?" he asked.

"The dark web," she corrected.

"That's what I said."

Rachel exhaled loudly. "No, you didn't."

Ria wanted to smile. Go on. Give it to him.

"They're two different things?" Jim frowned, then poked his knife in the air. "Whatever. It's not like you can hire a hit man."

As Jim wiped the cheese off the side of his mouth with his sleeve, she stabbed a carrot with her fork. The conversation went on. Rachel kept trying to explain the benefits of Blockchain and Jim kept asking her questions. He sounded like an idiot. Ria could barely keep up with them. Dear god, no more. Shoot me now.

She closed her eyes and harnessed every last ounce of energy she could muster so she didn't blurt out something brazen across the table. Anything to shut them up. Who was he sleeping with? Whoever it was, why should he go unscathed? She played the conversation she wanted to have in her head. She ached to say it out loud.

Excuse me. Have you heard Jim is sleeping with someone? she'd say.

Silence. There. That did it.

Who wears Hot Pink, or maybe Metallic Blush lipstick?

Everyone would turn to look at her. She'd lay her hands on the table and smile.

I don't know which, but if we put them side by side, we could play a game. We could all choose our favourite.

Another long, stone-cold silence. Surely, it'd be more interesting than discussing the inner workings of Blockchain.

"More potatoes?" her mother-in-law said.

"What?"

"Are you alright?" she asked her. "You're a little pale."

When Ria refocused, her mother-in-law's face pinched with concern. What tipped her off? Was it her skin? Her eyes? Her hollow cheeks? She held one hand with the other, to keep them from shaking. Ria hadn't slept in twenty-four hours. In fact, she hadn't had a decent night's sleep in six weeks. Her mother-in-law pointed to her bandage and said, "Maybe you should get that checked."

She scraped her chair back and stacked the serving dishes. Her head was spinning. Unsteady on her feet, she hobbled as quickly as she could to the kitchen. As she dumped the dishes haphazardly on the counter, an arm shot out from behind her. Jacob grabbed them before they crashed to the floor.

Ria could feel his eyes upon her. She pinched the bridge of her nose, pushing her anger away, begging him to stay silent. Not to ask any questions. She couldn't control what would come out of her mouth if he did. She didn't need him hanging on to her every word, repeating the string of obscenities she wanted to let rip. As her blood boiled, Jacob rinsed the plates and put them in the dishwasher. Then he folded and refolded the towels squashed up on the edge of the sink.

A minute later, Jim appeared. "Let me help," he said.

She held up her hand to fend him off.

"I can take in the pie," he suggested.

"Don't bother," she told him.

"What's with you two?" Jacob asked, his voice no more than a whisper.

After supper, Ria put on yellow kitchen gloves and swirled her hands in the hot, soapy water. The gravy boat. The glass Pyrex dish. The three-pronged fork. She laid each carefully on the counter and congratulated herself. She'd made it through dinner in one piece. Though she'd had nasty intentions, she reigned them in and there was no second body murdered.

She submerged the roasting pan, then set it on the stove to soak overnight. Still unsure what Jim did, she needed to figure out how to keep this marriage together. Losing control wouldn't help.

Back at the counter, she pulled the plug from the sink. A slick, beige fatty lump stuck in the drain. A sour smell billowed to her nose and turned her stomach. While marriage may mean little to him, it meant everything to her. The flaws in her parent's marriage and her father leaving almost broke her. She knew the scars, the cracks in her heart that couldn't be mended. Her boys required stability. She'd never subject them to the same heartbreak.

As she removed her yellow kitchen gloves, she locked away old memories. She needed to focus on the present. Be sensible. Solve the problem she now faced. Holding this family together was the priority. Her entire identity was built around this marriage. If anyone knew about her past, the whole house of cards would come tumbling down.

NINETEEN
Jim

Jim sauntered down Mrs. Pott's walkway to find Frank and Rachel standing on the sidewalk in front of the house.

"I thought I saw you sneak out," Frank said.

"I dropped a plate of food off for Lucy. She's going strong, but who wants to cook when you're eighty?"

"Who wants to cook at all." Rachel laughed. "I've got to go. We brought two cars." She pecked his cheek, then paused. "Are you okay? Ria looked spaced out tonight."

He didn't need to be reminded. After he found Ria with her head stuck in the basement freezer, they'd gone upstairs to talk. She insisted that she was fine, but he could tell something was off. Then when he asked her if he could assist with the cooking or set the table or clean the bathroom, she refuted his every offer. Her tone was angry, her body language defensive. No clue what had set her off again, he was certain there was another storm brewing on the horizon.

Once Rachel begged off and headed home, Frank stretched his arms over his head, then patted his stomach. Complaining about how much he ate, he asked if Jaylyn could cook like Ria. The question took Jim by surprise.

"About that." He blew out a long breath. "Let's go for a walk."

His brother glanced down the street. "Is she here? Am I going to meet her?"

"There's been a change of plans."

"What?" Frank's eyebrows rose. "The affair's over?"

Jim wouldn't describe what he and Jaylyn had as an affair or even as unconventional or exotic. Those words didn't do it justice. It was unlike anything he'd ever experienced.

After Frank disappeared into the house to get his jacket, Jim thought back to the day they first met. He'd turned from his locker when someone called his name. Who was she?

"I'm Jaylyn." She'd crossed the room, a hand in front of her. "I've been hired full time to assist with HR and provide sensitivity training for the station this summer."

Her hand was soft as warm butter. "That sounds interesting."

"It is," she confirmed, "but sometimes it takes years of work for people to uncover their biases."

He'd looked at her, not sure how to respond. Biases? Years?

She laughed. "Don't worry. I've got a great way to kickstart the process."

He'd asked when she'd arrived in the area. She'd explained she was brought up in Albany and she'd been at the station two days. Two days? She was someone he would've noticed. Why hadn't he bumped into her? Brown eyes the colour of melting chocolate. Long dark lashes.

"If you need any help settling in, let me know," he said. "Do you like Thai?"

"Thai?"

"There's a place down the road. We can go for a bite and I'll give you a few tips on how the station works." *We.* He imagined them lying side-by-side in the sheets together down the line, soaked in sweat. Stop. "Or maybe you want to go on a ride along to a call?"

She cupped a hand to her mouth. He nodded, feeling a

tingle of excitement. Faithful the last seventeen years, he was sick of fighting with Ria. With their marriage strained, he could use a bit of fun. That's all it could be. Ria was so wrapped up in her work, she wouldn't notice anyway. He glanced at his schedule on the desk as Jaylyn tapped the screen of her phone.

"How's a fast dinner tonight?" He gave her his best smile.

"That's kinda short notice." She placed a hand on her hip and batted her eyelids.

He ignored the setback. "Tomorrow maybe."

She smiled brightly. "That works for me."

That works couldn't have come fast enough. Unshaven, in a golf shirt and jeans, he'd arrived at the restaurant a half hour early. At the bar, he took a mouthful of his drink, the warmth radiating up in his cheeks. Another deep swallow loosened the knots in his neck. Then it all started to come back. He knew how the audition worked. He'd been there before. She'd need someone to listen. To understand her. To support the ambition, he knew she had. He'd seen it in her eyes at the station. By helping her, he'd feel needed, too.

When the front door of the restaurant opened, she tossed him a little wave. Dark shiny hair cascading down her back, she brushed by him as she sat down at the bar. He breathed in her scent. She reached across him, finished his drink, and left the empty glass on the coaster. When the bartender came over, she pointed to the back of the restaurant.

"Two, please," she said. "In a booth."

They'd slid into a brown vinyl seat, ordered dinner, and talked comfortably for hours. He hadn't remembered it being this easy. Next came lunch. Followed by a movie. A mid-week stroll by the lake. A blow job in the shadows of a park. Sex. After that, things blurred together. Hiking. A summer wine tour. A baseball game. He remembered it because the Yankees won.

Dinner in the New York City, the casino. The sound of the front door slamming shut yanked him back to the present.

He and Frank strolled past Mrs. Potts' house in silence. As they passed by 142 Highland, Jim noted the yellow police tape was gone. He'd have to remember to tell Ria. For the past week, she'd been going on about it, taking pride in posting all the news on Facebook before anyone else on the street. Frank spoke first, asking him what had happened with Jaylyn.

"I told her I loved her," he said.

"And?"

"I was ready to end it with Ria and move in with her."

"Don't tell me. She bolted." Frank laughed. "Burned."

"Fuck you," he said. "Do you think it's funny?"

"It's a classic. How'd you read it so wrong?"

He jammed his hands in his pockets. "I don't know."

"I'll tell you how," Frank said. "You were thinking with your dick."

Jim picked up the pace. That wasn't him. This was different. Frank was a straight arrow, a straight A student, not a parking or a speeding ticket his whole life. Sometimes his older brother pissed him off. True, initially he was looking for a quick lay, but over time he'd fallen in love with her. He kicked at a stone on the pavement. It shot through the air and pinged off a car. A hand clamped down hard on his shoulder.

"Slow down," Frank said. "This entire thing was a bad idea but I'm on your side."

"It doesn't sound like it."

"I am, but you can't believe this wasn't an affair," he sounded doubtful.

"Are you finished now?" Tired of being lectured, he couldn't believe his older brother saw what he didn't.

They walked along the sidewalk in silence again. They

passed the high school and checked out the new basketball courts that had been erected. The creaking of the branches and rustling of the wind hastened them home. Streetlights shone in front of them, casting a glow on the pavement. Before they crossed the street to the house, Jim turned to his brother. Frank was going to hear what he had to say whether he wanted to or not.

"I have no idea why it works," he said. "But we're good together. We have fun-"

"Had, Jim, had."

He held up a hand. "Jaylyn's smart. She's relaxed. She never rides my ass."

Frank nodded slowly. "Then this is about Ria?"

"No," he shot back. "She's got nothing to do with it. Jaylyn's grateful for any little thing I do, any gift I give her. She appreciates me. She's had a tough life."

Frank smirked. "All twenty-five years of it?"

He ignored the comment. "She grew up in downtown Albany, in a pretty rough spot. Her brother's been in and out of jail. She had an abusive relationship with some guy mixed up in a gang." He shuddered. He didn't want to think about what she'd told him. "But she's resilient. She's beautiful inside and out."

"Have you met her parents?" When he shrugged, his brother said, "Do you think they'd want their daughter dating someone the same age as her father? What about her friends?"

"Not yet," he said. "We were talking about it."

His brother swore. "Listen to yourself. You're in complete denial." When Jim pulled out his phone out of his pocket, Frank scowled. "Don't even think about it."

"I'm not." He was. Could it hurt to call her? They'd talked twice since the break-up. Those brief conversations had gone well. He was sure she wasn't truly done with him. She only needed a reminder of how good they were together.

Frank sighed loudly. "Delete the photos. Don't call. You can't handle it."

He returned his phone to his pocket. A lump rose in his throat. Frank may be right but didn't want to hear it.

"Give your head a shake, Jim. I know Ria's difficult, but you need to straighten yourself out."

Difficult? Is that what Frank thought? It was like living in a reality show. He was dead set against the idea of couples counseling. It wouldn't help.

Frank was relentless. "You think you're the only person on earth with someone who's smart. Who's successful? Look at my wife."

"You can't compare the two of them. Rachel's a keeper."

"She is, but there are days I could keep her somewhere else." His brother walked across the grass to the curb. "Before I go, remind me. Did you want to ask me something about money?"

Jim sat on the curb. He felt defeated. Chin in his hands, he told Frank about Liam and #TheFella's gambling debt. He let it all spill out. How the day they'd told him, he was nearly sick on the floor of the food court. How he'd promised he'd clean their mess up quietly. How he was going talk to whoever this Dirk was before he paid back the money the boys owed. When he finished, Frank was slumped on the curb beside him.

"Holy shit," he mumbled. "Does Ria know about this?"

"She's too stressed out," he said. "There's not a chance in hell I'm telling her."

"Is that because of her hand?" Frank asked.

He didn't want to talk about it. "She's been freaking out for weeks. Ever since that guy was shot on the street. She thinks we've got a prowler. First, she found footsteps in the backyard.

Then it was cigarette butts. Last week it was a man outside the house again."

"Again?" Frank looked straight at him.

"The first time it happened I was away in Seattle."

"Is there someone watching the house?"

Jim shrugged. "Who knows? Since the shooting, everyone's on edge. When we were walking home from the community meeting about it, even I thought there was someone following us."

Frank laughed. "Did the police find out what happened?"

"Only that it's not a case of mistaken identity. They told us the media was jumping at nothing. Anyway, Ria's been in a snit all weekend. She won't talk to me."

Frank ran hand over his face. "Do you think she knows? About the affair, I mean."

"How could she? The only person I told was you-"

TWENTY
Ria

It was nearing ten o'clock when Ria got undressed and nestled under the soft duvet. Given the circumstances, she was amazed how calm she felt. An hour later, the bed shifted. She flipped on the lamp. Jim was staring at her.

"Where were you?" All she could think of was pink lips.

"Out for a walk with Frank."

He smoothed the hair off her face and kissed her on the cheek. She was so surprised at his sudden display of affection, that at first, she hugged him back. Then, she quickly let him go and turned out the lamp. The ambient glow of the streetlight crept in through the slatted blind. Lying there, she could hear him breathing. She needed to know what he was thinking. She rolled over and asked him.

"Right now?" he said. "Nothing."

Adrenaline pumped through her veins. She weighed whether to talk about it now. She weighed whether to talk about it all. What to do? Start small. If he opened up, she'd persist until she got what she wanted.

She turned on the lamp. Stretched out beside him now, the shift that occurred in their relationship became even more apparent. They stared at each other in silence. Though she knew what she wanted to say, her brain was a jumbled mess. She forced herself to focus. "Are you okay?"

He sighed. "I'm tired."

"Me too."

"Then go to sleep."

She caught his forearm and felt the muscles tense as he pulled away. The bed creaked again, and the room went dark. She gritted her teeth and stared at the wall.

It was three a.m. when she slipped from the covers and limped to the bathroom. In the glare of the lights above the sink, she stared into the mirror. Lines were etched into her forehead. Her hair was thin and matted. Her lips were chapped. Neck wattle? She tilted her head back to examine it. Blue-green veins marbled her hands. Sausage arms? Dry patches of skin? Unfamiliar divots and dimples on the sides and the backs of her legs. She used to be in good shape. When had her proportions shifted? The extra layers of fat around her waist, impossible to lose after having Jacob, did nothing to protect her from the cold.

Back in bed, she eyed the lump sleeping beside her. After all the lies, all the information he was withholding, it didn't seem fair. She wanted to smack him with her pillow. What would she say if she did?

When sunlight crept through the blinds, she went over the phone call she'd made before Jim had returned home last night. Only one person could help her make sense of it. Aunt Beth.

After they talked for a few minutes, catching up with bits and pieces of news, she got to the point of the call. Whispering in the kitchen to avoid the boys eavesdropping, she'd outlined the reasons for her suspicion. Her Aunt agreed her reservations were worrisome and surmised if the evidence was accurate, she needed to keep a clear head as she'd likely lose sleep until she found out if her misgivings were true.

"It's too late," Ria'd told her. "I can't think. I can't work. I haven't showered in two days. After cooking family dinner, I don't even want to fry an egg. I want to disappear down a hole somewhere. Anywhere. Lie in the dark and be done with it."

In a gentle voice, her Aunt had talked her down. She'd told her to take a hot shower and to go bed early, then when she was feeling better, to grab a coffee and get out in front of it. Rather than drowning in intuition, she needed to identify the best way to talk to Jim.

It had all made good sense last night. Had it worked? No. She hadn't showered. She hadn't slept a wink. Coffee would only add to her already elevated heartrate, the stress, the complications. Tossing in the sheets, she had no idea how she was going to make it through the next week with the demands of work and the house and the boys. Without knowing for certain, without Aunt Beth.

For four nights in a row, Ria weighed her options. Monday, she considered turning on the light and dangling the pink-smudged shirt off her finger. Too dramatic. A low-key course of action was more his style. It was better to put the casino chip on his night table, so he'd find it when he woke up. Tuesday things shifted. She wanted to rip the sheets off the bed and scream at him. Still unable to sleep, she had all night to listen to him grovel and beg for forgiveness. Wednesday, she panicked. What if she tied him up and drove him to the therapist? Thursday, she had desires. Strong desires to choke him. They were living, swollen and sick, festering under the surface of her skin. She knew strangulation almost always left physical signs. Bruising. Fractures of the hyoid bone. Petechia in the white of the eyes. She pictured her hands wrapped around his neck. Would he wake up if she tried? Would he stop her?

By Friday, she was no further ahead. Exhausted, her mind refused to settle. There were some days Ria wished she was more like her aunt. Calm. Wise. Steadfast. Not her nature, she wondered if she'd grow into it, like cheese or fine wine that gets better with age. The same blood, if it was genetic, why wouldn't she?

Past midnight, she dropped to the bed like a stone. Tears flowed down the sides of her cheeks, creating a wet pool on the pillow. She squeezed her eyes shut and hoped for sleep.

Crumpled in the chair by the window in her office, Ria stared into the light of yet another day. There had to be a way to find out what was going on.

Outside her office door, Jim had left this phone sitting face down on the hall chair. She couldn't resist. His password had always been the same since he bought it, something easy and predictable. She tapped it in, and his home screen lit up. First, she checked his texts. Nothing unusual. His emails presented only ordinary messages; the captain's weekly message, one or two from Frank, a number from the crew, the ones she sent. No voice mails. She scrolled through his contacts, searching through the names. Then set his phone back, careful to position it the way it was, and wiped her sweaty palms on her pants.

Zoom video button rang. She stumbled to her desk.

"Bella," Marco said. "I haven't heard from you in a week."

Had it been that long? Days and nights had twisted and turned together in a fog. Her brain was too muddled to process what he said. She twisted the laptop towards her and peered into the screen. A white wall, a glittering crystal chandelier hung from the ceiling and behind it, a bank of windows. Behind the windows, a blur of green. Where was he? Come on. Step into view.

"Is there a problem?" he asked.

"No," she said. "I've been under the weather."

A shadow appeared on the wall. "You okay, bella? Il orologio-"

She closed her eyes. The words rolled off his tongue like music. Smooth. Flowing. Lyrical. She could listen to his voice all day long. She knew he'd grown up in a questionable family, speaking Italian. She guessed sometimes his past caught up with him. When he paused for a moment, she said, "I'm not sleeping. My whole rhythm's off."

She quickly pulled up an image on the screen.

"I did a dry run of the photo," she said.

His voice softened. "That's what I need to hear. It's looking good, yes?"

"It will be in about another week."

"Then you have until next Friday," he said. "I'll be waiting. And Ria?"

"Yes?"

"Stay in touch." The connection went dead.

TWENTY-ONE
Jim

The pager vibrated on the night table beside him. When Jim reached over and flicked the button on the side, Ria groaned.

"Good morning," he whispered.

"That's a matter of opinion."

After she pulled the covers over her head, he grimaced. They were the first words she'd uttered to him after days of stony silence, ugly looks, and the smacking of frying pans and saucepans. He grabbed his clothes and dressed in the dim of the hallway. Downstairs, the pager screeched to life.

Di-di-di-di-di-di-di

Five seconds of a stiletto of high-pitched chirps felt like an eternity. He hoped Ria hadn't heard it. If she had, he'd hear about it later. As he rushed to the car, the pager crackled again.

Catskill FD Station One, Station Two. Jefferson Heights FD Station One, Two, Hudson FD Station One, Two. Confirmed structure fire, 1754 South Service Line. Time out 5:15 a.m.

Six stations? Did he hear that right? He backed out of the driveway and sped along the quiet streets. At the station, he flung open the door and ran inside. The first one there, he barked into the radio. "Station five awaiting manpower."

He opened his locker door. Pants. Jacket. Helmet. Others rushed in. Within minutes, the driver pulled the pumper to the street. With his captain up front with an iPad, three crew huddled shoulder to shoulder in the back seat. They tore down the road, flashing lights, siren wailing.

"Pumper five responding with five on board," the captain said into the radio.

Jim was directly behind him. "Is it a commercial fire?"

His captain turned. Broad shoulders, a mop of blond hair, an easy smile. He was a natural leader. "Yeah, an auto shop."

"Fully functioning," the driver added.

Jim's heart raced in anticipation. The possibilities to fuel the fire were endless. Cars. Trucks. Machinery. Heavy equipment. Gas lines. Stuffed between him and one of his long-time buddies, two legs were jiggling a mile a minute. A rookie? He turned sideways in his seat to face him.

"Jim."

"Will." His eyes were wide.

"Is this your first call out?"

"No, I attended to a lady who took a fall."

He took a closer look at him, swore under his breath. Physically tough and aware of the rules, with no fire missions under his belt, the rookie had no muscle memory. More problematic was this recruit had seen he and Jaylyn duck out of work together during scheduled duty. What was the chance he'd turn on him?

Pumper four with three on board.

The recruit's face paled. "Why so many stations?"

Jim knew exactly what Will was thinking. Fifteen years had passed, but he could still remember the fear of his first big call. A small wildfire simmered for days before the winds accelerated its growth, driving it straight into a residential area. Embers carried on the gusts took hold of a woodpile, then a deck, then the shingles, transporting it in a full-blown apartment fire. With nearby houses evacuated, the team worked with the local wildland firefighters to battle the flames. When they called for a mandatory evacuation down the street, it had amazed him there was the same number of people running as those who refused to leave.

"We'll stick together." Jim forced a smile. "I've got you."

The rookie didn't smile back. Jim knew Will didn't trust him. Several hundred feet down the road, a massive black smoke plume curled to the sky. As the pumper covered the distance, the captain picked up the radio. His voice was calm and measured.

"Pumper five on scene. One story commercial building. Heavy showing smoke showing from the back. Pump five securing water and will assume command." The captain glanced to the back seat. "While he gets on the pump," he pointed to the driver, "Jim and Will can grab the packs and the cross lay of hose and," he nodded at his colleague, "you head around back with the next pumper in to get water on the fire."

When the truck stopped, Jim tumbled out the back. The smell of metallic sweat, gas and dead rot filled his nostrils. To determine what they were up against, he looked through the glass front of the shop. Six bays were positioned in the middle of the cement floor, their vehicle hoists empty. Air hoses and a waterline hung from a ceiling at least twenty feet high. To the right, a shelf of metal canisters, and beyond it, motorcycles in a corner. Six or seven cars in the space leading to the back. Piles of tires reached halfway to the ceiling nearby, smoke billowing around them.

"Mask up," the captain shouted.

A dozen trucks pulled up to the scene. Hoses snaked across the ground. Men and women ran back and forth, calling out between them. Jim pulled on his self-contained breathing apparatus and stomped his boots on the ground.

"Come on, come on," he said as he waited for the oxygen to flow through.

"The blaze is melting the siding at the back so six teams are taking it from there." The captain pointed to the hose line. "Go, go, go. It's connected."

Jim grabbed the nozzle in his right hand. He shoved his left arm through the hose, swinging the weight over his shoulder. As he advanced, the hose tightened. He dropped a loop. Two more steps. Tighten. He dropped another. Will was on his tail.

"Flake it out," Jim called behind him.

Will scrambled, close on his heels, bending the hose, releasing the kinks on the ground. A few feet from the garage, Jim stopped. He opened the nozzle and checked for water.

"Air's out," Jim said.

He pointed to the door. Will skirted around him and tugged the handle. It didn't budge. He raised an axe over his head. *Crack.* Metal splintered and chain links littered the ground. Jim nudged the door with his boot and stepped inside. He waited for his eyes to adjust to the darkness. As the gloom lifted and shapes formed, he surveyed the shop. A loud pop emanated from deep in the murky shadows. He squinted to the far-left wall. Nearby, spray-paint cans and one-pound tanks lay scattered across a table. Below them, a bench of hand tools. On the floor were a row of white twenty-pound BBQ tanks. His adrenaline surged.

Zzzzzzzzzz. A can of WD-40 flew by his mask.

"The tanks are venting," he yelled to Will.

As soon as his knee hit the cement, he turned the nozzle of the hose to straight stream. He aimed water at the base of the fire, protecting himself and the team behind. Then eerie silence. He held up a hand.

Suddenly, a floor to ceiling sheet of flame exploded. Glass

shattered. A screaming eruption of fumes threw the contents of the garage through the air. Blown on his butt to the floor, he felt something smash his shoulder. Pain radiated down his arm. He threw a jagged piece of pipe aside and staggered to his feet.

"Knock it down, knock it down," the captain yelled.

The crews went into offensive fire attack. Jim stepped toward the intense wall of flame. The first wave of noise swept over him, and heat seared though the layers of his uniform. His head pounded and his vision doubled. For a brief second, he thought of the boys. Of survival. How would Ria cope with them alone? Jacob was increasingly stressed out and Ria didn't even know about Liam's problem. He had to get out of here alive.

As embers and debris rained down, he held the hose tight. Gallons and gallons of water surged through. Only a minute in, the muscles in his arms ached. He couldn't see two feet in front of him. Though he couldn't hear them, he knew from instinct as tunnel vision set in, that the crew was beside him, around him, battling the flames, lurking in his periphery.

Behind him, someone yelled. Jim turned as Will dropped to the ground. Shadows surged forward. He passed a gloved hand the hose, then heaved Will up over his shoulder away from the flames and stumbled outside. He was soaked in sweat, his muscles screaming. Once he found a place to stop, he lay Will down. Slumped by the edge of the pumper, he ripped off his mask and gulped in fresh air.

"You okay?" Will didn't answer, so he gently removed his mask.

Once Will's eyes fluttered open, he sat up slowly and said, "I don't know what happened. I was dizzy, then boom."

"Who knows? The heat? The adrenaline? It had to be a thousand degrees."

Will huddled beside him, staring at the ground. "Fuck, my

first time out and I screw up."

After his breathing slowed, Jim scanned the area. Off to the side, the paramedics were attending to a colleague. "I told you I got you. Don't worry, it happens the best of us."

"Thanks, man. And Jim?" Will caught his eye. "I got your back, too."

An understanding passed between them. Jim pulled Will to his feet, assuring him he'd straightened up. He gave him a slight nod, then passed Will his mask.

For the first time that morning, he took a good look around. More than thirty emergency vehicles were parked haphazardly around the periphery of the containment area. He wiped the sweat from his face, snatched a bottle and emptied it over his head. Will did the same. He grabbed two more and they gulped them down, readying themselves to head back into the flames.

In the dying light of day, they returned knackered to their halls. Jim and the crew worked quickly to clean the hoses, the pumpers, the trucks, the bunker gear. With the equipment returned to the shelves, uniforms in lockers ready for the next call, they converged in the dining room.

"We're lucky the fuel load didn't blow us all to bits today," the captain said as he walked in. "Beers on me tonight at The Bonehouse."

Jim grinned, grateful to be alive. The first thing he thought of was his boys. Grabbing his phone in his locker, he sent them a text. Seconds later, the device pinged. Expecting it to be them, he glanced at the screen: *OMG. Saw the news. The building, the surrounding bush fire. Two hurt, one in hospital. Praying it's not you. J xo*

He hesitated, swallowed hard. Then he typed out a message, read it, and changed several words. As he recalled what he'd told Will earlier about Jaylyn, his finger hovered over delete. Before he could think more about it, he pressed send.

After a quick shower, he pulled up to the restaurant. Saturday night, the place was packed. Before he went in, he called Ria to let her know where he was and what time he'd be home. It was the first cordial conversation they'd had in while. Whistling as he got out of the car, he swung open the front door.

At the bar, the crew had cold beers in hand, as they relived the highs and lows of the call. This was the life. He found an empty stool between Will and the captain.

"That bush fire came out of nowhere today," his boss said.

Jim nodded. "Reminds me I've got to do the raking and eavestroughs at home."

He winced as he reached for the platter of wings on the bar. Could he clear them with the bruise spreading across his shoulder? He thought of the paint peeling around the windows along the side of the house and the upstairs hallway which was five years overdue for a paint job. Before winter, he'd take care of those too. Maybe he'd get Liam and Jacob out there to help. They needed to know how to do those things, in case he wasn't around to do them.

He stared up over Will's shoulder along the bar at the faces of the crew. Women. Men. Young and old. Laughing like a family, tight, yet hanging loose. That was what he wanted at home. How had he lost it all?

He'd always wanted the same things as normal people. Should he throw in the towel and start again with Jaylyn? He knew he could win her over. He'd done it once before. Or try to work it out with Ria? While there were days her excessive energy drove him nuts, he loved her dark eyes, her ease in the kitchen, the way they used to laugh together. She was charming one minute, explosive the next. Her damn shenanigans kept him on his toes. It wasn't boring.

One thing was certain. If he wanted his marriage to endure, he'd have to change. No more lying. No more screwing around. Do what Ria wanted, no questions asked. Either way, it was time for he and Liam to take a drive and visit with Dirk too. He'd avoided it long enough. He turned to the captain.

"Got any news?" he asked.

"About?"

"Demar Robinson." It felt good to finally do what Ria wanted him to do for her all along.

"The deputies and I were chatting about it last week." The captain waved at the bartender and shouted over the noise. "Three more here and give everyone another round of shots." As the crew cheered, the captain turned back to him. "Jesus. I'm getting too old for this shit. Anyway, the investigation's stalled. They don't know what happened. You live nearby?"

"We live on the same street. We're at 124. He was at 142."

"Cheers." The captain passed him a shot glass. "Good thing the shooter didn't mix up the address."

As Jim sucked back the brown liquid, it burned the back of his throat. *Jesus Christ.* He'd never considered it.

TWENTY-TWO
Ria

Ria awoke and felt Jim shift beside her. His hot breath at her face and the clothes strewn across the back of the chair hinted at how much he drank the night before. She turned over, pulled the twisted sheets from around her and flung them to the end of the bed. She couldn't look at him. She didn't trust herself to say anything either. She wanted to kill him.

Stop.

Her mother always warned her to be more careful with words.

They're powerful, she said, and you don't always need to sound so dramatic.

She slipped on her robe and crept out of the bedroom. Downstairs, the house was still. Face pressed to the pane of her office window, the rising sun seared the back of her skull, setting her teeth on edge. She could feel the onset of a migraine and the voices rambling in her head didn't help.

Stop.

She needed to be careful with that, too. There weren't voices talking inside her head, *per se*. It was more like white noise. Like the fuzz on the late-night TV screen. Like the buzz of hydro wires above a summer meadow. Like the sound of the radio stuck between stations. Yes, that was a better explanation. Her mother always said examples were helpful if you wanted to be understood.

She slipped behind her desk and rubbed the lumps at her temples. As she closed her eyes, a crystal-clear image appeared in her mind. Hair cut blunt to her chin, dressed in a bright yellow blouse and green skirt, her mother was standing in the doorway of the living room. Ria pressed her fingers against her eyelids and let out an angry shout.

Her mother called it the parlour. Red velvet curtains hung floor to ceiling. Blue flames rose in the fireplace, a deer head mounted above it. Her father's favourite hard-backed chairs with stiff upholstered seats sat on either side of a table covered with framed black and white photographs. Paintings and murals of dark forests covered the walls. Predators, eyes slit, stared back at her from the undergrowth.

She sized up her seventeen-year-old self, the one called Angel, perched on the edge of the sofa. Arms crossed, second-hand bell-bottomed jeans, red tank top. Long black hair held high in a ponytail. Multi-coloured painted toenails.

Ria's eyes flitted between her mother and Angel. What had they been arguing about that night? Everyday things. Normal stuff. School. But when their squabble turned to her future, things got ugly fast. The sharp crack of her mother's high-heeled shoes echoed as she stepped forward. She braced herself for the impact.

"What the hell's going on in that head of yours, Angel?" her mother had said.

"A lot."

"Good lord, don't give me an opening. There's not chance in hell you're going away to college to study photography. There's a fine line between creative and crazy. Trust me, I know. People think I am."

"Crazy?" Angel had said. "No, they don't."

Ria scoffed. Yes, they did.

"You can't drop math and science in high school because you want to take arts in college." She lit up a smoke, then she gave Angel *the look* Ria knew well. It was the silent one her mother used to tell her she was disappointed with all her choices. It had been seared into her subconscious.

"But I'm good with a camera," Angel had said. "I made a portfolio. Want to see it?"

"I don't."

When Angel turned away to hide the look on her face, her mother tipped her cigarette into the ashtray. Then she'd came around the edge of the coffee table and stopped in front of her, hands on her hips, feet spread apart.

"Let me be frank," she'd said.

Ria's migraine pounded. When had her mother not been? She couldn't recall an occasion when her mother wasn't blunt. She had no filter.

"This fanciful idea of yours? The logistics? The complications? The headache of it all? It's impractical. College? All to stay hidden behind the lens of a camera? What a waste of time and money."

Ria balked. Possessive, controlling, a parent who wouldn't let go. Her mother crossed the room, sank into a chair underneath the deer head, and took a drag of her cigarette. She blew three perfectly formed smoke rings. "You want a taste of the arts? Sign up for community theatre. You've always had a flair for the dramatic."

Ria wanted to reach out and snap her neck. Once her mother had gone as far to explain she wasn't simply fussy, she was bordering on neurotic. She had no clue at the time what it meant, but she guessed from her mother's tone that it wasn't something to aspire to.

"I've got the money," Angel said confidently.

"How?" Her mother snorted. "Did you rob a bank?"

Ria flushed. What her mother hadn't known was that her aunt had offered to pay her tuition.

"You're not going." Her mother's jaw hardened. "Who's going to take care of me? You are. Simple as that."

Angel exploded. "You are crazy. What do you think I've been doing the last ten fucking years?"

"Blame your father for that."

Ria winced. Her mother was always the martyr. If she were alive today, she'd still be playing that card.

Red faced, Angel jumped off the couch. "Ruin your life, but you're not gonna ruin mine. You and this shit hole place? It's killing me."

"Bravo," her mother clapped. "Such a performance."

"You can't tell me what to do. Wait until September. You'll see, I'll be gone."

Her mother raised her painted eyebrows and scoffed. "Please. You don't have the talent."

So few words, but the hurt went deep. How could her mother be so cruel? When Angel ran out of the living room, Ria wanted to follow and comfort her, tell her, if her mother were alive today, she'd have to eat those words. She'd choke on them. Then who'd be laughing?

Years later, her mother's opinions and emotions still hung in the air, like foul smelling smoke rings. Had her mother been right? She'd never been able to turn off her white noise, instead giving in to it as her mother suspected. As an adult, she learned to manage it, but her mother had been wrong about her talent. Her artistic venture had blossomed to full-time work and this year she was pulling in three times what Jim made without stepping a foot outside the house. If her mother could see her now.

Ria could almost hear her mother whispering in her high-pitched, squeaky voice.

I'm literally in bits, she'd have said.

Ria smiled. Her mother was, the old gasbag. She'd been resting peacefully for over three decades in a cemetery in Finger Lakes. Good riddance.

Ria could not settle her churning mind. The house was a disaster. Yesterday, Jim had stayed in bed all day hung over. The laundry basket was overflowing, Liam's floor a tangle of clothes hiding dirty cereal bowls. Downstairs, a thick layer of dust covered the baseboards and half-filled glasses littered the coffee table. Outside, the sun disappeared behind a darkening cloud. She could still see the dust. The whole place needed scouring. She couldn't stand it a minute longer.

Her hat rammed low as she could get it, she grabbed the garden shears from the kitchen drawer and stole out to the back deck. Down the steps. Past the terracotta pots, and across the backyard. She swung open the gate and walked at a brisk pace, shoes crunching on loose leaves and twigs on the ravine path. Twelve houses in, she stopped. Her palms pressed to the fence; she examined the space on the other side. Her neighbour's award-winning garden burst with colour.

The gate groaned and she scanned the house for any sign of life. No movement. Not a window open. She edged forward past the shrubs and crept to the end of the grass. She drew in the sweet smell. The flowerbeds were lush with black-eyed Susans, bright orange nasturtiums, blood red geraniums, chrysanthemums, and sunflowers. With one hand tight around the shears, she snapped at the stems. A mountain of blooms grew at her feet. When she was done, in large strides, she moved quickly to the gate.

Back in the kitchen, she removed the leaves, and created arrangements in complimentary colours. Once she inspected her work, she snapped a few pictures and set overflowing vases in every room through the house. Better. Everything in order, everything in its place.

From the couch in the living room, she sent the photos off to her Aunt. She knew she'd appreciate the artistry.

A few weeks after Ria turned fourteen, Aunt Beth came to visit the house. She recalled the gifts she brought, the lukewarm tea, the long stroll out in the back field. Her mother never joined them, which was fine by her. All she'd done was rage on about her stupid concerns. That the roof leaked. Where her father might be. What on earth they were going to do, on missed opportunities. How she failed to inspire much confidence because she bit her nails, picked at her eyebrows, habits she couldn't break. She'd laughed it off, but she didn't feel like laughing at all.

Alone with her aunt, she reveled in her stories, sharing secrets as they walked hand in hand. Stopping in the middle of nowhere, wrapped in sunshine and silence and the strong arms of her embrace. What her mother called obsessive; her aunt waved away as quirks. Her worries melted away. In that moment, she'd felt cared for, accepted, safe.

Ria went to the root cellar and rummaged through a box of old photos. A straw hat perched on her head, a dark bathing suit wrapped around her girth, Aunt Beth was sitting on the beach. Her purse, her shawl and a small glass bottle lay half-wedged in the sand. Coke? Sprite? Fanta? Behind her, the ocean spread out forever. The picture was faded with age, and Ria wondered if she should restore it. She flipped it over. Mexico, 1976. She was right.

That meant what? She'd have been six years old? Some

recollections of her childhood were sharp. Others she couldn't call to mind. The first day of Kindergarten. Her class trip to Niagara Falls. Grade Eight graduation. All lost. But she remembered the party afterwards. Magical. Fizzy fruit punch. Trays of vegetables and crustless sandwiches. A strobe light spinning from the ceiling and the silver circles of light bouncing across the wood paneling in a classmate's basement. She wore patent shoes that pinched her toes, and an itchy pink dress with sweat stains under the arms. It was the night of her first kiss. Taking care of her mother during high school left little time to hang out with her friends. There were no other kisses, no suitors, preserving that first kiss in a memory still as soft and tender and clear as the night it happened.

She took once last look at her aunt's photo and returned it to the box. A vague recollection filtered of walking along a hallway, doors to each side, the soft give of the carpet beneath her feet. Shadows. A hand. The creaking door. A voice. Distant and garbled, she knew she'd heard it before. Blood. The voice again. She hesitated. Aunt Beth? She struggled to identify it but came up empty. Her mind turned still and silent. Trapped inside her head, she wondered whether remembering things she didn't want to remember was a good idea. She'd forgiven herself. Why worry about things she couldn't change?

TWENTY-THREE
Jim

The screaming woke him. Jim jumped off living room couch and tore down the hall. Rooted to the spot behind her desk in her office, Ria pointed to the floor. There was a large red brick on the carpet. He glanced at the front window.

"Don't move," he yelled.

He ran to the front door, swung it open and scanned the street from the porch. Dark to the right, taillights to the left in the distance. Inside, he bundled Ria in his arms, placed her gently on the living room couch and wrapped a blanket around her shoulders. Footsteps clamored down the stairs behind them.

"What the hell?" Liam yelled. Jacob cowered behind him.

"Call 911," Jim ordered.

"Is Mom hurt?" Jacob said, his voice shaking.

"Honey, no," Ria said. "I'm fine. It's only a scare."

Jim looked her over. Drawn and pale, there wasn't a scratch on her. He smoothed a strand of hair behind her ear.

"Forget 911," he said, "I'll get hold of the detectives."

He left Ria with the boys and made the call. Twenty minutes later, Detective Singh and Detective Li stood at the front door. After he told them what happened, they entered Ria's office. They bagged and tagged the brick, took pictures and joined them in the living room. Detective Singh opened a notebook.

"Let's start with a few questions," he said, pulling out a

pencil he had tucked behind his ear. "Can you think of anyone who wants to hurt you or your family?"

Jim shook his head.

"What about you, Ria?" He tapped his pencil on the page.

"No."

"What about a grudge?" Detective Singh said. Tap, tap.

"A grudge?" he said.

"Neighbours. Family. Your social circle. Maybe a colleague at work."

Jim swallowed. "I don't think so." A message about Liam's debt?

He glanced at Ria. She was chewing a fingernail, staring out the window with glazed eyes. Jacob was perched on the chair beside her, his hands clenched hard on his knees.

"What are you going to do?" his son asked.

"Open an investigation."

"When?" he said curtly. "How long does it take?"

Detective Li explained all the details. They'd open a file with the date, time, and location of the incident. They'd fill out a form describing the account and how they'd add any evidence they collected.

"What about fingerprints off the brick?" Jacob asked.

Detective Li pulled a notebook from her pocket and thumbed through the pages.

"Do you watch CSI?" Jacob nodded. "Then you'll know friction ridge detail is tough."

"How about using forensic light?" he said.

Detective Singh looked up. "How do you know about that?"

Liam rolled his eyes. "Welcome to our life."

"The library," Jacob told him, annoyed. "It's basic investigative procedure. It increases the chance fingerprints are detected on textured surfaces. Plastic bags, foil, glossy magazines. Paper stuff."

Detective Li smiled. "You want to be a police officer?"

Jacob huffed. "No. Why would you think that?" As Liam laughed, he went on to suggest they collect door cam footage from the neighbours. "And pictures. See?" He passed them his phone. "I took these from the porch. To the left, straight out front, down the street to the right. It's important to be prepared for emergencies."

Detective Li took Jacob's phone, looked at it and handed it back. "Thank you." She turned to Jim. "Have you seen anything odd recently?"

"You mean strange?"

Detective Li nodded. "Suspicious"

Ria spoke up. "I found footprints in the backyard and cigarette butts by the fence." She paused. "But we don't know if they're Jim's."

Detective Li cocked her head. "How would you not know?"

"They're not." He'd already gone through this with Ria once, but he wondered whether he should have dismissed her so abruptly.

Ria talked over him. "And someone was prowling around the house too."

Lines appeared on Detective Li's forehead. "When was that?"

"Two weeks ago, when I was working late," Ria said. "I saw him outside my office window. I'm pretty sure he had a knife."

"What did your husband say when you told him?"

"To lock the door."

Jim cringed. When Detective Li turned to him, he caught the look on her face. She must have thought he was the most pathetic husband in the world. Or an idiot.

"Do you have something to add?" she prompted.

"I might," he told her.

"From that same night?"

"No," he said. "From after the community meeting."

"You were there? At the school?"

He nodded. "I got the feeling someone was following us home."

"What?" Ria's jaw tightened. "Why didn't you say something?"

When the detectives looked at him again, he sighed. He didn't want to relive it, but he had no choice. "I tried to afterwards on the sidewalk. Remember?"

"So between the cigarette butts and the footsteps, which may or may not be Jim's," Detective Li looked up, "the person at the office window, who may have had a knife," she kept reading from her notes, "and the feeling you were being followed, you didn't think to call us?"

Jim opened his mouth, but he had no idea what to say. He was pissed off that he hadn't seen the obvious. But with Ria off her medication, his breakup with Jaylyn, the nagging worry about how to best deal with Liam's gambling debt, he hadn't connected it all. His stomach tightened. Had Ria been right?

"Someone was murdered on this street," Detective Li said slowly. "Shot dead. You need to be more vigilant."

He'd had enough. "Us? Whose fault is it this guy's still walking around? We wouldn't have to be vigilant if you caught him."

"Or gave us any fucking information about it at all," Ria added.

"We're working every angle." Detective Singh said. "You got someone to deal with the front window?"

Jim ran his fingers along his forehead. Did he? He'd had to deal with hundreds of crime scenes before with his brothers in blue, yet not one in his home.

"Board it up for now. Hopefully, they can get out tomorrow. If not," he smiled, "you're ready for Halloween next week."

When Ria's eye's widened, Jim wasn't sure whether she was going to scream at him or throttle him. After the detectives got to their feet, Detective Li pulled a card from her wallet and dropped it on the table.

"We'll find who did this," she said.

Ria snorted. "Right. Like you found the guy who killed our neighbour?"

After the detectives left, they sat side-by-side on the living room couch. Ria crossed her arms over her chest, then turned to him annoyed. "Do you believe me now?"

He nodded. He did.

"I'm scared, Jim. For the kids."

He squeezed her arm. "It's okay," he told her. But he wasn't sure if it was.

Jim removed his jacket and hung it up on the peg in the station changeroom. Three calls to return, emails to answer, and he had a report due by the end of the day. At his desk, he opened a file to review the paperwork. The words all blurred together. He glanced at the clock and tossed it on the pile.

Last night as he boarded up the window, Ria asked him what they were going to do. He knew what she wanted him to say, but he still didn't want to move. They'd sunk a bundle into the last round of renovations. Once the boys grew up the house would be too big for the two of them anyway.

That morning, a new window in place, a deadbolt installed, a house alarm ordered, one comment she'd made left him unsettled.

"What kind of asshole throws a brick through a window?

It's like a message, you know. Something personal."

He picked up a pen and doodled. As a firefighter, he saw all sides of life. Calls took them where they were needed. Fires of course, but also heart attacks. Cats in trees. Domestic disputes. Drug overdoses. Problems didn't discriminate between race, age, religion, or postal code. Upon occasion, they got up close to some sketchy criminal activity. Tow truck fires and house bombs. He wondered if Liam's gambling debt was the reason for what had been going on the last few weeks. The mess #TheFellas were in would've started in September—right after the boys were settled into school. Had the footsteps and the cigarette butts showed up after that? The prowler and the brick through the window had. Was Ria right again?

It occurred to him it may be a good idea to share this information with the detectives. As he put the pen down, sweat gathered in the small of his back. If he did, the four boys could end up charged, their futures ruined. For one stupid mistake, he wouldn't risk it. He had to stop putting it off and visit with Dirk this weekend. It needed sorting out.

That damn report was waiting. He needed to refocus. Neck deep in paperwork, his phone skittered across the desk. When he checked the screen, there was only one text.

The message: *Leave her alone.*

He stiffened. No name, no number. But he knew what it meant. Jaxon. Had he intercepted the voice mail left for Jaylyn after the fire? Thrown the brick? Or was this simply a coincidence? A warning to stay away from his sister.

He recalled what Jaylyn had told him about Jaxon. They were inseparable as kids, but their relationship ended abruptly in middle school after the teachers found a gun in his locker and expelled him. With ample time to hang out with new friends, he'd drifted in and out of the house and spent a few months in juvenile detention. While she went to college, he served three years in an adult facility. What her parents must have thought of the two of them. Nature? Nurture?

He closed his office door and read it again. From the get-go, Frank had been skeptical about Jaylyn's family. The timing was right. Jaxon had got out at the end of August, before their neighbour was murdered. Beads of sweat broke out across his forehead. Was his brother correct? Then he remembered what the Chief casually said to him at The Bonehouse. *Good thing the shooter didn't mix up the address.*

His stomach lurched and he heaved into the garbage can. On his knees, he dry-wretched fumes until he was gasping for air, then he rolled over on his side and collapsed. Had he brought this on? Was he responsible? Had he put his family in danger? One thing for sure, this wasn't only about some neighbour now. This was aimed at him, at his family. If the cops started looking for suspects, would they uncover his relationship with Jaylyn? Maybe it was time to come clean with Ria about what he'd done. The consequences filled him with dread. Eyes closed; he blew out a long breath. He couldn't do it. He might not see her again, anyway. Best let sleeping dogs lie.

TWENTY-FOUR
Ria

Someone pounded on the front door. Ria squinted at her calendar on her desk. Friday. 12:30 p.m. She wasn't expecting anyone. The pounding continued. She crept to the window. A man she'd never seen before stood on the porch. With no progress reported about the shooting and the brick that was thrown through her office window, she debated whether to open the door.

She glanced at the street. Who, how, why, what was happening in this neighbourhood? There were so many possibilities her mind spun. It was clear as day the police were either not doing their job or had nothing yet to go on. In the front hall, she turned off the alarm and gripped the door handle. Open it? Yes, no, yes, no, yes, no. She peered through the pane and saw an envelope in the man's hand. At his feet, there was a large box.

"Can I help you?" she said, in a tentative voice.

The man held out the envelope. He was younger than their regular delivery person. Taller. Clean shaven. Dark hair, deep set black eyes. He wasn't just the best-looking man she'd ever seen; he was the best-looking man she'd ever seen, period. For a second, she wanted to pull him inside and jump his bones in the hallway. It would make her feel better. It would serve Jim right.

"Need a signature?" she asked.

He smiled. "No, Ma'am."

Ma'am? Every salty thought brewing inside her head evaporated. Was she the same age as his mother, or something? It wasn't like she was dead. She took the envelope, picked up the box and slammed the door in his face.

In her office, she opened the envelope. Five thick brown bundles of one hundred-dollar bills spilled across her desk. She picked one up. Fanned it. Held it up to her nose. Sniffed. Musky ink. A hint of fruit? When the phone rang, Marco asked if the money had arrived and whether she'd opened the box.

"Not yet," she said. "What's in it?"

"Something to cheer you up," he replied. "You're not the first person with problems on the home front."

Her eyes narrowed. "What the hell do you know about that?"

"My investments are important to me." He drew on his cigarette. "Not now, bella, but one day we'll talk."

Her arms prickled. Was Marco giving her an opening? If he was, she was going to take it. There was so much she wanted to ask. How he came into doing what he did. How he managed it emotionally. She hoped he'd tell her in Italian how they handled disloyal soldiers. Did they warn them? Maim them? Kill them? Did he order it or do the deed himself? After he hung up, she found the knife she'd stashed in her desk drawer. In one quick motion, she sliced the blade through the top of the box.

"Holy crap."

She picked each item up. A beaded Chanel purse. A black Balenciaga handbag. A health watch. She thought of her therapist. Perfume, three scarves, two sweaters. A little black dress. Marco must remember her this way, always at her best. Fanning a hand in front of her, she examined the labels. Gucci. Dolce & Gabbana. Versace. Like Rachel's, they weren't knockoffs.

She lugged the box upstairs. In her bedroom, she slipped on the silky, black dress. She ran her fingers along the fabric, imagining Marco's hands upon her, his voice low in her ear. The smell of cigarette smoke. She studied the shoes scattered on the floor of the closet. Flat and dark with thick, solid soles. Sensible, like footwear nurses wore to reduce the noise in a hospital. Not one heel. Not a chunky one, not a come-fuck-me one in the lot. What the hell had happened to her? Was she eighty years old? Afraid to slip and fall?

She flicked through her clothes. Beige linen pants. A modest knee length tweed skirt. White, cream, and camel blouses. The two black mock turtleneck sweaters she stole from Eddie Bauer. She thought of the neighbourhood clique. The tooth whitening, the prolonged tans, the waxing god knows where. It wasn't like she didn't have standards. Every woman did. But she dressed to blend in, not to look like a trophy wife.

In a fury, she ripped everything from the hangers. Then she scrounged through her dresser, plucking out old sweaters and stretched cardigans. She bundled up the pile in her arms, and downstairs, she tossed it all in the garbage. She spritzed a little perfume on her wrists and went back to work.

Later that night when she was reading in bed, she could feel Jim's eyes upon her. Sick of all the questions firing around in her head, she decided to ask him to go for a walk. To confront him. If she chickened out, at least it was exercise. When he propped himself up on his elbow, a sourness settled into her stomach. Before she could warn him not to dare say whatever he was about to, he spoke first, asking if she wanted to do something on Saturday.

"Like?" she said.

"How's the waterfront trail, then supper?"

Perfect. She'd ask him then. "Let's try the new place. The

Bonehouse."

"Sold."

After he lay back down, she put her book on the table. Before she shut off the light, all she saw was a lump nestled in the sheets, breathing deeply. She prayed he slept well, because if he'd done what she suspected, those breaths would be some of his last.

Ria stood beside Jim inside the front door of The Bonehouse. Music was pumping from the bar to the right and the restaurant was straight ahead. The hostess slipped through the crowd to a stack of laminated menus in a corner. After she tucked two under her arm, she weaved back through the sea of bodies to the reception desk and Ria and Jim followed her to the back of the restaurant. As Jim squeezed into a seat, Ria unwrapped the scarf from around her neck.

"That was invigorating," she said.

It wasn't. She knew it. He knew it. Their walk along the waterfront trail had been like a death march. She shook out her hair and slipped into a seat. He gave her a small, tentative smile. Was he gauging her temperature?

"We should do it again," he said. "I wasn't sure we'd remember how, without the boys." He laughed.

If he was trying to lighten the mood, he failed. She snapped open a menu and pretended to examine the mains.

"How was your day?" she asked.

"Good."

Of course, it was. He'd spent most of it with Liam. Popped by the station. Gone out for lunch. God knows what else they'd done.

"And work?" she said. "That new course you were asked to look into?"

The server appeared and introduced himself. He ran through the specials and Ria chose for them both. The server tapped the order into a tablet and wandered in the direction of the bar.

"This course. What is it?"

"It's focused on ship fire training."

As he explained a bit about it, she folded her menu and placed it on the table. Let him talk. Don't say anything. The server returned and put two beers on the table. Jim picked up his glass and took a slurp.

"There's a couple companies that offer it," he said, "but some of the modules are online. It's complicated and the training would be better if it was done real life." He waved a hand dismissively. "It's ridiculous."

She raised her eyebrows. Must be nice to feel so assured. Smug was the word that came to mind. She took a long slow mouthful of Mill Street Organic. Let it linger in her throat. It had a refreshing taste. A smooth, clean finish.

She half-listened as he went on to explain.

"These companies," she said, losing patience. "Are they in New York City?"

When he shook his head, she leaned back in her chair. Was that how he was playing this? She wasn't putting up with the answer. She flashed him a half grin as he took another slurp.

"What?" he said.

"I wouldn't have guessed that."

"What's the difference?"

"Details, Jim. Details matter."

He put the mug on the table. A frown flickered across his face. Their knees brushed up against each other underneath the table, and she felt him pull his back. Before the argument could escalate, the server reappeared and put a large two-pound basket of barbeque wings between them.

"Medium," he confirmed.

After he placed a pile of wet wipes beside the plate, Ria picked up a wing and blew on it. They might as well have been suicide. She didn't care.

"Have you been to the city lately?" she asked sweetly.

He took a wing from the plate and looked at the ceiling. She wondered what memories he was reliving.

"Not that I recall," he said.

"Try and think back. How about in September?"

He sighed heavily. "Want to check my calendar?"

Ria looked around to see if anyone was listening. If they could hear, they showed no sign. She put the wing on the side of the plate and licked her fingers. Struck by a certainty so strong, she sat straight up to make sure she had his full attention.

"Are you having an affair?"

"No."

Quick denial. Too quick. She wasn't buying it. She sat stone-faced and crossed her arms over her chest. Jim raised his glass to take a sip but gulped too much. He grabbed a serviette and dabbed at his face.

She dug into her purse and pulled out the plastic bag. She threw his shirt and the casino chip across the table. The couples on either side of them didn't move. Didn't blink. They'd heard part of the conversation. While their eyes were glued to the big screen, their ears were perked. The rosiness had drained from Jim's cheeks. He sat silent. Studied what lay in front of him. Had the contents triggered his memory? She wondered if he felt panicked or if his thoughts were crystal clear.

"I'm not having an affair," he repeated.

His sulky look wasn't convincing. His wounded integrity

didn't fool her either. Something was off. The words pricked her mind. Verb tense was critical. She clenched her fists under the table and lowered her voice.

"*Were* you?"

His hands trembled. He didn't deny it. The same dread she felt the day she stumbled out of the dry cleaners seeped back into her lungs. The gap between suspecting and knowing disappeared. Her throat thickened. She glared across the table.

"Who?"

He shrugged but wouldn't meet her eyes.

"Who?" she repeated.

"Someone I met at work."

As he did his best to conceal his emotion, a bitter taste filled her mouth. He wasn't saying anything she hadn't already guessed. She knew because two weeks ago, she searched the station's Facebook page, scrolled through the images, and catalogued the staff to consider the options. It was as if he read her mind.

"She's gone," he said softly.

"You were dumped?" She wasn't sure whether to cry or to laugh.

"No." He frowned. "She was part of the HR contract team doing training at the station and asked for a transfer."

Ria sucked cool air in through her teeth. A contract? Temporary? A first job. She glanced around the restaurant and jammed her hands under her thighs. When she opened her mouth, her voice was so strained she had to work hard to speak.

"She was a college student?"

Jim winced. "She graduated."

Her blood boiled. "You must be so proud! She graduated! Did you pay her tuition? Pay her bills? Were you her fucking sugar daddy?"

"It wasn't like that."

His faced reddened and he stared at the bones on the plate. Low mumbling followed. Ria leaned forward, straining to hear.

"Speak up, you cradle robber," she hissed. "Tell me. Does this thing have a name?"

"Ria, please." He shifted in his seat.

"Don't tell me it doesn't matter."

"Jaylyn Hill."

She heard it but didn't repeat it. "That's not a fucking name. Has she been tested?"

"Tested?" His eyes narrowed. "For what?"

"VD. Gonorrhea. I hear syphilis is on the rise." She jabbed a finger at him and listed off every other sexually transmitted disease she could think of. "God knows what else. Have you?" When he extended his arms across the table, she smacked his hands away. She backed out of reach. "Don't you dare touch me. If we weren't here, right now, in front of all these people, I'd wring your fucking neck."

"It was a mistake. I never meant for anything like this to happen."

"That's what you call it? A mistake?"

"You know what I meant."

"No Jim, I don't."

When she thrust her legs out, the table rocked sideways. The basket of wings tipped over, spilling across the table. A glass rolled along the wood, teetered on the edge, then fell and shattered on the ground. The pub went silent. She fumbled around the folds of her purse for her phone. When she found it, she pressed her finger to the app to call a ride share.

"I'm sorry," he mumbled. "I messed up."

"That's all you've got? An apology?" She couldn't believe it. "You piece of shit. You're not sorry. Look at you." She leaned across the table and slapped him across the face. He gasped, stood and stepped backwards, a palm to his cheek. Her phone buzzed in her hand.

"Ria," he said, eyes to the ground.

"Fuck you!" she shouted.

She jumped up and kicked the chair out from under him. It spun across the space between the tables, slammed into the wall and toppled over. Jim's face paled. Without waiting for a reply, she marched out of the pub.

TWENTY-FIVE
Jim

Jim picked up the blanket off the living room couch Sunday morning. He folded it and tucked it on the end of the coffee table. When he turned around, Ria was standing in the doorway. Her face was dead calm.

"Sleep well?"

He didn't respond.

Her eyes bore into him. "Get used to it." When the doorbell rang, her body tensed. "Are you expecting someone?"

He stepped around her and squinted at the two dark shadows on the other side of the glass. He opened the door. Detective Singh and Detective Li were on the porch.

"Good morning," Detective Li said. "Is this a good time to come in?"

It wasn't. Ria was beyond pissed off, his bladder was full, and his back was aching from being cramped on a six-foot pin cushion all night. He'd also promised Liam that today they'd deal with Dirk. The timing couldn't have been worse.

"We won't be long," Detective Singh said. "Five minutes at most."

Did he have a choice? He let them in, then followed them down the hall to the living room. They settled side by side on the couch. Ria was folded into a chair and looked like she'd rather be anywhere else.

"We have video we want you to look at," Detective Li said.

"It's door cam footage from one of your neighbours." She pulled a laptop from her bag and laid it on the coffee table. The blanket was gone. Where did Ria put it? She tapped at the keys and then patted the couch. "It'd be easier to see it if you're both over here."

Ria didn't move. He pushed himself up from the chair and thrust out his hand. Detective Li shrugged and passed him the laptop. Back in his seat, he balanced it on his knees. Ria rose from her chair and stood behind him, her hands on his shoulders, her nails sharp stabbing through his shirt. When she leaned forward, her breath stunk.

"What do I press?" he said.

Detective Singh got up and pointed. "That box."

He clicked the file and Highland Avenue came to life. An SUV pulled out of a driveway, cars passed both ways, and a small black dog ran across a lawn. Then a car pulled up the street, slow and easy, past the bicycles, the scooters, the tricycles, the basketball hoops. It passed 132, 130, 128 and stopped at 126. A man got out and walked into view. He glanced left and right, then tugged at the rim of his baseball cap and crossed to the other side. Detective Singh paused the image. The man on the screen was average height, the cap pulled tight to his head. A grey t-shirt, blue jeans.

"Recognize that guy?" he said.

Jim shook his head. "I can't see his face."

"Ria?"

"Nope."

Detective Singh pressed the keys. "Watch the way he walks."

Jim peered at the picture. Not fast, not slow. Straight ahead. Step-by-step. The man walked like everybody else did. What was he supposed to see?

"Who is he?" he asked.

"He was on the street the night your window was smashed."

"He did it?" he said.

"We wanted to see if he rang any bells."

"If you've seen him around," Detective Li added.

Jacob poked his head in the doorway. "Can I see it?"

When Detective Li nodded, Jim passed him the laptop. Jacob held it close to his face and examined the screen. He turned it to the left. He turned it to the right. Then he took his phone out of his pocket and snapped a picture.

"Whoa," Detective Li said. "You can't do that. Delete it. It's police property. Evidence in an investigation."

Before she insisted even more, Jacob quickly slipped his phone in his pocket and passed her the laptop. "I've never seen him."

Jim asked the detectives about the murder down the street, but they had no concrete answers. No updates. After they packed up and left, he followed Ria to the kitchen. He day had barely begun, and he was already exhausted. When she put a pod of coffee in the machine, he suggested they make a full pot. She didn't acknowledge his comment. Since the mess of their lives was all his fault, it was to be expected. Less than twenty minutes until he had to leave with Liam, he'd pick up a cup downtown. He opened a drawer, pulled out the cloth bags and sorted the coupons.

"That video," Ria said coldly. "Is it a friend of yours?"

"Pardon me?"

"Apparently you have new ones."

"Jesus, Ria." He shoved the coupons in his pocket and turned around to face her. "I said it last night. I'll say it again. I'm sorry I messed up."

Ria's chest rose and fell as she took short breaths. Her

throat reddened and colour spread up her cheeks.

"I hurt you," he said. "I know I did. I'll say it a hundred times if you want me-"

Hot liquid splashed across his face. He gasped. His eyes stung; his skin burned. Then something smacked him straight in the forehead.

When he opened his eyes, there was a cup on its side on the floor. Then she leaned in, inches from his ear.

"Trust me. If I'd wanted to, I could've really hurt you. Get out before I change my mind."

After picking up a coffee, Jim edged the car onto the highway. He turned up the radio. A foot to the gas, he passed the oil puddles and garbage dotting the shoulder of the road, then slowed and took the exit ramp for Albany.

"Where do we find this Dirk?" he asked.

"South," Liam told him. "In the older part of town."

He turned left and drove past the railway tracks, through a run-down industrial area surrounded by abandoned commercial structures that had survived the ravages of time. Skeleton trees lined the street. The buildings looked dark and quiet. At a red light, he searched for a street sign. Liam pointed and directed him towards a dead-end street. He pulled into an empty parking lot in front of a building. Five stories, graffiti covering the faded red brick. There was debris scattered across the ground. Tires. Clumps of metal. Old shopping carts. Attached to one side, a rusty fire escape looked ready to fall at the touch of a finger. Jim got out of the car. His palms left sweat stains on the steering wheel.

"Dirk?" he called out.

A rusty door swung open. A slim fellow in his mid-twenties stood there. His round brown eyes darted between them.

"Who's asking?"

Jim took a step forward and extended his hand. The man raised his in the air. The undersides of his arms looked like gnarled tree bark.

"Personal space, dude, back off."

The door swung open again. Three straggly-haired males, testosterone pumping, closed in around him. One dark-haired, one round-faced with deep glassy eyes and one with a rangy beard that was patchy and sparse. Jumpy. Then two girls stepped out. Close to identical, pink lip gloss, so skinny their hipbones jutted out from their skirts. The one with thinly plucked eyebrows and a little green gem in her left nostril waved chipped red nails.

"Hi, Liam."

Liam blushed. The conversation they'd had two days ago resurfaced in his head. Grateful he wasn't looking at his future daughter-in-law, Jim stepped forward again. The smell of weed, sweat and sleep filled his nostrils.

"I'm Jim."

"Dirk." The dark haired one. He was around twenty-five. Lean, oily lips, features hardened beyond his years.

"I understand my son owes you money."

"He does."

"We're here to see how to pay you back."

Dirk stood scratching his chin.

Jim tried again. "You know? To work something out."

"Listening."

His friends started to laugh. Jim's pulse quickened. The back of his shirt was wet, and his ears were hot. When Dirk stepped away from the doorframe, Jim could see a scar not yet healed above his left eyebrow.

"You're no fun old man." Dirk's voice was smooth but tense.

"This money," he said, tightly. "When are you expecting it?"

"Right now."

"Are you kidding me?"

"Why would I do that?" He jutted a finger at Liam. "You don't have to pay it. He does."

Jim's chest tightened. "He's seventeen."

"Then it's ten thousand next time."

Jim's mouth fell open. "That's extortion."

"No, it's interest."

"It's crazy."

"Crazy would be not paying it back."

Dirk's friends snickered. One of them flashed a knife. It was serrated with a curved blade and glistened in the light.

"Take it easy." His voice came out higher than he planned.

Dirk's larger friend moved forward. He had thick arms with scabs and a face full of acne. "You heard the man," he said in a husky voice. "Five now or ten later. Make the choice."

Jim's head spun. "We'll have to come back later."

"You'd better." Dirk dragged on his cigarette. "Or your son here sees a piece."

"We should leave," Liam said quickly.

"I'm not done," Jim said, trying to shush him.

Liam poked him with his foot. "Yeah, Dad, we are."

Jim could hear the panic in his son's voice. He glanced over. Liam's cheeks were flushed, sweat dotted his upper lip. He decided to make a quick exit. Trailing him back to the car, Jim pushed open the passenger door.

"Get in," he said.

"Nice work, Dad."

He shoved Liam into the front seat so hard that his head banged off the dashboard. Then he slammed the door. He walked around the car, got in and fastened his seatbelt. He breathed, held it, and slowly let it out. Through the rear-view mirror, he glimpsed back at the rusty door. They'd all gone back inside.

Jim cranked the engine, gunned the gas, and peeled out of the parking lot. As they approached a stop light, he glanced across the seat. Liam's lip was swollen, and blood dripped from tip of his chin. Jim looked away, overwhelmed with shame. He was no better than Ria. In fact, he was worse. He'd let the situation get the best of him. He pushed all this aside for too long, and now he was taking his frustration out on Liam. The adult here, he should have let it go. He sped along the quiet street and turned onto the highway. The car ride home was silent.

TWENTY-SIX
Ria

Ria stood at the kitchen counter. Her head was pounding. She took slow, steady breaths and poured a cup of coffee. With the boys at school and Jim finally at work, she was relieved to be in the house alone. She didn't have the energy, nor any desire to deal with them right now.

Two days after dinner at The Bonehouse, her nerves were still snapping too close to her skin. She walked a loop between her office and the kitchen over and over, trying to calm down. It was futile. She couldn't do it.

Jaylyn Hill. A bitter taste filled her mouth. She detested the idea of ambiguity. It got in the way of things. She knew what to do.

At her desk, she pulled up Jaylyn on Facebook. It wasn't long before she found what she was looking for. Sinewy and lean, long hair loose and down, nails buffed to a shine. Jaylyn looked so young she could have been a friend of Liam's. She hated her heart-shaped face. Her perfect smile. Her laughing eyes. Her wide full mouth. She wanted to break her slender button nose.

She wondered what the little tramp was like. What people present online is seldom true to real life. She understood that more than anyone. How did Jaylyn talk? Walk? Communicate? Was she conniving? Bitchy? Full of light? Ria visited her friends' pages, studied the photos, and searched for comments Jaylyn might have left on their posts. Heart. Smiley face. All Jaylyn spoke was emoji. She slammed the lid of the laptop.

Outside, a police cruiser drove down the street. She'd noticed them more since the in-group demanded increased security at the community meeting. She wondered where they'd been when the brick came through her office window? The video the detectives had brought over to show them yesterday was useless. The man's face was obscured, the picture grainy.

Yesterday, after Jim got home from doing god knows what with Liam, they'd sat together in her office with the image Jacob had captured on his phone. She knew he hadn't deleted it. Yet no matter how many times or how many ways she enlarged or manipulated it, they'd come up empty. She cursed Jim for his inability to provide any inside information. She doubted he'd even bothered to ask. He'd been too busy fucking his precious schoolgirl. Too busy to meet her demands.

Afterwards, Jim brought up his affair again. Stumbling over his pathetic explanation. Apologizing profusely. Rambling, trying to make amends. She'd turned to the window and refused to look at him. Then he had the gall to accuse her of not listening. But she'd heard him. She'd heard it all. Like her father, a man like him was never going to change.

Her stomach growled. She hadn't eaten since Saturday supper, though she wasn't hungry. She grabbed a cup of coffee and for the rest of the day, she worked on Marco's photo. She checked blogs describing gunshot wounds and their residual effects. Skimmed law enforcement and court records. Reviewed videos and audio recordings of serial killers on Youtube. Drug users, sex workers, runaways. Deaths that went unnoticed. Deaths that stirred little outrage. She scoured images of strangulations. They were haunting, yet familiar.

It reminded her of the time she'd babysat at one of the big

houses when she was a teen. Amazed by the space, the light and all the food packed in the fridge, she hadn't noticed when one of the kids ran out the back door and fell in the pool. She'd found the little one in the nick of time. But Ria vomited so hard afterward, she had a subconjunctival hemorrhage for weeks. She'd never forgotten how it looked.

She pulled up the photo and went to work. Tearing and destruction of tissue helped produce a permanent round cavity around the eye socket. Laceration on the upper lid. Back splatter of tissue surrounded the entrance wound. Eyeballs hung down two centimeters underneath, bordered by bruised skin. Then she gently brushed on layers of bright red colour across the slivers of the whites where the eyes had once been. She zoomed out and took a look. Not yet satisfied, she continued. By evening, the second proof of the bullet-ridden holes was near perfect.

Then *Grrzzzz*.

She bolted to her feet. The chair toppled behind her. Her eyes darted around the office. To the window. Nothing. She skirted around her desk to pick up the photos scattered across the carpet.

Grrrzzzzz.

The rattling noise was coming from inside the vent.

He's watching you.

She'd been four years old the first time her mother said it. She'd laid in bed deep under the covers and prayed her mother was wrong. "Who's watching me?" she wanted to ask. But before she could, her mother turned out the light and closed her bedroom door. Her heels *click, click, clicked* as she descended the hardwood stairs. She'd trembled all night. How did the man get in the vent? When would the man come out?

For years after, she woke up panicked, convinced she saw glowing eyes. His crooked fingers. A boney hand. A hairy arm, reaching out to find her. But each time she screamed, nothing happened. The man didn't take her away. No one ran to her room to console her. Only Lexie barked.

Her stomach coiled into a tight knot. Her skin hummed, her thoughts whirled. It was like she was reliving the same thing all over again. Who was watching their house? Watching her? The police investigation was hanging by a thread. Nothing new reported about the shooting. No progress. No arrests. Who, how, why? There were so many possibilities. She clenched her fingers together in her lap to stop them from shaking.

It was too late to call her aunt again, so she opened her collections of images. As she clicked through, her breathing slowed. When she brought up the last one, she leaned in and studied it. A hand. Her hand. The creaking door. The voice. Raspy, muffled sounds. A gunshot. Memories seared. Fear gripped her and her breathing turned ragged. Demons and monsters flooded her head, burning hot as coals. They hurt. What had she done? In her chair, she pulled her knees to her chest and rocked back and forth. She'd never felt more alone.

After another restless night, Ria was barely able to concentrate sorting through the requests in her inbox. Some from regulars, others from new customers. Keepers. Considers. Rejects, with a kind, yet firm message. She spent the next couple of days focused on small restorations with big returns. Larger projects to showcase her creativity. She kept her eyes open for an email from Marco but found herself disappointed.

Late Thursday afternoon, she got the call. White walls, the chandelier, the same blur of green behind. She thanked Marco for the package then she flapped a page in the space between them.

"The photo's done," she said.

"You'll send it, yes?"

"Tomorrow. I want to look it over one more time."

A finger appeared. Then the screen went dark. Muffled sounds. Low murmuring. The shuffling of papers. Who was he talking to? One minute passed, then two. She picked at her nails. What was keeping him? A moment later, the screen lightened.

"Sorry about that," Marco said.

"Was that your assistant?"

"No." A click of a lighter.

"Your wife, then?"

A deep drag. "Stella passed."

Her eyes widened before she could stop them. The wife of a mobster? That couldn't be good.

"No, bella. Cancer took her, six years ago. Sometimes life doesn't turn out how you think."

Jim had made sure of that. "I hear you."

"This is what's happened?" Another deep drag. "To you, I mean?"

She slumped in her chair. Images of Jaylyn filled her head from her search online the other day. She didn't want to think about her. But she and Marco had shared something special. It'd be nice to talk to an adult.

"Ahhh," he said, after she told him about Jim's affair with the douchebag at work. "I don't remember you being the forgiving type. So, why don't you strangle him."

She hesitated. It wasn't like she hadn't thought about it.

"I'm kidding," he said. "Strangling someone is intensely personal."

"I'm better with a knife anyway."

"Amateurs lack discipline."

She frowned. "You're saying I'm an amateur?"

"It needs to be one strike. Clean. Efficient. Unemotional.

The uninitiated lose it and hack up their victims."

She gaped. "Says who?"

"You're not the only one watching Netflix."

She laughed out loud. Marco was a smooth liar, and there was so much more about his lifestyle she wanted to know about.

"Back to before," he said. "Don't think about the affair. Think of happy times. You and your husband are together for a reason."

"It's a lot of work."

"Every marriage is."

When Marco asked whether she'd ever had someone on the side, she snorted. "You've remarried?"

"No. Only Stella. How long has it been? The affair, I mean."

"It's over."

"See? Marriage is an unbreakable bond. Forgive him. Nothing to worry about. Take a little trip, do the counselling. He's not a sleazeball. Only cowards leave."

Sleazeball. The word fit. Then she froze. Balked. Leave? Leave her? She hadn't even considered it. She didn't hear another word Marco said. Her father left her. Her mother left her. Jim might try and leave her too, but she'd never let that happen. Whoever Jaylyn was, she was not going to bring down her house. She'd die first. Him too.

TWENTY-SEVEN
Jim

"Get up."

Jim cracked an eye open. Ria stood in front of him. Her lips were curled, and the blanket was in her hand. It was still dark outside, save for a few streaks of dawn. What was she doing up this early? It was Saturday morning. He wanted to sleep in.

"Now."

He scooted upright. In the kitchen, he slunk down the back of a chair. She splayed her hands on the table and leaned towards him. Her eyes were glacial.

"This thing," she said. "It's over, right?"

He nodded.

"You're sure."

He nodded again. "Trust me."

"Trust?" She laughed. "Like you'd know anything about that."

Heat rose in his cheeks. It was an unfortunate choice of words. He raised a hand, his fingers spread an inch apart. "I do, a little." When her face flattened, he retreated. "And I've lost yours."

"That's right," she confirmed. "And now you're going to earn it back."

He grimaced when she told him how. "Couples counselling?"

All he could picture was sitting in a stuffy room talking with a stranger who used the same new age mumble-jumble she did. He'd rather have a root canal. Did he have a choice? Before he could respond, she waved an arm in the air, and said, "Why are you still sitting there? Out of my kitchen."

In the living room, he wrapped the blanket around his shoulders. Friday night's shift had been long, and he hadn't gotten home until after midnight. Although Ria had been in her office and the bed upstairs was empty, he'd curled up in a ball on the couch. He was relieved Ria hadn't set up the counselling for today. He'd made plans to meet Frank at noon to pick up the money Liam and #TheFellas owed Dirk. As he dozed in a chair, footsteps pattered down the stairs. First Jacob's light footfalls at seven-thirty, then Liam's thunder, two hours later.

"Dad." Jacob said. "Let's go. I want to get to the library."

He heaved himself up. He was in desperate need of coffee. His head was pounding, his back cramped. Every movement felt torturous. After he trailed the boys out to the driveway, he swore out loud.

"What happened?" Jacob asked.

"I don't know." He squatted at the side of the car next to a clean, one inch slit in the front tire.

Liam pointed to the back. "That one's flat, too."

When he went around to the other side, he couldn't believe what he saw. Jacob's face turned beet red. Breathe, he told him. Then he ran back into the house.

"All four?" Ria said, after he told her. "That's horrible, honey."

Honey?

She continued to stare at him blankly. "Who would do something like that?"

The dark thoughts crawling through his head appalled him.

She was up most of the night. She was angry enough this morning. His scrotum tightened. She dug through her purse, handed him her car keys, and said, "Take mine."

He hesitated. She couldn't be behind this, could she? Why?

Outside, he slipped behind the wheel. A foul smell filled his nostrils. He spotted a carton of chocolate milk wedged in the cupholder and rolled down the windows. After a stop at the coffee shop, he dropped Liam off at his friend's place and Jacob at the library.

Stopped in the community centre parking lot, he scrounged around Ria's vehicle. Cups and cans and fast-food wrappers and paper towels covered every inch of the floor. In the glove compartment, he located maps, the car's instruction manual, insurance documents, a tire gauge. But no sharp edges. Finding nothing to support his suspicion, he collected all the trash and walked to the street. He jammed the lot in a garbage bin.

A couple blocks down, he dropped by the hardware store to pick up a shovel and a bag of salt for Mrs. Potts. He felt bad about leaving it for so long, again. At least she'd be prepared for the winter now. Outside, the rain fell in torrents. He sprinted to the car and headed across town to meet his brother.

Jim slipped into a booth at the restaurant. When the coffee arrived at the table, he filled a cup to the rim and guzzled it. Last week when he'd called Frank to tell him about the confrontation at The Bonehouse, he'd also told him he and Liam were going to pay a visit to Dirk. With this morning's incident to add to the mix, they'd have a lot to talk about. He was topping up the cup a second time when his brother sauntered between the rows of tables.

"About bloody time," he said, as Frank slid into the seat

across from him.

"You look like shit."

"Thank you."

"You're welcome. I couldn't find parking. What's going on?"

Jim had no idea where to start. He poured his brother a coffee. As he told Frank about his morning, his brother clasped his hands and listened to every word he said. When he finished, Frank's glasses were still fogged, but he was staring intently across the table.

"What are you basing your suspicions on?" he asked.

"Nothing. I have no proof. It's only a hunch."

"If she slashed your tires, holy crap," Frank said. "That's serious anger."

He nodded. He didn't know what else to say. After the waiter came and took their order, Frank put his glasses on the table, then swiveled slowly and removed his coat. Jim stared at him. He did not seem himself.

"What's up with you?"

"I pulled something in my back," Frank said.

"Try sleeping on a couch."

"Go get a massage."

They both laughed. Jim could only imagine the trouble he'd be in if Ria found out he was lying half-naked with someone, anyone's hands all over him right now. He needed to get to the gym to stretch everything out. To burn off his energy. Frank's smile faded into a look of concern.

"What're you going to do?" he asked.

"What can I do? I have to sit and ride this one out."

"For how long?"

"However long it takes."

Frank took a sip of coffee. "Can I help?"

"Thanks, but no." He shrugged. "I don't think anyone can."

The young man in black pants and a white apron brought their plates to the table. As he set them down, Jim looked at his lunch. Soup. Corn beef piled high on rye. A pile of coleslaw. A dill pickle on the side. The smell made him nauseous.

Frank picked up his sandwich. "I'm not saying it's her," he said with his mouth full, "and I'd have a hard time believing if it was. But after everything that's gone on, if it's the worst thing that happens between the two of you, you'll be fine."

Jim sighed. Frank was right. Their marriage had survived a lot. It would survive again. His cream of broccoli soup had formed a thick skin. He dropped a spoon into the middle of the bowl and stirred it around. Frank stopped chewing.

"What?" he said, putting the sandwich down.

"This morning Ria announced we're going to couples counselling."

Frank barked out a laugh. "That oughta be fun."

"A whole fuckin' bundle."

"No, that's what it's gonna cost you. Speaking of which," Frank pulled out an envelope out of his pocket and pushed it across the table. "Ten thousand. It's all there. When are you going to do it?"

"Tomorrow."

"Want me to come?"

Jim shook his head. "I'm good."

Frank lifted his chin and scratched his neck. "Have you considered that between the brick, your prowler, and the slashed tires, that maybe this is all about this gambling debt?"

"You mean because of Liam?" He felt sick.

"I don't know, it's-"

"Come on, Frank. First, it's me. Now it's him."

"Or maybe Ria."

"For fuck's sake" he said, angrily. "Make up your mind."

When his brother glanced around the restaurant, Jim had no idea his voice had been so loud. Frank fell silent.

Sorry," he said. "I shouldn't have snapped. I'm tired."

Frank held his palms up. "I'm only trying to figure it out."

"I don't know what's going on. I need to sleep in a bed. Have a normal family. I need my old life back."

"Which one?" Frank laughed. But then he stopped. "I love you, but what family is normal? I'm not helping either reading into all of this."

"I appreciate it," he said, "and I appreciate you too. It's all been so crazy since the killing on the street. I don't know if all this is connected, somehow."

"That shooting? You hear anything more about it?"

Jim shook his head. He relayed to his brother what the captain had told him at The Bonehouse. When Frank asked whether he'd poked around at the station or with his brothers in blue, he cut him off.

"Of course. I've asked my EMS buddies too. All anyone says is the investigation is still active."

"How about the brick?" Frank asked. "Any follow up?"

"From the police? Crickets. Ria asked Jacob for the picture he took."

"He kept it? It's got to be someone."

"She did whatever she does with her stuff, then we both looked at it. The guy's wearing a ballcap, and his face is turned away. We have no idea who it is."

The clouds were gray and heavy when he left his brother a few minutes later to walk back to the car. The street was cast in pools of light and shadow. He passed by the busy stores and slipped into a laneway between two buildings to take a short cut. Near the end of the alley, a voice rang out. He stopped and eyed two smaller walkways that went off to the left and right.

Nothing.

After he rounded a corner, he combed the space behind him. There was nothing. At the end of the alley, he came to a stoplight and listened again.

Still nothing.

Beads of sweat broke out on his forehead. When the light turned green, he stepped off the curb. That's when he heard it again. A man's voice, from somewhere in the shadows. It was low and quiet. *I know where you live.* His blood went cold. Jim spun around to face him, but the man was already gone.

TWENTY-EIGHT
Ria

Mrs. Potts opened the front door and stared out from behind thick-framed tortoise-shell glasses.

"Ooooh." She smiled. "That's a nice one."

Ria smiled back. The old bat was crazy. It was a shovel. A red scoop, a wooden neck, a metal handle. Jim had dropped it off and then gone to run more errands. Or so he said. Ria couldn't stand to leave it cluttering up her hallway so here she was delivering it to the old busybody in person. She heaved the bag of salt from the front step and swung it over the threshold. When it landed less than an inch from the toes of her fluffy pink slippers, Mrs. Potts scrambled back.

"Sorry Lucy." She glanced up. "I misjudged it."

"Jim wouldn't have," she said, a cool edge to her voice.

Ria held her gaze. The next time Jim could deliver it himself. She was sick of the neighbours fawning all over him. All they saw was his calm, cool exterior, not the cheating bastard with four flat tires that he was.

"Something's not right with you,' Mrs. Pott's pursed her lips. "What do I owe?"

She had no idea, so she made something up. When Pebbles appeared in the hallway and growled, Mrs. Potts waved him off.

"Wait here," Mrs. Potts said.

After she disappeared to the living room, Ria stepped inside. The hall was dark. A mirrored closet door was half open, and a small table was cluttered with junk. Flyers and a couple of dog-eared books. A wooden bowl sat in the centre containing a tarnished pocket watch. She slipped it into her purse. Who knew? One day it might be useful.

On the front step, she glanced at her phone's notifications. Her pulse quickened. *Bella. The photo's perfect. Will call in ten minutes.* Leaving Mrs. Potts' door wide open, she bounded down the steps, crossed the grass and burst inside the house.

In the powder room, she raked her hands through her hair. She'd kept it the same way for years, but the cut last week gave it a more modern shape. She'd asked for auburn highlights, three tones richer than her natural colour. She ran a silver tube around her lips and smiled in the mirror. Thank goodness the boys were out—Jacob at a rare playdate and Liam...well, who knows where? At her desk two minutes later, she answered Marco's call on Zoom.

"Tell me more about your husband. Is he still alive?"

His comment caught her off guard. The knife? She thought back to their last conversation. The gun. The affair. She stifled a laugh.

"Did you use it last weekend?" he asked.

"I can assure you he's still walking and breathing." She recalled the night Jim came home drunk from The Bonehouse after the big fire. If she was going to kill him, she would've done it then.

"I'm glad it all worked out," he said. "You look rosier today."

"That may be a little optimistic."

Monday morning, she'd downloaded Jim's credit card receipts. She opened June's first. Nothing. July was no different. When she skimmed through the next two months, she found what she'd suspected. A three-hundred-dollar charge for a wine bar. Yankee's tickets. An obscene charge from Piper's Jewelry in

September. In a huff, she called the jeweler and the woman who answered described the sale. Distracted all day wondering what that silver necklace looked like, she decided to keep it to herself. Until they got to counselling, it was all best left alone.

"The photo is exquisite." The click of the lighter. "My people will drop off your second payment next week."

"What people?"

"Are you asking who they are?"

"No. How many there are."

"Lots." Marco blew out a breath. "All are respected and powerful."

"Meaning what?"

She waited. Now the job was done, she wanted to know everything about him. But especially, would more business come her way?

A shiny silver watch on a wrist came into the picture. The view shifted. She stared at the screen. A leather chair. Behind it, a framed picture and a pair of boxing gloves hung on a wall. Save for the circle of beads hanging loose from a bookshelf between them, what she assumed was his office was immaculate. Then Marco stepped into the frame. Dressed in a golf shirt, his face was obscured by sunglasses and a baseball cap. He lowered himself to the seat. She studied his face. Sharp nose. Strong jawline. She could still see him as he was, but he'd grown into his looks. He was a handsome man.

"Loyalty is the only currency I know. It provides safety. Security. Status. On a good day, it brings rewards."

"Like in prison?"

"You've been doing your research. Yes, I've been in prison. I've done a lot of things, lived a lot of lives since we last saw each other."

There were sounds on the other side of the screen.

Muttering. Laughter. Footsteps. A high voice. Two low ones, arguing. Marco shifted his weight and moved out of sight. He swore. Repeatedly. Then the screen went black and silent.

As she waited, she dug through her purse. She picked through candy wrappers, the pens, her sunglasses. At the bottom, she found the silver tube and ran it around her lips. A little more charm never hurt. She needed to keep him talking. She liked this. She wanted it. She needed to know more. After Marco sat down heavily in his chair, he apologized, then he asked where they were.

"Prison." Straight to the point.

"I was charged with manslaughter in 2000." His expression sobered. "Eight years of my life for a set up."

They were different yet so alike. Blood coursed through her veins. She used to think they were made for each other.

"Do you remember Paris?" she said.

They reminisced about the old days. How she was hired to coordinate the coffee station in the bowels of a hotel, where he often ate breakfast in the lounge upstairs. How after six months, she got promoted to room service, then salads and sauces, then mains. Within five years, she was the sous-chef for the formal dining room, cooking a line-up of black diamond dishes. Spanish Seafood Paella. Thai Massaman Curry. Singapore Chili Crab. Vietnamese Goi Cuon. Drawn to the kitchen, it was a chance to work quietly behind the scenes. How she'd fallen in love, lived in her own flat, and spoke fluent French. How he'd run into trouble with drugs and the police, then they'd broke up, all before her return to New York.

"The drug trade," she said. "It's big money in there, too?"

"The screws have eyes everywhere, but the market is extensive. I ran a small ring, a profitable one. Your value is measured on what you can get your hands on. A toothbrush to carve into a shank. A magazine to pass time. Though I never touched contraband, a hit of anything non-prescribed to forget about life for a couple of hours. Inside, you do what's needed to survive."

She could picture it. Respect and fear were deadly narcotics. They were clearly his drug of choice. His voice was low and calm. He was a man who never had to raise it, because he knew how to take charge.

"And after you got out?"

Marco's voice took on a mechanical tone. "Describe your daily activity, whether you've consumed any alcohol or non-prescribed drugs, been in contact with other felons or associated with anyone involved in illegal activity."

She laughed, figuring he must have heard the same thing a hundred times from his parole officer.

Marco spoke again. "Then I married late, had kids, and the business to take care of. When the kids moved out, Stella passed."

Stella again. And the way he brushed by thirty years made her doubtful. Did he kill her? "What about the guy who framed you?"

"You really want to know?"

"Yes, or I wouldn't be asking."

"Indisposed."

"Permanently?"

When he gave her a slight nod, a shiver went up her spine. She could picture his body tucked tight into a drum of lye and acid.

"Tell me the truth," she said slowly. "You murder people."

"Dead bodies are bad for business."

She dropped it. "Tell me about the photo. Why did you want it to look like you're dead?"

"For assurances," he said, matter-of-factly. "In my business, they're needed."

"The man in the picture's you."

Once she hung up, the day flew by. Though her workload was heavy, she felt lighter. Not once did her mind fixate on the unsolved shooting on the street or Jim's affair. She moved quickly through what needed to be done.

Midafternoon, the sky darkened. Waiting for the boys to arrive home, she curled up in her chair by the window.

She mulled over the conversation she had with Marco. His voice. His sharp features. Had he removed the sunglasses; she could have stared straight into those bright, blue eyes. From the moment she first saw them, she'd dreamt about them. Windows to his soul, no doubt about it.

Fat drops splattered her office window. She'd always loved the rain. It brought memories of simpler times. The row of black rubber boots lined up on the plastic mat by the back door. The crisp smell of the air before a storm hit. The worms, swollen and wrinkled, inching over the patio stones in the backyard. Her parents, inside hurling insults at each other. Neither noticed when she slipped outside, nor cared when she cut the worms in half with rusted garden shears and lit them all on fire. The smell had never washed away. It filled her nostrils every time she thought about the screams, the tears, and the incessant wail of the fire trucks the night the house she grew up in burned to the ground.

TWENTY-NINE
Jim

Jim kept an eye on the GPS as he maneuvered in and out through the late Sunday morning traffic on the highway. November now, the colder weather was rolling in. The escarpment stretched out in front of him looked dull and raw in the light. The last time he was at the Catskill Mountains was with Jaylyn. Thoughts of her still pursued him in his dreams. He still missed her, felt they were edging toward a reconciliation after she'd called him. It showed she still cared, at least a little. Yet he was still planning to go ahead with the counselling with Ria. Nothing wrong with having a back-up plan.

Last night, Ria had seemed less combative, more even keeled, humming to herself as she cooked up a storm. Pork roast. Maybe it would be possible to get things back to normal. Maybe couples counselling wouldn't be so bad.

When a sign for the speed limit appeared on the side of the road, he eased off the gas. With ten thousand dollars on the front seat beside him, the last thing he needed was to be stopped by the police. As he passed the exit to Frank and Rachel's house, the words he'd heard in the alleyway after he and his brother met for lunch echoed through his head.

I know where you live.

He turned down the radio. After what he assumed was Dirk's voice calling out from the shadows, maybe he should have taken his brother up on his offer and brought him. Too late now.

This was his fight, and his alone.

Ten minutes later, he turned off the highway and drove up the mountain road. Thick trees lined either side and the tires crunched on the gravel. He punched the gas. Around a bend, the outline of a shabby little box appeared on the horizon. The final leg of the journey took him down a long narrow dirt road. As he slowed, he passed three dark-coloured trucks parked in a laneway. He pulled the car up at an angle along a patch of weeds and got out.

The place had seen better days. Wood logs criss-crossed the front of the building, and the first-floor windows were broken. In front of the sagging porch, the same two girls he'd seen outside the deserted building a month before sat in white plastic chairs. Despite the cold, they were dressed in t-shirts and were sharing a tall-necked brown bottle. They ignored the skinny mutt with wiry black hair, whose tail thumped the ground in front of them.

"Hi, Jim," one called out.

"Where's Liam?" said the other.

"Doing his homework," he said, trying to be polite.

"Maybe you can bring him next time."

There wouldn't be a next time. When he didn't respond, she hooked a thumb over her shoulder. She snapped pink bubble gum. "They're inside."

He took the steps up to the weathered slats of the porch. The screen door was ripped, and the wood door behind it rotting. As he entered, he was hit with an earthy smell of dead animals. Thick dust floated in the air as light filtered in through the broken windows. Through the gloom, a staircase stood out in the far corner. Caked in dirt, there were dark red stains and drag marks across the floor. His eyes narrowed and a lump rose in his throat. What the hell had gone on here?

After he eased the door shut, he crept forward, testing each floorboard as he went. In the kitchen, the ceilings were low and stained. He found peeling linoleum, an ashtray full of cigarettes, discarded fast food wrappers. A half-drunk glass of something on the counter. Plates and forks encrusted with food sat stacked in the sink.

"Got the cash?" a deep voice called out behind him.

He spun around. A large man with a purple mohawk and a deep scratch running down his cheek leaned in the doorway. He was covered in unruly black hair. There were multiple chains around his neck and thick gold hoops hung from his earlobes. Jim pulled the envelope from the pocket of his jacket and passed it over. The man looked at it, then him.

"Feels a little light," he said.

"It's what we agreed to."

The man shrugged. "Up you go, then."

Jim didn't move. From behind, an arm gripped his shoulder, jerking him from the depth of the kitchen. He lurched forward but tried to remain on his feet. Someone caught him and flung him face first to the floor. A rough sack was jammed over his head. Then two strong arms picked him up, hurled him over a shoulder and carried him up the stairs. He could hear the steps creaking under their weight. At the top, he landed hard on his back on the floor. Unable to catch a breath, he kicked out at anything he could reach. His wrists were bound in front of him, then he was dragged to his feet. He stumbled along, nearly tripping, swearing. Six steps. Right. Four steps. Stop. Something squeaked.

"Jim."

He turned to the voice. It was the same one he'd heard in the alley. When the burlap bag was ripped off his face, he gasped for air.

"What the fuck?" he screamed.

He ignored the chatter behind him and took a quick look around. Between cobwebs high among the rafters, two bulbs hung from open light sockets in the ceiling. The ground was littered with discarded needles. Pieces of wood, plastic milk crates, broken glass. Dirk stepped forward and grabbed hold of his wrists.

"String him up, Jaxon," he said, laughing.

Jaxon? Over his shoulder, all he could see was dark hair, dark eyes, and a crooked nose. It looked like it had been broken many times. The sound of the clang of chains scraping across the floor echoed through the space. He braced himself. Lifted off his feet, he was suspended in midair. His heart was racing. He swung back and forth from a silver chain hung from a distressed wood beam. Drenched in sweat, he kept his eyes glued to Dirk.

Neither spoke. He waited.

"Let's see what he's got."

The blows came relentlessly. His chest. His back. His legs. His knees. Clouds of dust flew up, choking the air off around him. The cool metal rubbed his skin raw. His lungs burned and his muscles screamed. When the room narrowed before his eyes, Dirk appeared from the shadows. Everything ceased.

"You've got a wife, two boys, a nice little family. And you still won't leave Jaxon's sister alone."

Jim tried not to vomit. Thank god he hadn't brought Liam with him. Dirk stepped around him, furled his hand in his hair, and jerked his head backward.

"You're lucky the count's good," he snarled. "Or your boy would've got hurt."

The chain loosened and he fell to the floor. Dirk pulled a knife from the waist of his jeans. He fingered the sharp edge, then slid the blade through the plastic wrapped around his wrists. As Jim rubbed the skin to get the blood circulating again, Dirk crouched beside him. His sour breath prickled his neck.

"Now get outta here."

Jim clambered to his feet and staggered down the stairs. He didn't look back. The only direction he had in mind was away. Outside, he ran to the car and stomped on the gas. He tore down the gravel path, then turned hard left onto the road. He was safe. For now.

At his brother's house, Jim stripped to his underwear and threw his clothes in the washing machine. He ran a finger across his ribs and winced. Only a half hour since the beating, the welts on his chest had already turned purple.

"What the hell happened?" Frank hollered.

"Things got out a little of hand."

"Out of hand?" His brother's face went scarlet. "I told you I should have gone with you."

"Then you'd have bruises too," he replied. "If you want to help, find me something to wear. I'm freezing."

Frank's voice rose again. "Are you out of your mind? That's shock, you fucking idiot. It's twenty-two degrees in here."

When his brother stormed off down the hall, Jim limped from the laundry room to the kitchen. After he'd arrived at the house, Frank had insisted they call the police, but Jim talked him down. It wasn't an option. He'd do anything to protect Liam from this mess.

He pulled two beers from the fridge, uncapped them, and slid onto a bar stool. One long swallow, the first was finished. He was nursing the second when his brother reappeared. As Frank grabbed a beer from the fridge, Jim slipped on the clothes he'd given him. The kitchen stilled. Then Frank took a panicky breath.

"Tell me everything," he said.

"I think you've seen it."

"What'd they say?"

"They know where I live."

Frank's eyes bulged. He held the bottle mid-air. "Shit. This is serious. At least we know Ria had nothing to do with slashing your tires."

"Don't remind me." He shifted on the stool. "You know what freaked me out the most? Jaxon was there."

Frank's mouth dropped. "Jaylyn's Jaxon?"

He nodded. "He must know Dirk."

"Those clowns are connected?"

"Or in on it somehow, but it sounded more like they were friends."

Frank slammed the bottle on the counter. "Criminals hanging out with criminals. One big, bloody, gang." His voice rose again. "Great. This upped the whole fucking ante."

The kitchen stilled. A coldness stole into his bones. He'd seen the look in Jaxon's eyes the day he picked Jaylyn up outside the restaurant. Though the relationship was over, it gave those thugs another good reason to kill him.

Was Frank right? Should he go to the police? If he did, it was their word against his. Those scum bags would twist the story around to try and make it look like he was the initiator. He knew his friends in the service would never believe them. But he'd had an affair. Drove to the farmhouse. His fingerprints were on the cash. And when he left, what did he do? Rather than call them right away, he stripped off his dirty clothes, removing any evidence that may have been on them. Then had a beer.

Frank ran a hand across his face. "Anyway, what are we going to do?"

Jim looked at him. "We?"

"Yes, we. Last time I said it, you refused."

He pretended not to hear the emotion in his brother's voice. The welling in his eyes was more difficult to ignore. He didn't look away. "Frank. I'm fine."

"These people? They're criminals."

"They're low life wanna-bees," he stated.

"Between the guy murdered on your street and now this?" Frank's voice cracked. "You're scaring the shit out of me. Money is the least of your problems."

Tired, it took him a minute. "You mean if they keep coming back for more?"

Frank looked frustrated. I'm talking about the threats to you. To the kids. To Ria."

Jim stood and walked slowly across the kitchen to the window. Wind thrashed against the side of the house. In the backyard, raindrops fell in the puddles on the pool deck and made circles on the surface of the water. When he turned around, his brother was fiddling with the coffee machine. He took the filter from his hands, filled it with grounds and punched in the settings. For a few moments he stood with him, saying nothing, as the scent of the beans filled the kitchen. Frank swiped a hand to his cheek. When the pot was full, Jim passed him a cup. He laid a hand on his shoulder and gave it a little squeeze.

"You holding out on me?" Frank said softly. "I hate when you do that."

"I'm thinking."

"What about?" His brother grew very still.

"If they ask for more," he lightened his tone, "if they make one single threat, we'll go to the police."

Frank blew out a breath. "Together?"

He turned. "Yes, together. I promise. You and me."

THIRTY
Ria

Jim showed up at her desk soon after the kids got home from school. Neck deep in work, Ria ignored him. Out for most of the weekend at Frank's place, he'd spent the evening soaking in the bathtub and talking in hushed whispers to Liam. She was sick of his silence, his continual brooding, the never-ending secrecy.

"What time is the counselling appointment?" he asked.

The calendar he held trembled in his fingers. She told him and took it.

Well behind what needed to get done, her fingers flew across the keyboard. In addition to new clients, Marco's final payment hadn't arrived. Earlier that morning, she'd sent the photo again with a read receipt. A gentle reminder.

"Bella," Marco said, after the phone rang ten minutes later. "Did you forget me?"

He shushed her. "There's a lot going on. I need to lay low for a bit." Then a fist hit something. The desk? The wall behind? The line disconnected abruptly. All morning, she'd wondered what happened.

As they debated the best route to take to the counselor, she spotted the photo of the night of Liam's grade eight graduation. She'd dressed up. Gold hoop earrings. Little black dress. High heels. She sat up. Perfect posture. Surely there was someone who'd find her a catch. Marco would.

She picked at her fruit salad, angry red raspberries among the green grapes. It was time to shut this conversation down.

After she closed her files, they put on their coats and headed out. A full snow had fallen, and the ploughs were out, cleaning up the roads. Her patience was waning. They only had a few minutes before their appointment. It was close to four-thirty when she spotted the brown squat building.

"There." She pointed.

In the lobby, the elevator doors yawned open. On the second floor, a receptionist sat behind a desk, her brown hair sprayed in place, her lacquered nails tapping on a laptop.

"Hello," she said. Her glasses sat too far down her nose.

"The Stiles for Dr. Segal."

The receptionist picked up the phone.

"Don't bother." A tall man dressed in khakis with a practical haircut and horn-rimmed glasses appeared around a corner.

"Efram." He held open a door. "After you."

Ria stepped through. Dimly lit, drab green, it looked like the room had been painted fifty years ago. The odour of pipe smoke clung to the walls. Faded bobo dolls and a pile of yoga mats were stacked under the window. In the centre, a small wood table was surrounded by three overstuffed patched leather chairs. She lowered herself into one and Jim sat opposite.

"Welcome," Efram said. "Are you comfortable?"

She glanced at Jim. Hands fidgeting in his lap, he was staring at the carpet. She pulled her coat tightly around her. Maybe the chill was a deliberate move to keep them all alert?

Efram took a moment to adjust his tie, then he picked up a clipboard. "Today is simply about information gathering. Mostly, getting to know each other. I've got a few questions, but perhaps first you could give me a sense of what brought you here. Who'd like to start?"

When Jim's cheeks reddened, Ria raised her hand.

Efram smiled. "It's not school."

"He had an affair."

"Alright," Efram said. "Let's unpack that for a moment. Have either of you put any thought into why?"

"He's an asshole." A stupid question. Why else? She tried to catch Jim's eye. On the one hand she wanted him to respond, but on the other whatever he said would make no difference.

"I imagine it's been very difficult-"

Ria huffed. "And your point?"

Efram's face grew serious. "Often in these situations, the actual affair, what's called disruptive behaviour, is a symptom of deeper-seated issues." He looked at Jim. "How long have you been married?"

"Seventeen years," he replied.

"Good," Efram said. "That's a strong base to work with." After he scribbled on the page, making notes, he glanced up. "Is this a first marriage for you both?"

"Me? Yes," she said. "He had a starter marriage that flamed out."

Efram shot her a look she couldn't interpret. "Do you have children?"

She nodded. "Two boys."

"Are they aware you're here?"

"No," Jim interjected. When she rolled her eyes, he shifted in his chair. "She's talking about Jacob. Our youngest is pretty observant, but I don't think he knows."

Ria took it all in but didn't respond. She wasn't giving him an inch, yet for once, she agreed.

"Kids are perceptive." Efram leaned forward. "Jim, have you put any thought into why you had the affair?"

His cheeks reddened again. "I wish I hadn't."

Ria snorted. He sounded like a paid advertisement.

Jim continued. "Maybe we drifted, maybe we took each other for granted. We don't do much anymore because Ria's always working. It's like she lives in a world of her own creation."

Her jaw dropped. "Are you fucking kidding? You're trying to pin your affair on me?"

"No," he shot back. "I'm answering the question."

The last grain of her patience dissipated. Jim was lucky Efram was in the room. She pictured Demar Robinson lying in a thick pool of blood on his driveway where no one saw the shooting unfold or could explain how the shooter vanished into thin air. If someone did it, she could too.

Efram held his hands up. "Alright, everyone. That was uncalled for. These are tough issues to deal with, but we'll do it calmly. Let's start with some exercises to release the tension between you."

She glared. Exercises? If she wanted exercise, she could've gone for a walk. As Efram explained what they were to do, he spoke slowly like he was talking to an elderly relative. She wanted reach over and rip his tongue out. Instead, she sat on her hands and gazed at the icicle fangs hanging from the eavestrough outside the window. Inhale. Exhale. Calm. Calmer.

"Ria?" Efram said. "Are you ready?"

She forced herself to smile. The first exercise was to open communication. While Jim was able to rhyme off six or seven things he appreciated about their marriage, she could only come up with one. He was a good father to the boys. Next, a trust task. They sat knee-to-knee, eyeball to eyeball, during which all she could think about was how much she hated him. Minutes ticked by and the heaters placed throughout the room did nothing to dispel the chill. She turned to Efram, who said, "Do you want to stop now?"

She nodded. Efram picked up a sweating pitcher of water on the table, filled two glasses and passed them over. She raised the glass to her lips. She would have preferred alcohol.

"Well done." Efram smiled. "You kept eye contact for over five minutes. It's an important skill to have in order to listen to each other."

Ria choked. Jim hadn't listened to her for five seconds the last six months.

Efram spoke again. "It's a signal you're engaging with the other's opinion."

Ria stabbed a finger across the table. "He lost the right to one the moment he started the damn affair."

"Which must've made you angry."

No shit. "Wouldn't anyone be?"

"How have you been managing that anger?" Efram asked.

She bristled. Heat flooded out through her pores. It wasn't like she cut Jim out of their wedding photo like her deranged client had. Like she no longer hid razor blades to slice up the inside of her arms. 'For fuck's sake, relax,' she told her mother the day she caught her in her room pouring lemon juice over the open wounds. Before she could answer, Efram said, "What about intimacy?"

She barked out a laugh. "Like sex? I stopped offering."

"I stopped asking," Jim added.

She exploded. "You were getting it anyway. If you took me to the winery or bought me the necklace from Pipers, we wouldn't be sitting here."

Jim's face paled.

Victory. What an idiot. Hadn't he considered she'd find out about what he and Jaylyn did together? Didn't he think she'd do her research? His life did not belong to someone else. His life belonged to her.

"Would you like to respond?" Efram urged Jim.

When Jim folded his arms over his chest, the entire mood of the conversation shifted. Ria knew this was her chance. She would not back down.

"Should I start with the lies? His secrets? Or that he doesn't talk? Is it that goddamn hard to say hello? Or I love you? Does he love me? I wouldn't know." Her eyes stung and the lump in her throat grew. "Me? I cook. I clean. I make way more money than he does, but I'm invisible. He doesn't listen to a bloody word I say. He takes no initiative. A husband? It's like living with a third fucking child."

When she finished, Efram passed her a box of tissues. "That was great," he said. "Next session, we'll hear what Jim has to say. Once he explains what he's feeling, we'll start to bridge the issues between you."

Ria glanced across the table. Jim's jaw was twitching and the look in his eyes was sadness. She had no sympathy. For the past few months who she truly was existed in the world she built. She'd clawed her way into the life she wanted. He was not going to take her down.

THIRTY-ONE
Jim

Jim tiptoed past Ria's office, pulled on his coat and stepped outside. His breath hung in clouds in the air. A half-finished glass of scotch on the bench beside him, he stretched his arms. There was a loud popping sound as his tendons and muscles loosened. It had been weeks since the beating on the mountain, but his body still hadn't recovered.

From the front porch, the cars lining the street looked like giant snow globes. Wreathes of gold and red ribbon adorned every door, eavestroughs glowed with colour, and trees were wrapped with white sparkling lights. He couldn't look at them. For as long as he could remember, he'd never missed a holiday concert and helped bake platters overflowing with loaves and pies and cookies for the school bake sale. Not this year. Ria did it all herself. Her demand for perfectionism without excuses excused him.

She hadn't said a word to him, nor he a word to her since their last counselling session. Efram had asked him to share *his feelings*. It hadn't been easy. The words didn't come naturally. Yet during two torturous sessions where Ria sat glaring and wringing her hands, he'd finally done his best to explain through his tears how he was lonely, that they were stuck in a rut and how he felt taken for granted.

Everything exploded in the car on the way home. What was he supposed to have said? Efram had asked the question. He'd answered. Explained his perspective. How could she tell him those feelings were wrong? While he'd been careful with how he said what he had, the feelings were real. They were his.

Relegated to sleeping on the living room couch since then, the holidays had been a disaster. Ria refused to acknowledge him through Christmas and New Year's. Now, a week later, it was more of the same. He knocked back the scotch, ignoring the burning in his throat. Then he heaved the glass, losing it in a snowbank, and stomped inside.

The house was quiet. Jacob was in his room, Liam out on a first date. He'd spent half the afternoon assuring his son his clothes were crisp, his hair looked good, his breath was fine.

With everything at a standstill, he got out two slices of bread and scraped the bottom of a jar of peanut butter. Afterwards, he dismantled the Christmas tree and wrapped the ornaments in tissue paper, stacking them in a neat pile in the plastic tub. This was usually Ria's job. She was particular about it and had informed him a dozen times he'd yet to master the art of swaddling precious glass. As she was on another tight deadline, at least he could be helpful.

In the root cellar, he edged along the narrow passage between the shelves to find a space to place the tub. Nothing. He bent down and pushed his hand farther back on the shelf, his fingers finding a box. He pulled it gently forward and lifted the lid. Dead mouse stink wafted upward making his stomach turn.

Crouched on the floor, he sifted through the items inside. What was this? A silver dollar. A pack of matches from a bar called Mona's. A photo of Ria's family, he assumed taken outside their house in Finger Lakes. In it, Ria was frowning at the grass. Her stern-faced parents stood beside her, cigarettes dangling off their fingers, each with a hand on her shoulders. Also in the box were two rings, a silver necklace, a faded driver's license, a set of keys.

Cold and heavy in his hand, he examined them, trying to recall why they looked so familiar. Then it hit him. They were the keys to the apartment Ria rented in New York City when they first met. He grinned. Saving them was so Ria. On top of the world then, she played by her own rules, took what she wanted, kept what she believed was hers. Guess she never gave them back.

He pulled two more photographs from the box. The first was of a young Aunt Beth sitting on the sand, the sun shining, the ocean in the background. The second was of Ria. Arm in arm with a tall man, she was laughing, her face flushed, the blue sky and the Eiffel Tower behind them. When he turned it over, the inscription read Marco. She'd never mentioned him. Examining his face, he noted the dark eyes and white smile. He presumed he was an old boyfriend. Wedged along the side of the box was a plastic bag with something heavy inside. After he carefully lifted it out, he unwrapped it on the floor. When he saw what it was, his heart lurched. A gun? He reeled backwards, a hand against his mouth.

Blood rushed to his head. *Fuck.* Two kids in the house and she'd never disclosed this? His mind raced back to the summer and the man shot down the street. Did Ria know more than she was letting on? Was she hiding something? He checked for bullets, thumbed the gun's safety, and shoved it into his coat pocket.

Three yellowed envelopes lay flat in the bottom of the box. Two return addresses from somewhere in Aurora. He pulled them out, scooted sideways, and leaned his back against the wall. He opened the first, unfolding the paper inside it. It was written in block letters.

KAREN GROSE

YOUR ANGRY AND EXPLETIVE-FILLED LETTER ONLY CONFIRMS WHAT I SAID IN MY REPORT TO THE COURT. PLEASE CEASE AND DESIST. ANY FURTHER COMMUNICATION OF THIS NATURE WILL RESULT IN SERIOUS CONSEQUENCES.

DR. GIBSON

He ran a hand across his forehead. He turned it over. Nothing on the back. If it was Ria's, he had no idea what this man was talking about. He opened the other. It was written in Aunt Beth's loopy handwriting.

How are you? it began.

He blew out a breath. At least he knew who she was. While Ria and her aunt hadn't visited since a falling out a few years back, he was aware they'd patched things up and emailed and talked regularly on the phone.

> *Miss you, but it's lovely to hear about your life in Europe. You clearly don't miss Aurora. Loved the photos you sent. Italy looked beautiful. Old, all stone, so different from everything at home. It must have been nice to see the vineyards. It made me laugh when you said people drink wine like water there. Hope you're settled in France, now. I can see from that photo you've been shopping up a storm. The new haircut looks great, too. You fit right into the fashion mecca.*

He recalled what she wore when they first met in New York City. The boots, the scarves, the hats, turning heads wherever they went. He read on.

Glad you met someone. I know it's early days but keep me posted.

He grunted. Must've been Marco. He flipped the page. As he scanned the other side, there wasn't much to hold his interest. Until he got the bottom.

Congratulations on your new job at the hotel. Love you, Angel.

Angel? A nickname? A term of endearment? If it was, he'd never heard her aunt use it. He dug into the box again and pulled out the driver's license. He held it up to the light. *Angel Calarco. 27 Highbank Avenue, Aurora.* The accompanying faded photo barely resembled Ria, her cheekbones, the haircut. His arms prickled. It was her aunt's address; he recognized it from what was written in the top left corner of the letters she sent.

The last envelope was the largest. It bore no postage mark, in fact, the whole front was blank. He tore it open.

Dr. Jack Gibson. Another address in Aurora.

His eyes widened. It was addressed to a judge. By his estimate, there were fifteen typed pages in the document.

As per your direction, the psycho-assessment is complete, and I am submitting my final report to the court.

His chest tightened. He leafed through the paper.

I've been seeing Angel Calarco, nineteen years old, on a weekly basis the past six months.

Sweat dotted his upper lip. It was possible the first letter was Ria's. He glanced at the gun. What had she done? At the very least, she'd threatened the doctor.

> *Angel has been in the care of her aunt since her mother's death. Recurrent and serial pattern of misbehaviour including lying, stealing and aggression. Appears to have a history of conduct disorder. Due to time limitations set by the court, unable to determine conclusively whether clusters of behaviour represent a narcissistic, borderline personality disorder or sociopathic personality.*

Bile rose in the back of his throat. What was the doctor insinuating? It made his skin crawl, like something was watching him through the crack in the door. She was a psychopath? A sociopath? No, she was his wife, for Christ's sake. Did she have narcissistic tendencies? Maybe. Definitely. The more he thought about it, the more he became convinced it had all been there right in front of him from the beginning. The need for a bigger house. The drive to build her business. Everything was always about her. But she was a good mother, if a little overprotective at times. What mother wasn't? His was still protective, even after all this time.

What about lying? He thought back to last fall. The footsteps. The prowler. A wave of nausea washed over him. Was it possible Ria made it all up? What about the brick through the window? Did she do it herself and run back inside all for attention? For years, he'd overlooked Ria's behaviour. The incessant mumbling as she wrote letter upon letter to her Aunt Beth. Her need to be right, to control him. Her bursts of rage. The scalding coffee she threw in his face.

FLAT OUT LIES

Recommended course of action includes daily medication and ongoing psychotherapy.

His hands trembled. All he could think about was the unopened pill bottle they'd fought about last fall. How long had she been off her meds? Back on them? Had she been taking them at all? Too busy with Liam's mess and missing Jaylyn, he hadn't followed up with her. God, he was so negligent. So checked out. He needed to confront her and demand she tell him the truth.

And what had happened years ago? Head in his hands, he searched for an explanation. There had to be one. If there wasn't, then who was she? Ria? Angel? The mother of his children, whatever her name was. His stomach tightened. After everything she put him through? After all the shit she said in front of their couples therapist? *You lie. You cheat. You turtle. You need to open up and communicate. I need you to talk to me right now.* He shoved everything back in the box and stormed upstairs. She was about to get her wish.

In the kitchen, the fridge door was open. Pieces of lettuce, tomato, cucumber and chunks of feta cheese lay spread across a chopping board on the counter. He held the box in front of him.

"What the hell is this?" he shouted.

When Ria spun around, her face went white. She held up a knife. Fear soured his gut, but he didn't move a muscle. He waited. And waited. And waited. When she finally put the knife on the counter, he stepped forward and grabbed her elbow. She stiffened at his touch.

"Who the hell are you?"

She yanked her arm away. Then she started to pace, back and forth, back and forth, walking the length of the kitchen. She mumbled to herself in a low voice. Over and over. Suddenly she stopped dead in her tracks, inches from him. She reached out and took his hand.

"Come." Her fingers were cold. "There's something I need to tell you."

THIRTY-TWO
Ria

Ria glanced over her shoulder. With the box still clutched in his hand, Jim followed behind. It was hard to walk forward, harder to breathe. She wanted to run, to hide, to escape the questions she knew were coming.

When she was a child, she simply covered her face with her hands. As she grew older, she hid behind her camera, invisible to her classmates and the cliques and the teachers. Since then, she'd left all the questions behind, moving steadily forward. To her aunt's house. To college. To Europe, then back to New York, where her past had been erased. She'd claimed a fresh outlook, a fresh new persona. A girl gone for good, a woman returned.

In the living room, she sat in a chair to put as much distance between her and Jim as she could. When he dumped the contents of the box on the carpet, she didn't need to look. She knew what was in there. But she looked anyway. Her old driver's license. The letter to her aunt. The doctor's report. When she glanced up, her gun was dangling off his fingers.

"That's my father's." For one brief moment, she wondered if there was a bullet left in the barrel.

"Right." Jim picked up the license. "Angel Calarco."

"That was my former name." But Angel was there, inside her all the time.

"That's comforting because in the documents?" He pointed to Dr. Gibson's report. "It says she's a psychopath."

"A sociopath," she corrected.

Jim's voice rose. "What the fuck's it matter?"

She folded her hands in her lap to keep them from shaking. "A psychopath is conniving and calculated. A sociopath just has a temper-"

"I don't care." His voice quivered. "What matters is I'm living with her."

"She, I mean me, is neither." She kept hers steady.

"So, normal, healthy people go around threatening their doctors?" She shook her head. "Then start explaining this, Ria."

She took a shallow breath. Where to begin? "Unlike you, my early days weren't idyllic." Mired in memories, she reminded him about where she'd lived. The house in the middle of nowhere, her father's gun, growing up hungry.

His face reddened. "Everyone has crappy childhoods. Half the population is divorced. What they don't have is boxes hidden in the basement with guns and fake names and medical records." He jumped out of the chair. "I'll ask again. What the hell is going on? Answer my questions or we're done here."

She put her hand out to stop him, and he stayed where he was. She told him that her parents had no money. How her father drank every night. How when he left, her mother preoccupied herself with her collections, ignoring her. How her daily theatrics, swings in personality, inability to hold a job, cruelty, and neediness, her demands to be taken care of, had nearly killed her. She kept her voice as breezy as she could, but hated the sound, the shaking in it.

"No wonder your father left. I would've too." He looked straight at her. "If your father's alive, do you have a family in Wisconsin?"

She nodded. "But I've never met them."

"Does your father keep in touch with your aunt?"

She knew the question was coming. There was a burning sensation in her nose and throat. She swallowed to give herself some time to think. "Aunt Beth died three years ago."

His jaw dropped. Speechless, he shifted in his chair. He didn't say anything right away. She knew it was a lot to take in. Then his eyes bulged. "But you still call her! You write to her all the time! What's wrong with you? What's the hell is the point of this whole charade?"

She stopped, composed herself, kept going. "I was lonely. I missed her. I needed connections outside the house. It makes me feel normal."

"Normal?" His eyes bore into her. "What about this report? The letters? Ria. Angel. Whoever you are. What happened?"

She clamped her lips shut, then blew her nose. With the tissue balled in her hand, she could feel him tracking her every move. It was time to fill in the holes of her past.

"My mother died in a housefire," she said and told him the story of that night. The smell of the smoke. The black tendrils curling up the walls. The heat searing her skin. Her body shaking uncontrollably as she ran. The firefighter who had found her, head in her hands, sobbing hysterically, sitting outside in the laneway. With his flashlight shining down on her, he'd swept her into his arms and wrapped a foil blanket around her shoulders. He'd made her feel safe.

"We'll take care of you, miss," he'd said as he placed her gently on the back seat of the pump truck.

She'd opened her eyes and clutched at his collar. "My Mom. Is she okay?"

His expression had been grim. Two strong hands squeezed her shoulders. A fresh stream of tears poured down her cheeks and she'd collapsed in a pile on the seat. Through the cracks in her fingers, she'd looked up through the window, past the smoky air, at what was left of the house.

"It burned to the ground?" Jim asked. When she nodded, he continued. "And you went to your aunt's in Aurora?"

"I lived with her through college. And... the trial."

His face paled. "The trial? They charged you?"

She stiffened. Her eyes welled. She'd been eighteen years old at the time. Speculation about her mother's death had been rampant. The family's problems were gossiped about, and half-baked theories and wild questions circulated in the media as the police conducted their investigation. One theory was that it was a house invasion and arson, but others suspected Angel, the strange daughter of a controlling mother. Was she hiding a history of abuse? Or was she an opportunist, not wanting to wait for her inheritance?

"I was there when the fire started and was the only one who made it out alive."

At the trial, her aunt described her as an independent young woman, who until tragedy hit, was starting what would be a successful life of her own. When Ria took the stand, her motives were questioned, her theories denied. Yet she still had no explanation for what happened. Backed into a corner, she'd cried and proclaimed her innocence. Some questioned her performance for the benefit of the jury. Jim's jaw twitched as he listened.

"But you were innocent, right?" he probed when she was finished.

"Of course, I was."

"What about the doctor's report?"

"All bullshit. Even the jury said it was. That man talked for hours, but I barely spoke to him."

"And your aunt? Who's dead-"

"She's my hero, Jim," she said softly. "She sacrificed

everything for me. Do you understand now?"

He grunted. "Not really."

Her pulse quickened. He was making this difficult. "I couldn't let her go. When she died, I needed her to stay alive. She's a piece of me."

He held his head in his hands. "That's fucking creepy."

"To you, maybe, but you have Frank and your parents. She's all the family I had."

"You write to her, you talk to her." He paused. "On the phone."

"I don't expect you to understand. I know she died, but I can't accept it. I need to keep her alive." Why couldn't he understand this?

Jim ran a hand over his face. "This is too weird. For starters? You need to go back on your medication."

She agreed. It was best to let him believe she would, but she wouldn't. She was happy to be herself.

"Why didn't you ever tell me any of this before?" he asked.

"That I'm damaged goods?"

"But Ria," he protested, "a jury found you innocent."

"Like you would've married me?" When he didn't respond, she sniffed. "See? I changed my name to put my past behind me. I wanted to have a smaller life, to be with you and to be the mother I always wanted to have." She hesitated. "But I'll pack a bag and go. You stay here with the boys."

He frowned, then crossed the room and sat beside her. When she took his hand, he flinched, then pulled away. "Did anyone determine how that fire started? It couldn't be smoking in bed because burn patterns would've told them that's what it was."

She swallowed. Of course, he would know about fires and burn patterns. The conversation was proving more difficult than she thought.

In her mind's eye, she saw the house she grew up in with perfect clarity. The main floor was a show home. The kitchen always bright and sparkling, liquor bottles hidden in cabinets, magazines fanned an inch apart, tight stacks of coasters on the table. The living room, a formal dining room, an avocado-green phone, its tangled cord hanging on the wall between them. Her mother taught her the importance of appearances downstairs, and the importance of secrets upstairs. The three tiny bedrooms, with piles behind every door, pressed right to the corners of the walls. Sagging bookshelves of newspapers, chipped bowls, dishes, boxes upon boxes of cereal. Folded blankets, dolls without eyes. Tattered coverless books. Packages of toilet paper. All belonging to her mother, who guarded her horde like a dragon.

"I'm sure you've seen it all on your calls," she said, wiping the tissue to her eyes. "People with collections."

"Collections," Jim said slowly. "She was a hoarder?"

"Love to shop, she called it. It was why we couldn't eat."

"I'm surprised the crew, or the police didn't realize."

She turned to face him. "Thirty years ago? I wasn't going to tell. All I wanted was to get out. I was embarrassed."

"It wasn't your fault." He frowned. "You were a kid."

"That's what my aunt said," she confirmed.

Images of thick black plumes of smoke filling the sky swirled through her mind. Though she'd never forgotten the smell of burning flesh and hair, or the sight of her mother's charred clothes, she'd forgiven herself. He leaned over and hugged her, then pulled away, holding her at arm's length.

"Do you understand now?" she whispered.

"It's a lot to take in." He pulled her back toward him. "Maybe Efram can help."

She nodded, leaning her head against his chest.

For the rest of the evening, Ria skittered around upstairs, refilling empty paper toilet rolls, scraping toothpaste off sinks, straightening shoes in closets, plumping pillows lined up in rows on the duvet. Later that night in bed, with Jim's arms wrapped around her, she stared through the slats of the blind. She passed the test. She told the truth, save for one small detail no one would ever find out about.

After she'd shot her mother, she'd known better than to use a lighter. The summer she spent with Aaron at the campground at Sandbanks Provincial Park taught her that much. As flames caught the curtains and spread, dancing across the carpet, she'd stood for as long as the heat had let her, mesmerized by the strength of the fire. Then she'd backed slowly away and threw the pack of matches over her shoulder behind her. Her first kill. Stone cold focus. The most gratifying.

THIRTY-THREE
Jim

Headlights swept across the dashboard as Jim pulled up in front of the familiar squat brown building. Dusk hung ugly in the snowy landscape. A cold wind slapped his face as he hurried across the lot, Ria trudging behind.

For the past two weeks, things between them had thawed considerably. He was no longer eating sandwiches for supper. He wasn't sleeping on the couch, his body wasn't aching, the dark circles under his eyes were almost gone. While he didn't understand Ria's behaviour, now he knew more about her past, he wondered about their future. Was their relationship done or could they make a run for it?

"We've got something we need to discuss," he said, once they were seated in Efram's office.

After he explained how Ria's mother died in a housefire, how her aunt had taken her in and how, though she'd died three years ago, Ria was still talking to her as if she were alive, Efram tented his fingers.

"Wow," he said. "You two have had an eventful holiday."

Efram had no idea, but he'd promised Ria before they came, he wouldn't divulge any more than he did. "I know it sounds odd-"

Efram agreed. "That's one word for it."

Ria leaned forward and frowned "It's not that weird if you think about it. My aunt is my rock. She was always there for me."

Efram considered it. "And you're saying Jim hasn't been?"

"Come on," he said. "This is nothing to do with me." The idea was ludicrous.

Efram shook his head. "I'm not saying that at all. What I'm wondering is if it's a contributing factor to Ria's need to continue communicating with her aunt. The letters and the phone calls. A break, or on some level, a sort of a psychosis."

Jim's stomach clenched. His greatest fear, beside Jaxon and Dirk's threats about knowing where he lived, was that there was truth to the doctor's report in the box in the basement.

"Psychosis a very broad term," Efram explained. "False beliefs or seeing or hearing things. It can mean thoughts and perceptions are altered for a minute, or a lifetime. But with you two? My sense is it's not the root of the problem."

"Then what is?" he asked.

Efram shrugged. "It's stuff I see in my practice all the time. Taking the relationship for granted, drifting apart, miscommunication, or no communication at all."

"The imbalance of work around the house," Jim pointed out.

Ria glared. "Not listening to anything I say."

They began to argue. Efram nodded and shifted in his chair, his signal to go on. As the argument intensified, Ria's leg bounced, and she stabbed a finger in the air.

"All his damn secrets. What else is there?"

Liam. He didn't have the nerve to tell her. She shot him a look. It was a nasty one that took practice. He groped for an excuse but didn't have one. If they were to get everything out in the open, have any chance of moving on, he knew he needed to be honest.

He cleared his throat and the story of Liam and #TheFellas came tumbling out. The online gambling. Direct Lend Express.

The money the boys owed. He omitted the trip to the farmhouse at Dundas Peak in November. There was no benefit to sharing, it would only make matters worse. It'd been easy to hide the bruises back then because Ria would barely look at him. When he finished, the colour had drained from Ria's cheeks and the lone noise in the room was the humming heater.

Ria's eyes narrowed. "Help me understand this." He started to reply but she started talking again. "How could you think I wouldn't want to know?"

He averted his eyes. The answer seemed obvious. For a moment or two, they lapsed into silence. Then her lips drew into a blade thin line, and she slammed her fist on the table.

"He's my son," she yelled.

"Yeah, well, your son confided in me. I'm his father, remember?"

The argument escalated. On and on, round and round. He wondered if she'd ever get to the point or if there was a point at all. Give up? Or carry on? After what felt like an eternity, she stopped screaming and looked away.

He gripped his hands in his lap and stared at the carpet, the faded purple yoga mats in the corner, the fat white flakes falling out the window. He wondered what Frank would say if he was here in the room. He'd tell him to let her think, let the storm rage itself out.

He waited. Across the table, Ria's eyes were closed. Her jaw was clenched, her expression tight. Was this the last straw? Was she ready to pack it in? He recalled his last divorce. He'd done it once; he was going to do it with Jaylyn, and he could do it again if he had to. Finally, Ria looked up.

"Is there anything else you're hiding?" Her tone was icy.

"No," he said. "It's all out in the open."

"One more question. Jaylyn. Were you planning on leaving

me for her?"

A pause. He didn't want to lie, not now, after all the truths had come out, but he also didn't want to destroy her. *Yes,* he turned his face away. *Yes, he was*. He tried to respond. Didn't have a voice. Finally found it.

"No, never," he said.

"Alright." The frown faded from her face. "How about we go on a trip? The two of us. We'll start again and wipe this whole mess clean."

He breathed a little easier. An abrupt change of subject was one of her longstanding ways to call a truce. He played along. When he suggested they go to Florida, she proposed Aruba.

"Can we afford it?" she asked.

"How can we not?"

"And the boys?"

"I'll call my parents."

She smiled for the first time that morning. The conversation eased, flowing more freely, and he smiled back, a new commitment before them. At the end of the hour, as they stood at the elevator, Ria batted him on the shoulder. When he turned to her, she said, "I'm thinking of you and I lying on a white sand beach."

He grinned. "And a midnight dip in the ocean."

As the elevator doors slid open, she threw her head back and laughed. "You and me swimming alone in the dark? You have no idea how much I'm looking forward to it."

That evening, after he shut off the TV, he passed by Ria's office. He poked his head inside. A shaft of light poured across her desk, illuminating her closed laptop. No piles of paper signaled no project in progress. He wondered where she was.

After everything they'd been through the past month, he still had niggling concerns. Wary, the last thing he wanted to do was ask Ria a stream of questions. He felt guilty for even thinking about it. She'd been through so much. What had she said happened after the trial? For twenty years, she'd been on the straight and narrow. Adapted, cleaned up her act, made better choices. Had she? Answers were the only way to smooth out the wrinkles.

Alone in the front hall, he pulled out his phone and googled her name. *Ria Stiles* only drew up a link to *Pixel-by-Pixel*. When he did the same for *Angel Calarco*, stories filled the screen. Articles from local newspapers and short clips from local TV stations. He read about the trial, which offered little more than Ria had already described. Next, he typed *fires at Finger Lakes, Dr Gibson* into the search bar. All that flooded the page was a series of house and forest and commercial fires, the dates jumping from year to year.

When his name rang out, he locked the screen and pocketed his phone. If he was going to put his lingering apprehension to rest, he'd need to be more resourceful.

Upstairs, a glow shone from around the edges of the doorway of their bedroom. He eased along the unlit hallway and pushed the door open. His eyes widened. Tea lights in jam jars flickered on every surface. On the dresser, on the windowsill, on the night tables at each side of the bed. Between them, Ria lay smiling.

"I love you," she said.

Before their counseling, he'd had trouble rarely returning the sentiment. But he sat on the edge of the bed, brushed the hair that had fallen across her forehead and took her hands in his. Then he pulled her into a long, warm hug and whispered in her ear.

"Me too."

THIRTY-FOUR
Ria

Ria sat ramrod straight on the edge of the bathtub. She should've known it was too good to be true. What Jim disclosed about Liam's gambling debt in Efram's office was shocking, but the lie about Jaylyn stunned her. She'd held herself perfectly still. She didn't respond. So much left unsaid, so many scabs unpicked, so many jagged edges.

The terms had changed. He'd chosen the wrong path. He wasn't going to try to be honest. He'd crossed the line from useful to problematic. What mattered now was what she was going to do about it.

As Jim snored softly from the bedroom, she slipped downstairs to her office and fired up her laptop. Her mother's words echoed through her head. *Never waste time on anger.* To still her mind, she put in ear buds and listened to music. Humming, she surfed through the news. When she clicked onto the News10 website, her jaw dropped.

"Oh.....my.....god..........."

Two puckered eyes stared out at her. She peered at the photo. She'd created those eyes. The headline read 'Upcoming New York Mob Boss Found Dead.' She fought the nausea building up in her throat. Mob boss? She knew Marco was connected, but he'd suppressed his affiliation. After she locked her office door, she scrolled through the story.

> *This week a photo surfaced on the dark web suggesting emerging mob boss Marco Galante is dead. Galante has been on America's most wanted list for nearly a decade. The image reveals he was shot in an unknown location in northern New York. Police remain tight-lipped. Though his body has not yet been found, an undisclosed source close to the investigation has confirmed Galante was murdered by a rival crime family.*

Except Marco wasn't. She clicked on another site. A craggy faced man with a shiny bald head was talking into a microphone.

> *The Galante family's impact in the world of organized crime was unprecedented. They controlled most of the drug trade flowing in and out of the country and operated an extensive network which flooded the US market with counterfeit luxury goods. Galante's father, a powerful mob boss in northern Italy, moved his young family to New York in the 1960s to establish a global network. He was a ruthless boss from the Old Country who kept his house in order. Not so much his younger son.*

She wondered what the man meant. Shouting erupted from the crowd of reporters around him. The scene was all too familiar to her, so she clicked off the live stream, scanned news sites and read through old articles.

A long piece in the New York Times described the charges and time served she knew about. Underneath, it detailed a third charge. Murder? Marco denied all accusations, claiming his innocence. She quickly scanned the article about the investigation, the trial, the acquittal. Guess that was why he hadn't mentioned it?

She flipped to a couple of blogs. One said Marco's death was long coming, an act of retribution, the other, an emerging power struggle between families.

She pulled out her phone and thumbed a text. *What the hell?* Backspaced. Too confrontational. A thought struck her. With whatever was going on, what if someone was monitoring his messages? Instead, she hit videoconference. It rang and rang and rang. With reams of paper spread out on the desk, she went through the fine details of the article. Two o'clock in the morning, her calls had been going to his voicemail for an hour. Finally, Marco picked up. She watched the slow sweep of his eyelashes as he blinked.

"Bella," he said. "You've heard?"

She snorted. "The whole country has. The photo's everywhere."

On the screen, the skyline burned a deep shade of red. Rows of glass bottles, a line of old leathery guys sitting at a bar, bald heads encircled by gray hair. Behind them to the left, white houses, thatched roofs bathed in shadows. The ocean. To the right, rows of shops crammed together on a cobblestone street. Marco's tanned faced was relaxed, his disheveled hair blew gently in the breeze. He glanced around to ensure there was no one within earshot. Ria listened as he explained his situation. His voice was low and calm as he took hard pulls on his cigarette. When he was finished, there was a long pause. She raised her eyebrows.

"That's complicated stuff," she said, firmly. "You *might* have considered mentioning it."

"It was always the plan." Cold and detached.

The way he said it infuriated her. She tried to keep her voice steady, not wanting to ruffle his feathers. "We both need to scrub our tech."

"Come over and do it for me." He held her gaze, revealing he'd lived in Capri ten years.

To Italy? She bit her bottom lip. For a split second, she thought about it. There wasn't time. She'd never leave her boys.

"It has to be done now. Before you get rid of your laptop, we need to process it, sanitize it, and remove all the identifying information. Then remove the date on the file of the photo and whatever program your people used to send it."

For the next hour, she worked with Marco, guiding him through what to do. After the job was completed, adrenaline coursed through her body. She never should have taken his job. He'd put her at risk. For years, she'd been so careful. Thanks to him, now everything would go to waste. After decades of impunity, the rise of cold-case units and advances in DNA technology scared the shit out of her.

She cursed herself for ever returning to New York. After the trial, the countless months of venom, she'd had enough. It left her angry, desolate. She'd taken the cowards way out, calling her aunt from abroad. She was happy there, living a life of anonymity. Twenty-five years later, she was back in the same position, forced to tie up loose ends.

A hand to her throat, she sat for a moment to gather her thoughts. Inhale. Exhale. Focus. A plan to get her out of this mess once and for all materialized in the dark recesses of her mind. She could not save Jim. She could not save their marriage. But she could save her children and herself.

She opened her laptop and dragged all Marco's work into the trash. The preliminary art. The trial runs. The final pictures. Before she deleted them, she clicked through her collection of images. Reminders of her history, years of precious memories, pieces of unfinished business.

Her heart pounded when she pulled up the one picture she still struggled with. A head on a pillow. Through thin gray hair, a dark, raised bump. Slightly swollen lips. Beyond the head, a pile of books and a set of false teeth lay on the night table. Shadows. Footsteps. Her hand. The plastic bag, the cool thickness molded between her fingers. The creaking door. Aunt Beth's voice. She pressed a finger gently to the screen. She could almost feel her aunt's last breath. The burst blood vessel in her left eye was from a prior fall. Faint red petechial spots on her eyelids. Fortunately, no one had noticed.

Unlike her mother's death, it wasn't the same. At the last minute, she'd turned her face away. Though she couldn't remember the exact day or the exact look on the face of the only woman who loved her just before she died, she sure as hell remembered planning it. Starting to slip, she'd called her Angel in front of the staff at the retirement home, the boys, in messages left on voice mail. There could be no stone left unturned.

In the basement, she retrieved her box on Jim's workbench. Then she shrugged on her winter jacket and trudged to the driveway. Cold air slivered her lungs. At the end the street, she turned right, drove past the high school, then a mile past a row of townhouses in a new development. Farther down the road, she slowed at a patch of fenced off land and swung into a deserted parking lot.

Once her eyes adjusted to the night, she exited the car. Her breath hung in clouds in the air. With the box tucked under her arm, she stepped into the thick of the forest. Through the brambles, past the bushes, she crossed over a metal bridge, the sound of snow crunching beneath her feet. Halfway up a hill, she wandered along a path well behind a row of houses. Some were lit up, their shadows rolling out across backyards, others shrouded in darkness. When she came to a small clearing, she dropped the box at her feet.

The moon shone down between the gaps in the foliage. She pulled the hard drive from her laptop and SIM card from the back of her phone and reached into the pocket of her pants for her mother's lighter. She ignited the flame. The metal blackened and warped and then melted and fell to the ground. She carved out a small hole, buried them inside and covered it with snow.

Next, she snapped the wheel of the lighter and held it to the corner of the box. The cardboard blackened, then flames surged across the bottom. She gasped, released it, and quickly stepped back. Sparks and fragments and embers filled the air. She could hear the beat of her heart as her former life popped and sizzled until it was reduced to ash. Then she darted along the path, down the hill, across the bridge, hands out to fend off branches, and stumbled out of the forest.

At home, she filled a glass of wine and returned to her office. Settled at her desk, the glass shook as she took a sip. The smooth, earthy fruit felt good on her throat. The trembling slowed, then stopped. Before the house stirred, she searched through a drawer in her desk and removed the burner phone she'd found hidden underneath a pile of clothes in Jim's dresser last fall. She punched in Marco's number.

"Is it done?" That voice.

"It is, and in lieu of the final payment we discussed, I have a proposition."

"What's your pleasure?"

Arms wrapped tight around her chest, she told him what she wanted.

He kept his voice low. "You can't be serious."

"I'll get back to you with a time and location. I need to take care of something first." When she started to tell him what it was, he drew in a sharp breath. "Jesus."

"Trust me, you don't want to know any more than that."

A week later, Ria threaded through the aisles of the grocery store downtown, examining the shelves, poking at packages, peering through the glass in the freezer. Her cart full, the final details of her plan in place, she checked out. When she arrived home, Jacob was waiting at the door.

"Did you get it all?" he asked.

She held up the bags of groceries. With Liam holed up in his bedroom and Jim not due home from work until after five, they spent the afternoon baking tarts and cookies and banana bread. As Jacob watched through the glass oven door, she puttered around the kitchen. After they lay the desserts on the counter to cool, she sent a fast text to Marco from her office, while the soundtrack from *Pitch Perfect* blared from the living room.

Late afternoon, she pulled out the cast iron Dutch oven from the kitchen cupboard to prepare dinner. After she turned the oven on to warm, she rough chopped the vegetables, washed the goose, and patted it down with a paper towel. When it was dry, she sprinkled it with salt, pepper, rosemary, and thyme and placed it in the oven. Then she added onions, carrots, new baby potatoes and celery around it. She splashed it with a generous dose of white wine and set the oven for three hours.

In the living room, she collapsed on the couch. She dozed, despite the TV still blaring and Jacob laughing. Shortly after five, Jim came home, showered and joined them. Then she heard a strange noise.

Hissssssssssssss

"Mom?"

Ria looked up, stalled, then she jumped to her feet. "The goose."

In the kitchen, flames danced behind the glass oven door. She ripped it open, grabbed the cast iron pot and tossed it on top of the stove. She fought back a wince.

"Mom, your eyebrows," Jacob hollered.

Pain seared her fingers. She held up her hands. Angry red blisters covered the skin. She stumbled to the sink and plunged them in the water, screaming as they popped. The room spun. Strong fingers gripped her firmly under the arms as she fell in a heap to the tile.

Slumped against the counter, she heard the oven door bang shut. Then yelling and crying. Off in the distance, sirens pierced the air. A door slammed. Then footsteps thumping, pounding closer. Low voices, hot breath in her face. She felt herself lifted up, and then the cool air of an oxygen mask. This was it. The end of her old life and the beginning of a new one.

THIRTY-FIVE
Ria

Ria woke up with a start. Her eyes were unfocused, her back was soaked in sweat. A thick, plastic smell hung in her nostrils. She tried to move left. She tried to move right. She was trapped, stuffed between the pillows packed around her. Machines whirled and hummed and thunked, a cacophony of sound coming from somewhere. Her first thought was that she was dreaming, but as her mind cleared, the blurry outline of a room confirmed otherwise.

She lifted her head. It was a small, rectangular area. Apart from the bed and a window to her left, the walls were white and stark. A tiny closet. Fresh white sheets were tucked around her waist, and she discovered she was wearing a blue gown. She squinted at a woman wheezing in the bed to her right. Hair fine as mist, the folds of saggy skin. A green blob of Jello in a plastic cup on the table sat beside a silver kidney-shaped bowl, sour with reek, splattered with bile and vomit.

A few minutes later, a doctor in a white coat strolled into the room. He stopped at the end of her bed and put down a clipboard.

"Quite the accident you had," he said.

"I did?" Images flitted through her mind. Cookies. Banana bread. Vegetables. Fire.

"You don't remember?" he said. "The paramedics who brought you in-"

"Yesterday?"

He looked at her strangely. "Three days ago."

She drew in a sharp breath. She'd been out that long? Where was Jim? The boys? It was as if he read her mind.

"Your family's fine." He ran a hand through his thinning hair. "They've been in and out, but I told your husband to go home for now."

"What happened?"

He picked up the clipboard and flipped through the notes. "It says here you were in the kitchen and there was some type of explosion."

She looked at her arms. The skin was raw and pink. Oozing blisters spread up from the gauze bandages wrapped around her hands. She suppressed a smile. She'd done a good job. There was no doubt her fingerprints were gone.

The doctor moved closer to her bed. "Can you lift your arms?"

After she did what she was asked, he pulled a pen from the breast pocket of his checkered shirt and scribbled on the page. "The early movement is promising."

"Will my hands heal fully?"

He gave a slight nod of his head. "In time. Until then, we'll do everything we can to make you as comfortable as possible."

The IV tugged at her arm. "Can I get this out?"

He frowned. "That's where your meds are coming through. If you need a little extra, let the nurse on duty know. For now, rest to let your mind and body heal."

When the doctor left, she rolled over to the window. Her body would heal. Her mind? Not so fast. She'd escaped the past once--changed her name, her appearance, her identity—and now that her fingerprints were burned off, the last connection to Angel Calarco was gone. There was no longer any chance of anyone figuring out everything she worked so hard to hide. Angel and Ria. Ria and Angel. Two halves of a fractured whole. Why did it always come back to this? Could she ever let them go?

The last light of the day was fading. The sun, a low ball of flame in the sky, stared back at her. It withered and sank to be replaced by night. Hard rain tapped the window as the pain spiked. It was unbearable and she had to call for help.

"Nurse! Nurse!" she hollered.

Footsteps rushed down the hall. A short man in scrubs came into the room, shuffled around the bed, dragging equipment with him. He picked up the end of her IV, pulled out a syringe from his tray and pricked it with a needle. A warm rush flowed through her veins.

"You're awake." A woman's voice. Sickly sweet. "How's the pain?"

Ria rolled her head to the right. Masks, bright lights, tubes. Behind her, another bed, another body. Beyond it, a door out to the pale blue hall and a crooked picture frame. She felt the urge to get up and straighten it.

"A pill, then?" the nurse asked. "To help you sleep through the night?"

"Yes, please."

The night? She struggled to sit up. Every movement hurt. She'd been asleep nearly twenty-four hours? The woman in the bed next to her moaned. As the nurse counted out the pills, Ria hoisted herself up a few inches in the bed. She looked out at the courtyard below. It was lit up, illuminating a light dusting of fresh snow on wood benches and large empty terracotta pots. The sight of them made her long for her summer garden. Roses. Sunflowers. Lilies. The sweet smell of lavender and hyacinth.

The woman in the bed next to her moaned again.

"It'll be hard to sleep with the noise," she said. The nurse cocked her head, seeming not to understand her. "The next bed."

The nurse smiled. "I've been here so long I don't even hear it." She turned to attend to the woman and then left the room, her tread soft on the tile.

Ria stared up at the television suspended from the wall. *Click, click, click.* Friends. Big Bang Theory. When the woman in the bed next to her whimpered, she turned up the volume. Brooklyn 99. How I Met Your Mother. Out of the blue, the woman cried out, a dry and ragged howl. She turned it up again.

Doctors and nurses trickled through the room. From time to time, there were voices in the hallway, but they faded and disappeared for good. Near midnight, Ria turned the TV off and pushed the covers from her legs. Moving slowly, she crossed the room. She stepped around the curtain hanging from the metal track on the ceiling. With her closed eyes, and her mouth pinched tight, the old lady reminded her of the dolls in the antique stores. Their wiry hair, their vacant smiles, all in oversized dresses, fascinated her. What harm could come from looking? She moved in closer until she could smell the stale stink of the sheets.

The woman moaned. Enough already. She examined the white machine at the edge of the bed. A plastic tube secured to the bottom ran down a silver pole, snaked along the floor, and disappeared up under the bottom of the blanket at the middle of the bed. It reappeared again, inserted in the old woman's nostrils, helping her breathe. Ria coiled the breathing tube gently around her slipper and stomped her foot down hard.

The woman's eyes fluttered open. She gazed up, raised a veiny hand, her breath wheezing and laboured. Ria held the woman's gaze, until the woman's eyes rolled to the back of her head and slowly flitted shut. Then she stepped off the tube and eased away. She made a quick trip to the bathroom and averted her eyes as she passed. Settled in her own bed, she swallowed her pill and lay back on the pillow.

Hell. That's where she was headed. It wasn't a surprise. As a child, her mother had told her she was destined to get there.

One afternoon after coming inside from playing in the back yard, she'd asked her mother why she was so certain. A glass hanging from one hand, a cracked crystal decanter in the other, the woman who gave birth to her, raised her, and ignored her day and night, turned from the kitchen counter.

"Because you're your father's child." She'd stood, her sweater pulled over her chin, waiting for her to continue. Her mother hadn't missed a beat. "If you must know, you were an accident."

Angel thought she knew what that meant but wasn't sure. Her mother knocked back the remainder of the brown liquid left in the glass and sighed impatiently. "It can't be a big surprise. Look at me. It's not like I'm mother material."

She hadn't argued. "Wasn't there something you could've done?"

"By the time we realized?" Her mother filled the glass again. "It wouldn't have mattered anyway because your father refused to give you up."

"But he did," she'd told her. "He left."

Her mother took deep swallow. "You think you're the only one he left? While he was out galivanting around, I went out of my mind. Do this. Don't touch that. Walk, don't run, dear." Liquid sloshed from the glass as she waved it around. "Staying home with a kid is a boring life. Nothing like the thrill of the theatre."

"Then why don't you go back?"

"It's too late now." Her mother slammed the glass on the counter. "In one reckless night, my future was ruined. You ruined my life, you little shit."

Those words, coupled with the look on her mother's face, left her shattered. The pain she felt that day, a child in her mother's kitchen, sowed a seed her mother would reap later. Determined she was better off alone, confident she'd be happier without her, Angel thought about killing her mother then. But thinking and doing were two different things. It took her months to work up the courage.

There were times she still wondered if what she did could be justified. Marco would say yes. Dr. Gibson would say no. Society? Who the fuck cared? The jury made their decision. Slumped on a pile of pillows, she considered what she'd want as a last meal if she were put on death row. Steak? Lobster? More likely something home cooked. Comfort food. Mac and Cheese, meat loaf, a simple roast chicken. She took her pill and gazed out into the dark winter night. Soon, she was fast asleep.

Ria awoke the next morning peaceful and rested. Her breakfast was already on her tray. The oatmeal was lumpy, the toast burnt, the coffee cold. She didn't care. For the first time in days, she was starving. She ate it all.

In the bed beside hers, a leg was suspended inches above the sheets in a metal sling. Gauze crisscrossed a face, and a ponytail of brown hair was singed at the end. She wondered what happened? A car accident? A domestic dispute? A house fire? The new patient's breakfast sat untouched on her tray. She glanced toward the hall. Morning rounds wouldn't start for an hour, and she knew hospitals were expensive to operate. She had time. She crossed the room, exchanged the plates, and polished off hers as well. No one likes waste.

Right on schedule, the door to the room opened. The nurse came in, followed by two women in white jackets. They stood on either side of the new patient, poking and prodding, speaking in low whispers, while one took notes. When they finished, they stepped away, conferring in hushed tones. The tall, thin woman snapped the notebook shut and approached the foot of her bed. She looked like she needed a meal.

"Good morning," Skinny Doctor said.

"Morning."

"How was your night?"

"Fine." She'd slept well.

After the nurse picked up her glass to refill it and scuttled away, the other woman came in and stood behind her. She wore round wire framed glasses on her high cheekbones. She smiled at them. There was an awkward silence. Did they know what she'd done? She kept her mouth shut. This was not the time to give the doctors any information they could use against her. They observed her coolly. She considered what to say, reminding herself they had nothing to go on.

They examined her hands, turning them this way and that, and talked between themselves in terms she couldn't grasp. Medical mumbo-jumbo.

"Everything is progressing nicely," Skinny Doctor said, without looking at her.

The other agreed. "There's no need for you to stay here any longer, so we'll be discharging you today."

Ria lay her head back and took a deep breath. Finally, she was going home.

THIRTY-SIX
Jim

Jim nosed into a spot in the hospital parking lot and opened the back door of the car. Jacob tumbled off the seat. His hair was a mess and the white mask covering half his face accentuated the dark circles under his eyes. He had on the yellow rubber gloves Ria kept under the kitchen sink for scrubbing pots and pans.

After they approached the building and brushed through the revolving doors, Jim pressed the elevator button. On the fifth floor, Jacob stood at the end of Ria's bed.

"Dad didn't tell us we were picking you up today." His tone was sharp.

Jim raised an index finger to his lips. "I only found out two minutes before you did."

"Where's Liam?" Ria smiled from her bed.

"It's ten in the morning," Jacob said, annoyed. "Has the doctor signed you out?"

Jim gave up. He'd already explained to Jacob that he wasn't the only one caught off guard when the hospital called to tell them Ria was being discharged this morning. The last few days, he'd done his best. Juggling the boys, making school lunches, the cooking and cleaning. Phone calls from Frank and Rachel and his parents. It had helped Jacob stayed close on his tail ensuring almost nothing had been forgotten. At home, the blue box was overflowing and there were two empty pizza boxes on the counter. Had he received a little more notice from the hospital than he did, he'd have had the time to clean them up too.

Jacob turned away and paced the room. As he passed by the adjacent bed, he stopped rigid at the end. His eyes flicked back and forth. Wrapped like a mummy, a new patient slept soundly. He looked to Ria and frowned. "Where's the other lady?"

She shrugged and mouthed, "Out to pasture."

Jim stared at Ria. Since their last session with Efram, she'd withdrawn. Now her eyes were bright. She sounded so calm. Was it the morphine? After she swung her legs out of the sheets and pivoted to the floor, he took her by the elbow. He steadied her, imagining the highs and lows of what lay ahead. He had no clue what to expect.

While she was in the hospital, he'd gone into her office to take a quick look around. At first glance, there was nothing of the ordinary. He sat at her desk. The only thing he found odd was a shiny new laptop, beside it a new phone. Ria hadn't mentioned anything about replacing her technology. He fiddled with both, punching in his birthday, her birthday, the boy's birthdays. Combinations of each, coupled with their anniversary. Nothing worked.

Jacob gathered his mother's things in a pile on the bed. Slippers. Two clear bottles of coloured pills. As he and Ria caught up, Jim crossed the room to the bathroom to collect what remained on the shelves. Behind him, a heated argument spilled through the half-open door to the hallway.

"My mother doesn't imagine things."

"I'm sure she doesn't but-"

Jim turned, pushed the bathroom door closed a few inches with his foot and peered through the crack. A woman, sandy-haired with a narrow angular face, was talking to a nurse. There was an electricity in the air he couldn't pin down.

"That woman did something to her," the woman insisted.

"We have no reason to suspect her of anything," the nurse explained politely. "The female patient beside your mother is in considerable pain. Her hands are bandaged and-"

"I know my mother." The woman jabbed a finger at the nurse. "Do you have security video here?"

The nurse confirmed they did not. The woman threw her arms in the air.

Jim swallowed. When he arrived, the bed beside Ria's was empty. Was the old woman okay?

The nurse spoke up. "We understand your concern and take it seriously. Since you reported it this morning, we immediately moved your mother to another room down the hall. We also casually asked the female patient a couple of questions, and we have no reason to believe anything untoward happened."

Tension flowed around them. Jim puffed out his cheeks. He wondered how well that went. His stomach sunk. Under normal circumstances, he wouldn't have been worried. Ria always got up in the night. But this felt different.

He recalled what Mrs. Potts told him had happened when Ria dropped off the bag of salt at her house last fall. He replayed the awful, awkward conversation over in his mind. If she was in one of her moods, she was capable of cruelty. Still, she hadn't said a mean thing to him when he'd called earlier to let her know he and Jacob were leaving the house.

He needed to get Ria out of here. Word spread quickly. He pressed a sticky palm to the door, wondering what lay on the other side.

After they arrived home from the hospital, Jim made grilled

cheese sandwiches, then he quickly tidied the kitchen and joined Jacob and Ria in the living room. As the soundtrack from the movie blared, he checked the time. He leaned over and whispered in Jacob's ear.

"Where's Liam?" It was four p.m.

"In bed."

"Why would he still be there?"

Jacob looked at him like he was an idiot. "Do you want the list alphabetically or categorically?"

He laughed and ruffled his hair. Upstairs, he knocked on Liam's door. No answer. He knocked again, then pushed it open. He peered at Liam in the shadows. Head down, eyes closed, not a sound.

"Mom's home. Come and see her."

As soon as he said it, Liam lay back on the bed, curled into himself and stared blankly at the wall. He stepped inside his room. There were textbooks lying around, a phone on the unmade bed, beside it a wad of balled tissues. He sat beside him.

"Hey, bud. What's going on?"

As Liam wiped his cheeks with the back of his hand, Jim's stomach tightened. He'd seen Liam's many moods. Cocky after getting caught by the principal smoking pot, livid in the course of the conversation with #TheFellas in the food court, anxious during the confrontation with Dirk outside the deserted building, unsettled the day Ria was rushed in the ambulance to the hospital. But not once had he seen him cry. Not even when he'd lost his temper last fall and slammed his son's head on the dashboard.

"Liam." He softened his voice. "What's wrong?"

"Nothing."

"I don't believe you." He touched his shoulder. "Tell me."

"There's not much to tell. #TheFellas and I had a fight."

Jim put his arms around Liam and held him hard. His son didn't move, but his shoulders shook, and he could feel tears soak into the front of his shirt. He stared out the window, giving Liam as much time as he needed. When they pulled apart, Liam rubbed his face with the sleeve of his shirt.

"They wanted to go back to cards like nothing happened, so I lost my shit on them. I dunno what I did wrong."

"Nothing, son."

"They've ghosted me two weeks."

Jim stared at the floor. His heart pinched. For a tight-knit social support group, two weeks would feel like a lifetime.

"What do I do now?" Liam pushed the bangs back from his eyes and took a shaky breath. His mouth opened, closed, then opened again. "It's like I don't exist. They won't return my calls. They won't even talk to me."

"You need to give it time."

A few second passed and when Liam held up his phone, his fingers were trembling. "How can I? They blocked me on Instagram and texts." He thumbed his screen until a new page appeared. "On Snapchat and TikTok, too."

Jim recalled the way he'd felt last fall when Jaylyn did the same to him. Shut out. Distressed. Lonely. The anguish had followed him for weeks. While he couldn't tell Liam a thing about it, he understood exactly how he was feeling.

Liam's face darkened. "Everyone's talking about it at school. Everybody." He gripped the phone in his hands as if he could snap it in two. "They're all taking sides. Mostly theirs, and they're posting all sorts of shit on social. I'm such a fucking loser."

"No, son. You're not. One day-"

"Stop it," he snapped. "You know and I know it's true. I don't have other friends. I don't play sports--I hate them, and

I'm not in the band or in any clubs and I suck at school. I don't fit anywhere." He dropped his phone in the sheets.

"It'll blow over." In time, #TheFellas would be back on his side. Liam's voice was tied up with so much grief he could hardly bear it. He swore under his breath. They better be.

Liam seemed unfazed by the information. "Between the fuckin cards, the online thing and the money we owed? You can add all that shit to the pile too."

"Hey," he said, calmly. "I promised you we'd deal with it, and we did."

Liam's voice rose. "You did, not me, and do you think I'm stupid?"

"No," he said firmly. "Why would I think that?"

"Last fall?" He rubbed the side of his head. "Dad! I saw those bruises all over you."

Jim held his son's gaze and swallowed. There was no chance he was going to tell Liam the details that still haunted him at night, but he wasn't going to lie to him either. He took Liam's chin in this hand. "First, I need to apologize for smacking your head on the dashboard. It was a stupid, immature thing to do. And all this? Yes, you're right. I got a bit roughed up, but I'm okay now."

Liam nodded slowly.

"If it makes you feel any better," he said, "you should've seen the other guy."

Liam's eyes widened. "Was Dirk a mess? Did you give it to him?"

Jim grinned, then he looked away. Though he hoped Liam had forgiven him, it didn't absolve him from the consequences of making a poor decision. That he'd have to live with.

Liam regained his composure and looked down at his bare feet. "I'm so sorry, Dad," he mumbled. "I didn't mean to. I mean,

I didn't realize-"

"We're good, son. It doesn't matter now." Jim leaned sideways and wrapped his arm tight around Liam's shoulders. "You're gonna be okay. I've got you."

"Dad?" Liam let out a long breath. "I love you."

"Thanks." He squeezed Liam tighter, then met his son's eyes. "I love you too."

THIRTY-SEVEN
Jim

For the next month, Jim spent his days working, taking care of the boys, and driving Ria to physical therapy, which left no time for much of anything else. But as Ria healed, things slowed, and eventually returned to normal. When she started working again, he often passed by to find her at her desk, staring at the wall. Other times, she wandered the house increasingly restless. She was clearly not herself, but he didn't know how to address it.

There was something about the situation that was wrong, but he couldn't put his finger on it. He tried to bring up what he'd overheard regarding the older woman at the hospital, but Ria shrugged it off and refused to discuss it. Was it a drug-induced delusion or was Ria involved in something more sinister? Recently, he'd found her in the den watching PVRed clips about a mob boss' death. He wasn't sure what to believe or why she was so interested, but he was certain of one thing. He wasn't safe investigating any of it at home.

Sitting at his desk at work the next day, he typed Angel Calarco into google. The headlines of several old articles appeared: *Young Woman Acquitted. What Will She Do Next?* The accompanying images were haunting. News vans packed bumper to bumper on the street, hordes of reporters jostling on the courthouse steps. Aunt Beth guiding a body, head covered by a bulky coat, giving the media a middle-finger. Ridiculed, reviled, and ostracized for days, new stories emerged. Over time, he guessed they lost interest.

It all weighed heavily on his mind. At the bottom of an article was a familiar name. He googled Dr. Gibson and found his office address. Under the guise of training purposes, he sent an email to central office requesting final reports of fires involving hoarders. Frustrated by Ria's secrecy, he was determined to uncover what she was hiding. If she refused to tell him, he was going to find out himself.

One evening, he stole out to the front porch. Huge drifts thrown up by the snow plough shimmered in the glow of the streetlamps, the stop sign a snow-covered lump. He edged toward the window. Frosted patterns etched across the bottom of the glass. Her laptop pushed aside, Ria was at her desk, her phone held out in front of her. He caught snippets of the conversation.

"...good together, don't...."

"No.....understand each other.....the money."

"Probably more accurate.....the deal."

None of it looked right, sounded right, felt right. When the called ended, Ria threw her phone down on her desk. Then she rifled through a drawer and pulled out a silver lighter. A yellow flame shot up in the air. He watched in horror as she pulled it forward and held it less than an inch from her face. Suddenly, she hurled it across the room. After it hit the wall, she laughed out loud, softly first, then louder and louder, until she grabbed the sides of her waist and doubled over.

Jim backed away from the pane. A sinking feeling washed over him. What was he supposed to do?

That night showered and wrapped in a towel, he looked out the window to the street. The sky was black. The wind was fierce. His head was spinning. He stretched, working out the kinks in his neck and shoulders, then he plucked the blanket folded neatly at the end of the bed. Thick and warm, he wrapped it around his shoulders. Their bedroom was tidier than usual. The bed plumped, the smell of fresh laundered sheets. Sex? Whatever she thought may happen tonight wouldn't. After what he'd seen earlier, he couldn't think about it. Couldn't do it. He knitted his fingers together and stared at them. He needed a plan forward. He did not want to be here.

When Ria joined him a few minutes later, she didn't say a word. He slipped into bed and turned against the wall. Warm fingers caressed his shoulders. He wanted to say something, but his tongue was glued to the roof of his mouth. He rolled over to find her lying beside him, framed in the darkness.

"What?" She stroked his hair. "What's wrong?"

His thoughts were heavy, but he kept them to himself. He felt sick even thinking them. He turned around and lay awake in the darkness. Minutes crawled by. Should he bring it up? What could he ask her? He couldn't bring himself to speak. Not because he couldn't find the words, but because he was afraid of what he might find out if he did.

The following weekend, Jim blew into his hands as the wipers flicked snow off the windshield. Sunlight flooded the front seat. When he flipped on the radio, music blasted uncomfortably loud. He snapped it off. Liam.

He travelled through the city streets, quiet for Saturday morning. He picked up a coffee and set off to visit Dr. Gibson. An easy drive two hundred miles west, he had a strange feeling of being trapped that was at odds with the wide-open space of the six-lane highway. Earlier that week when his cell phone buzzed, he'd quickly picked it up, listening and nodding as their appointment was confirmed. He hadn't exactly been forthcoming about the reason for his call, and afterwards, he'd pulled a bottle of beer from the fridge and guzzled it.

An hour and half and a stretch of side streets later, he arrived at the Ithaca Wellness Centre. Housed in a three-story brown brick building, the parking lot was crowded with SUVs and police cruisers. On the second floor of the Wellness Centre, he pushed open a door to a suite. The waiting room was empty, but there was a narrow hallway that led to an open door of a windowless office.

"Jim Stiles," he said, as he stopped in the doorway.

"Grant Gibson." He gestured to a seat.

Dr. Gibson had a long, narrow face, and a head ringed with gray hair. He took out a key, rifled through a cabinet drawer and dropped a file on his desk. He sighed heavily, flipped through it and pulled out a piece of paper.

"What do you want to know?" His tone cold and clinical.

Jim scooted his chair closer to the desk. "I'm a firefighter. I respect you're bound by doctor-patient confidentiality, but I'll take whatever you can give me."

Dr. Gibson's voice sharpened. "Not much."

"Ria—Angel—is my wife," he pressed.

His bushy eyebrows rose.

Jim looked at him, trying to determine what to say. "We have two boys. I need to know they're safe."

Dr. Gibson grew quiet, even solemn. The paper trembled in his hand. He put it on the desk and looked over the top of his glasses. He stared with such intensity Jim struggled not to blink or look away.

"Alright," he relented. "I'm a father too. Between the kids, we've got four grandbabies, and a fifth coming along soon." He paused. Mouth grim. "Here's what I can tell you."

As Dr Gibson talked, Jim gritted his teeth and listened. The pit in his stomach grew. Everything about Ria's life was phony, built on lies, constructed like fake news on Facebook. Fragments of their marriage, outings, restaurants, friends, family trips, swirled through his mind. The uncomfortable feeling in his stomach worsened. That was it, he thought. His suspicions were confirmed.

"I don't mean to frighten you," the doctor said.

"I'm not scared," he said, although he was. He could barely breathe.

Dr. Gibson held his gaze. "You should be. For whatever reason, good care under a new psychologist, maybe medication, she's held it together thirty years. But Angel is smart. She's organized, she's manipulative and she's ruthless."

He cradled his head in his hands. His skin was hot, his forehead damp, a muscle twitched in his cheek. How did he get this all so wrong? Chilled to the core, he thought about his boys. If Dr. Gibson was right and Ria had killed an innocent person—her mother--was there a chance, she'd kill him or the boys too?

He'd never let it happen. He needed to act, and he needed to act fast. Tomorrow, he'd talk to Frank, and they'd determine how to get Liam and Jacob safely out of the house. Then he'd get out too. There was no other choice. He was finished. This marriage was done. When Dr. Gibson ceased talking, he eased from the chair. He shook his hand, slipped out of the room, and closed the door behind him.

Outside, the sky had turned dirty yellow. He dreaded the long drive home, but the trip had been more than worth the time. On the highway, Ria called twice, her voice echoing through the car, increasingly annoyed, asking him where he was. He ignored her calls and focused on the road and the horrible thoughts in his head.

At home by suppertime, they had a quick family meal.

Afterwards, he stretched out on the living room couch. Gusts of wind rattled the window and flakes of snow fell from the sky. He was tired, but he couldn't sleep. He put the game on the TV on mute to rest his mind.

"Are you okay?" Ria said from the doorway, her hair tumbling over an oversized sweatshirt.

Jim shifted slightly. When the cushion sloped beside him, he stiffened.

"They just announced a storm tracking in," she said. "Fifteen centimeters of snow by tomorrow morning. If you don't get a call from the station, you can sleep all afternoon."

It wouldn't be what he'd be doing. After he left Ithaca, he'd made a call to Frank to arrange to meet him for lunch. But he chatted a bit, polite conversation about who needed to do what before the boys' activities the next day.

"If we get a big dump tonight, it won't matter because we'll all be snowed in anyway," Ria said, when they finished. "Which reminds me, we need milk."

"Now?" The last thing he wanted was to go out.

She shrugged. "Only if you want coffee or cereal tomorrow."

Now that he knew what he did, his stomach rolled at the thought of leaving the boys alone in the house with Ria. But he didn't want to raise suspicion either, so he got to his feet, put on his jacket and scarf, and headed out in the dark.

Too late to hit a grocery store, he drove across town to the 7-11. Lights shone brightly from inside and he could see a lineup of people at the cash. Not a spot available out front, he guided his car to a stop in the adjacent strip mall. As he jogged back to the entrance, a truck rolled down the street. It stopped and made a u-turn. Bright lights blinded him. His eyes watered, and he had to squint against the glare.

Inside, he picked up milk. After he passed a row of garbage bins along the edge of the lot, he returned to the car and pressed the fob. A man wearing a black coat and a toque pulled low over his ears stepped out of the shadows.

"Jim."

Something clicked when he heard the voice. He peered over the roof. He could see the man's breath in white clouds as he approached. Tall, a chiseled face, long strides, confident swagger. Marco was exactly how he looked in the media.

"Aren't you, like, supposed to be dead?"

Marco only smiled.

"What do you want?" he asked.

"Your wife is a real character."

Wasn't that the truth. "You don't know the half of it."

"I know she has a relaxed relationship with the truth." Marco took a step forward.

He snorted. "No, she's a monster."

"Who's left quite the dirty legacy."

When Marco raised his eyebrows, Jim felt chilled to the bone. He knew? Holy shit. Then Marco knew everything.

"Get away from me," he yelled. "I want her gone. You gone. Both of you, get the hell out of my life. Get away from my kids and my family."

"The way she's built?" Marco stepped forward again. "That's not possible, Jim. Think about it."

His pulse was beating a mile a minute. He could feel it through this jacket. "What the hell do you know? For a dead guy, you're pretty fucking arrogant."

A flash of anger crossed Marco's face and then was gone. "We're both supposed to be dead, but my situation is looking a lot better than yours is."

All Jim saw was a tiny flash of light. The carton of milk

slipped from his hand and fell to the ground.

"What the-?" he stammered.

He staggered backwards and sucked in a breath. An intense burning sensation, then a deep ache filled his chest. He reached for the side of the car to steady himself, and then brought a hand up to his jacket. When he glanced down, there was a red smear across his palm. Unable to catch a breath, he could hear the squeak of the snow as Marco came around the hood of the vehicle. Images crowded his mind. Liam and Jacob's faces. His parents' place. Frank at the kitchen table. Jaylyn. When he looked up, it was into the muzzle of a gun. Marco's dark eyes were beyond it. Silence. Then another quick flash.

THIRTY-EIGHT
Ria

Ria woke up to pounding on the front door. She glanced at the clock. Three a.m. Before the boys stirred, she scrambled out of bed. Downstairs, there were two shadows on the other side of the frosted glass in the hall. She cracked open the front door. In the glare of the porch light, she stared at the faces of Detectives Singh and Detective Li.

"Odd time for an update," she offered.

Grim, neither spoke.

The sharp wall of the deep freeze they'd been in for weeks made it painful to breathe. The door had only been open five seconds and already the snot in her nose had frozen, pinching her skin. She shielded herself behind it from the cold.

"May we come in, please?" Detective Li said, her breath in white clouds.

Ria stepped back and let them pass through. In the hallway, they removed their coats and boots. As Detective Singh pulled out his phone and contacted dispatch, letting them know they'd arrived, Detective Li put a hand on her shoulder.

"Is there somewhere we can talk?" she asked.

Ria looked at her. "It's three o'clock in the morning."

"How's the living room?" she insisted.

"What's this all about?"

"There's been an accident."

"What do you mean?" She frowned. "An accident how?"

Detective Li cleared her throat. "We're sorry to be the ones to have to tell you-" Detective Singh took the lead. "We found your husband's body tonight on the Catskill escarpment."

She shook her head in disbelief. "That's not possible," she heard herself say. She peered up the stairs, as if Jim might walk down them any second to see what the commotion was all about.

"He was shot," Li went on.

"Shot?" She lifted her hands to her chest. "What? Are you sure?"

"I'm sorry, Ria." Detective Li said softly. "He didn't make it."

Adrenaline pumped through her veins. She fought to keep the relief from her face. A sorrowful moan followed only seconds later. She swayed forward, then downwards, and ended up in a crumpled heap on the floor.

Detective Li crouched beside her. "Can we call someone? Someone who can be here with you?"

She mumbled Jim's parents' names and their phone number. She started to speak again but couldn't remember what she wanted to say. When Detective Singh reached out to hand her Jim's soft woven scarf, she didn't need to take it to know it was his.

"When did this happen?" she cried. "How?"

"We're not sure," he said.

"You must have some idea."

"The coroner will know."

"You don't have a clue?" Her throat tightened. "Anything?"

Detective Singh glanced at his watch. "We got the call at 1 a.m. from the responding officers."

"And?" She wanted all the details.

"Your husband's body was still warm when they found him. We spent a couple hours processing the scene."

She knew what that meant. Bagging and tagging evidence. What evidence? She hoped the tech crews didn't find any.

"Once we finished," he confirmed, "we came straight here."

"Ria." Detective Li rocked back on her heels. "Why was Jim doing out that late?"

She shrunk, unable to process the information. She scrambled to recall everything she and Jim did together earlier. Dinner. The game was on TV. He was lying on the couch.

"The milk was low, so I asked him to go pick some up. The last thing I remember, we were talking on the living room couch." She replayed every word of their conversation, buzzing with adrenaline. Not the correct reaction. She was tired. So tired. "I was fading. I must have fallen asleep. Oh my god." She rolled to her side, wrapped her arms around her head and wailed. "He left without a last goodbye kiss."

Twenty minutes later, Ria stumbled into the back seat of the black sedan parked at the curb. The boys were still sound asleep in their beds and her father-in-law had his arms wrapped around Jim's mother as they stood shivering at the front door. Though they looked weak and frail in the moment, they were strong. She knew they'd get through this.

She pressed her hands between her thighs as the car sped through the neighbourhood. The houses on either side were dark, SUVs still in the driveways. After they swerved tight around a bend, they ascended the ramp to the highway. The headlights of the oncoming vehicles blinded her. Clouds of white smoke billowed from her mouth, and her fingers and toes were so numb they were starting to itch.

"Can you turn up the heat, please?" she asked.

"It's on high." Detective Li glanced through the rearview mirror. "It takes a while to come through."

"Then I need coffee," she told him.

His eyes turned back to the road. "There'll be some at the morgue."

Slumped on the seat, she laid her head back. She wondered if her mother would've thought her acting Oscar-worthy. She thought so. Her mother once told her: *Details matter, so whether you're on or off stage, pay attention until the curtain falls.* She had and she would.

Those sessions she was forced to endure years ago with the police taught her how to play this game. Unlike last time, she wouldn't make the same mistakes. To get what one wanted, to get out *unscathed*, it was important to be polite.

Her head spun and she closed her eyes for a moment. When a cold burst of air hit her face, she sat up abruptly. *Shit.* Had she drifted off?

"Let's go," Detective Li said, holding open the car door.

Her breaths were white bursts that dissipated into the darkness as they crossed the parking lot. She swiped a hand across her face. Get a grip. Wake up and focus.

Detective Singh fell in step beside them as they entered the heat of the building. They led her through the lobby, past a reception desk and swiped a card to a door. Behind it, a dimly lit hallway gave way to a series of closed offices. At the end, Detective Li flicked on a light in a room.

"I'll get something hot," she announced.

Ria stepped inside. It was scarcely big enough to hold a desk and four chairs. She fell into one and Detective Singh sat opposite. He looked at his partner slowly making her way from the kitchen across the hall, with three Styrofoam cups balanced between her fingers.

"Sorry," she said, as she joined them. "It's not Starbucks."

What Ria really needed was alcohol. When Detective Li

placed them on the table, she took the cup anyway. She forced herself to shiver, projecting it was the only thing that could take the numb from deep down in her aching, frost-bitten bones.

"Why are we here exactly?" She knew why.

"Like we said back at the house," Detective Li explained, "we need you to identify your husband's body. It's standard procedure."

She shifted her butt on the seat. As the threads holding her together unraveled, she pinched the skin on her arms. Hard.

"I can't do it," she blurted. A reasonable response.

"Let's start with a photo instead." Detective Singh suggested. "It may be easier."

Ria warmed to the idea. A knot formed in her stomach as he took out his phone, tapped the screen and passed it over. She removed her glasses from her purse. Her hands shook as she studied the image.

A body lay in the snow. A man, a tangled mess, twisted and bloody, his face almost unrecognizable. Someone had done a good number on him. A gunshot wound had taken out most of his right cheek and the gash around the bone was slightly open. Blood congealed around the edges of the hole, but the entry wound looked raw. She pinched at the screen. The photo was almost identical to the one she did for Marco. Damn, he was right. She'd done a masterful job doctoring his photo.

Horrified, she dropped the phone on the table. She turned away and did the best to find the right voice.

"From this?" Her voice wavered a little, then she said firmly, "I can't tell. I need to see him."

"You're sure about that?" Detective Singh picked up his phone.

When Ria pushed herself up, he put a hand at her elbow. He guided her from the room, down a flight of stairs and along a labyrinth of hallways. Detective Li followed and they stopped in front of a window.

She dropped her hands to her waist and peered into the morgue. It was a large white room with six polished steel tables under bright lights that didn't allow for shadows anywhere. Metal cabinets lined the outside walls. At a table, the short man with red hair snapped on a pair of regulation latex gloves.

"Can't be a robbery," he informed the others in the room. "He's still got his wedding ring on." He patted the pockets of Jim's black overcoat, then moved his hands to the front pant pockets.

Detective Singh banged on the glass. "I've got it," he called out to the tech crew. He extracted Jim's wallet from his jacket, walked down the hall through another door and passed it over.

The coroner plucked the driver's license out of the clear plastic window and held it up to the light. "Jim Stiles. 124 Highland Avenue. 1966." The tech crew waited for him to do the math. "54 years old."

The coroner stared into the shadow of what was left of Jim's face. Ria studied his expression as he leaned in closer. Impressed with his cool, detached professionalism, she figured he must've seen thousands of mangled, dead faces through his lifetime. What a job. It would be interesting work. Voices behind the glass rang out.

What the hell was a well-dressed middle-aged man doing at a strip mall?

In the dead of the night?

Alone. And on that side of town with so many abandoned buildings?

Nothing good.

He obviously wasn't by himself.

When the coroner began to unbutton Jim's shirt, Ria said,

"Tell me this isn't happening."

Detective Li banged on the glass again. The coroner's eyes widened. A red colour rose up his neck and into his cheeks. He pressed a button on the wall. All she could hear of the conversation was urgent and hushed, clipped tones. After the tech crew scampered out of the room, the coroner pressed the same button.

"Sorry about that," he said. "Come on in."

Ria took a deep breath and walked through the door. The room smelled flowery, but not strong enough to mask the faint smell of lemon cleanser. She stared at the body on the table. The stubble on Jim's chin and the hair on his chest looked longer. She thought back to the research she did for Marco. Rigor mortis would be setting in. Every bruise, every mark on his body would give the coroner clues. Vital clues. A strange hissing sound escaped from his lips, like fingernails scratching their way out of a coffin.

"What the hell was that?" she said, wide eyed.

"It's totally normal," he explained. "It's auscultation."

Ria swallowed. She needed a moment. When Jim's fingers twitched, she froze.

"A post-mortem spasm," the coroner explained again. "It's a result of the change in body temperature."

When Jim's fingers twitched again, she jumped back. Everything swirled around her. She didn't hear the shouting. She didn't feel her knees buckle. She never felt the edge of the table.

"Ria?" A male voice. "Are you with us?"

The lights were bright. Blood coated her mouth. The sickly smell of lemon clung to the back of her throat. Someone was crouched beside her. Was she in the hospital again? Sounds returned. Squeaky wheels, the hum of the lights, muffled voices.

Detective Singh's face came into focus.

"Are you okay?" he asked, gently. "I thought we lost you."

Lost me? Her mind a muddle, she sat up slowly. She turned to the left, working hard to blur the memories rushing back. Her head hurt. The morgue. Jim.

"My boys," she barked.

"They're with their grandparents," he said. "Remember?"

She heaved a sigh of relief. Unsteady, she sat for another moment. Detective Li passed her a tissue and a glass of water.

"If you're feeling up to it," Li informed her, "we'd like to swing by the station."

She nearly choked. "For what?"

"We just have a few questions."

Her blood boiled. When Detective Singh held out a hand, she slapped it away. She'd nearly brained herself and they wanted to talk to her now? She gripped the glass in her hand so hard her fingers went white. *They know,* she thought, *they know.* Inhale. Exhale. Then she lost it.

She hauled herself to her feet and hurled the glass against the wall. A rainbow of shards bounced across the floor. The coroner and the detectives stepped back, visibly perturbed.

"Are you crazy?" she yelled. "My husband was murdered. I need to be with my children. Take me home!"

THIRTY-NINE
Ria

The next morning, Ria sat in a cream-coloured plastic chair at the Police Service Headquarters. From outside, the building was monstrous, an ugly architectural smattering of black glass and beige stone. Inside, there was no warmth, no colour. Institutional. She tried to recall what Jim had told her. The headquarters had always been in downtown, but five years ago it had moved here. No wonder he missed the old one.

She checked the time. She wondered how Liam and Jacob were doing back at home. After the detectives had dropped her off at the house, she'd found them huddled together in the living room with Jim's parents. Their faces were pale, their eyes red and swollen. Unable to answer their stream of questions, she'd squeezed between them on the couch to console them as best as she could. Sending them to school this morning wasn't an option. Grateful Jim's parents had offered to stay, she'd taken a quick shower, then drove directly to the station.

Last night at the morgue wasn't her finest moment, so she'd arrived as early as possible to make amends. The offices were abuzz, phones ringing, radios squawking. Uniformed officers walked briskly back and forth along the hall, badges hanging off their hips, guns glistening in their holsters. She glanced at her wrist again. What was taking so long? Patience.

From her perch outside the conference room, she twisted

around and watched Detective Singh and Detective Li through the crack at the bottom of the bank of windows. They were slouched over a laptop, pointing to the screen. A man in a shiny blue suit rushed by her, nearly tripping over her feet. For the first time, she knew how women over fifty felt. Invisible. He tapped his knuckles twice on the door and entered.

"Heard you had an interesting evening, folks," the Suit said.

"We sure did." From the look on Detective Li's face, Ria could tell she loved working homicide.

"DOA male?" the Suit asked them.

"The call came in shortly before midnight. He was shot three times," Detective Singh confirmed. "Twice to the chest and once to the head. The third was the one to kill him."

"What type of weapon?" the Suit inquired.

"It's MIA," Detective Singh told him. "The recovered slugs indicate it's a small caliber handgun."

"A nine-millimeter?" The Suit sighed. "They're a dime a dozen, so it won't help narrowing down a search. Get to the paperwork. The phone's been ringing off the hook."

Ria gathered they were talking about the media. Word spread fast. When Detective Singh groaned, she knew it must be part of the job he hated. Damn reporters. She knew all too well.

"I'll walk the preliminaries to your office in an hour," Detective Li said.

The Suit scowled. "Not good enough."

Detective Li's cheeks reddened but she didn't argue. Young, ambitious, and smart, Ria guessed she couldn't afford to piss him off. When the Suit left the conference room, Detective Singh flipped him the finger. Ria almost laughed.

"You start the paperwork," he said to Li. "I'll check for a sheet."

"A sheet?" Detective Li looked skeptical. "You've met him.

He's a firefighter. Half his friends are cops."

Detective Singh shrugged. "You never know. I've been surprised before and I'll be surprised again." He tapped a password into the computer and waited. "You're right. He's clean as a whistle."

Li silenced her partner with a look. "Type in his address," she suggested. "See if you get anything there."

Detective Singh tapped at the keys. As he leaned back in his seat, waiting for the database to do its job, Ria imagined it was so much easier now with everything online. The officers who investigated her mother's death would have been in the file room for days.

"What'da you know?" He pointed at the screen. "124 Highland has a history. Ten years ago, there was a 911 call. A man in distress. Something about a curling iron and a bathtub."

"Did it end well?" Li asked.

Detective Singh leaned forward. "The note here says concluded and closed."

"Check the in and out."

He squinted. "It looks like it was all signed off, from the call in to response out, within an hour."

"An hour?" Detective Li frowned. "That's a lifetime for a 911 occurrence. Check the wife."

Ria snorted. Who was sitting right here? She thought of sticking her head around the corner and introducing herself, but she didn't dare. A muffled voice. A pause.

"Nothing," Detective Singh said.

Ria rolled her eyes. What did they expect? Of course not.

"The wife?" he said, "To be honest, she's kind of frumpy. She looks pretty harmless to me."

"That's not what the neighbour told the officers this morning," Detective Li informed him.

Ria frowned. They were already canvassing the street? After the shooting last fall, no one had showed up at their door looking for information or asking questions. Why now? And which neighbour? Although the women on the street never included her in anything, she always went out of her way to be kind to them. *Fuck them all.*

As she turned around, there was a scuffling sound. Chairs scraped the floor, and someone appeared around the corner. Ria picked at the fluff on her pants and pretended not to notice.

"Ria?" Officer Li's voice. "What are you doing here?"

She looked up, feigning surprise. "Oh, hi. This is where they told me to sit."

"Who said that?"

"I don't know." She pointed in the general direction of the duty desk. "Someone out there."

Officer Li looked down the hall and sighed. "That's not standard procedure. I'll deal with it later, but now you're here, you might as well come in."

She stood, shoulders tense, her stomach unsettled. In the conference room, they sat around the table, Detective Li in front of the laptop, Detective Singh with his notebook on his lap. He smoothed the paper with the palm of his hand.

"Alright." He smiled. "Let's get started. Do you mind if I tape this?"

"Go ahead." She'd done this before. If she did mind, it wouldn't make a hill of difference.

Detective Singh pulled a small black tape recorder towards him. He read out the date and time, the reason for the interview and declared the people in the room. His questions were brief. Was Jim having trouble at work? Problems with any members of his family? Difficulties at the station? Had he any enemies she knew of? No. No. No. And no, not that she knew of. Unnerved at first, put off by the detective's sudden changes in direction, she became more comfortable. Detective Li tapped on the keyboard, taking notes.

"Was money tight?" Detective Singh said.

She paused, trying to determine whether to explain the history of Liam's debt. She doubted Jim had mentioned it to anyone at work, but if the officers interviewed Frank or Liam, the story would come out. Should she tell them first? If she did, it would lead them on a wild goose chase. They'd dig further into Jim's entire life. Yes? No? Maybe? She felt dizzy. It was complicated. A can of worms.

"No," she answered.

"One last question."

Ria picked at the thread on her jacket. There was always another question.

"What about affairs?" he asked.

She looked up. Waited. Said nothing.

"Were either of you unfaithful?"

Not again. Another complication. What to say? If she said, yes it could direct them away from her. But frankly, it was none of their bloody business. "No."

Detective Singh scribbled the answer in his notepad followed by a question mark. Unease ate its way from her stomach to her chest, worming higher and higher, until it became a hard lump in the back of her throat. Was she going to vomit? Oh god. The mess. *Get a grip.* There was a moment's pause before Detective Li responded.

"Are you sure about that?" Her tone indicated she wasn't.

"Yes." Ria wouldn't be rattled. She waited to see if she'd past the test.

Detective Li held her hands still over the keyboard. "Your neighbour said she thought there might be something up."

She stalled, surprised by the response. "What neighbour?"

"Mrs. Potts." Detective Li looked at the screen. "Lucinda."

Her temperature rose. Lucy. That woman was always watching everything on the street. And her damn, yappy little dog. Puddles? Pebbles? She should've shut it up for good when she had the chance.

Detective Singh looked at his notebook, leafing through the pages. "I'd like you to clarify what Lucy described as…" he read directly from the page, "a loud argument you had with your husband." He glanced up. "It occurred last fall, she thinks."

Which one? Pick one. There'd been so many. "Alright," Ria zeroed in. "We were talking about those footsteps in the backyard. I saw them, but Jim didn't. We fought about it and then he stormed out of the house. End of story."

"How did you resolve it?" Detective Singh's eyebrows rose.

Why was he asking such a stupid question? "We didn't," she said coolly. "You know that from the night the brick smashed the window. You were there."

"Right." His face relaxed. "Tell me more about the 911 call."

"The one from ten years ago?" She looked at the ceiling. "Let me see. Jim was in the bathtub and something," she paused, pretending to think, "maybe the curling iron fell in?"

"Can you share a few more details, please."

She sighed. "There was a broken shelf in the bathroom. I told him a thousand times to fix it. He was too busy, was what he said. The shelf. Do you need to know the type?"

"I find it strange the curling iron was plugged in." He leaned forward. "For someone who works for the fire department, don't you think he'd move it?"

The look in his eyes gave her a first indication of trouble. She held his gaze, but she could feel sweat in the small of her back. "I can't remember now why he didn't. Maybe he didn't see it. Maybe he was tired. It could've been after he worked a double shift."

"It's still kind of odd, don't you think?" He let the question dangle between them. Then he leaned in so close she could smell him. "I'd like to take you at your word, Ria, but your husband was murdered. Your neighbour told us something about your marriage was off, yet you're insinuating you had a perfect relationship."

She stiffened. She knew where this was going. "I was home when it happened-"

"Frankly," Detective Li interrupted, "there are very few cases where the perpetrator doesn't have some sort of connection to the victim-"

"I was asleep. You saw me come to the door." Though she tried to cut Detective Li off, she could hear the desperation in her voice. She hated it. What did Detective Singh call her earlier? Frumpy. She rubbed her nose and then licked her fingers slowly and smoothed the hair that had fallen across her face. Let him judge.

Then she turned to Detective Li. With her ramrod posture and smug little smile, the detective was becoming someone she disliked. Curious. Suspicious. Observant. Arms crossed over her chest, the detective was watching, waiting for an answer. Ria braced her feet against the chair. If there were any way to get out of this, she'd take it.

"Fine." She dabbed her eyes with a tissue. Sniffing, she plastered a withering look on her face. Took a shuddery breath. "Jim was having an affair."

"Thank you," Detective Li said, calmly "So, why lie about it?"

"It's embarrassing." She looked at her hands. "Humiliating, you know?"

Detective Singh nodded slightly, but his frustration was clear. "I hope you realize, Ria. Lying about these types of things, these details, can get you arrested."

FORTY
Ria

The six long weeks after Jim's murder were a blur. Ria was exhausted. Facts and moments and emotions were lumped together in an unruly pile in her head. The funeral arrangements. Consoling Jim's family and colleagues. The phone calls, the awkward condolences, the insurance policy. After her mother's death, she'd dealt with the same, but with Aunt Beth by her side, she pulled through. Like she'd done after she'd killed her aunt, this time she was doing it alone.

The tension in the house was palpable. Dealing with the kids was draining. Liam oscillated between swearing at everyone and bouts of sobbing upstairs in his room, blaming himself for his father's murder. Jacob stuck to his routines, yet the odd day he spun like a tornado, culminating in a complete, mind-blowing meltdown.

She hadn't anticipated the full impact of Jim's death on the boys. While she'd never fully connected to Liam like Jim did, she could usually handle Jacob, but even this was too much for her. She hoped everything would calm over time and longed for a return to the general rhythm of daily family life.

Work was busy, too. New clients, new demands, new projects, anything to take her mind off what was happening around her. She was at her desk late one morning, when her phone rang.

"Ria?" Detective Singh's voice. "Are you free to come down

to the station?"

"Can we do this over the phone?" She had work to finish.

"I'm afraid not." He sighed. "We've got a new development on Jim's case."

Ria's pulse quickened. Finally. It was about time. She had no idea what had taken so long. Although Detective Singh and Li had been in touch with her regularly, she'd been expecting *this* call for weeks. She reviewed the two late-night emails she'd received from clients who wanted tighter deadlines. They could wait.

Humming, she hopped in the car and took the highway to the station. At Jim's wake, the Highland Avenue in-group revealed they had archived doorcam leading back to their system's installation. Though she couldn't stand their fake togetherness game, the casserole swaps and the holiday drop-ins, those women came in useful. One look at the link to the tape was all she required to set things in motion. She gave the police the evidence on a silver plate. All they needed to do was connect the dots. It'd turned out better than she ever could've hoped. Sweet revenge.

Before she approached the constable on duty at the front of the building, she ducked into the main floor washroom. Quick pit stop. She reapplied her lipstick and checked her hair in the mirror. She half-smiled. Nothing between her teeth. She took a deep breath and swung open the door. It was show time.

"Detective Singh and Li, please," she said to the uniform at the desk.

The constable picked up the phone and a few minutes later, Detective Li appeared. She slid a card through a reader and the door clicked open. Down a hallway, they were buzzed into a secured part of the unit. It stunk of burnt coffee and onions. Tables filled the centre, cubicles lined the outside, some with a laptop, others scattered with papers and family photos. Detective Li weaved across it and Ria trailed behind. Smile. Look up. Make eye contact. On the other side, the remains of the detective's lunch were sitting on her desk.

"Have a seat," she pointed. Frosty.

Detective Li disappeared and Ria closed her eyes. She tried to imagine herself stretched on the yoga mat in the kitchen at home. Every morning for the past two months, she'd been practicing those poses, keeping her anxiety at bay. She breathed in through her nose. Slow release out the mouth. Calmer.

When Detective Li returned, Detective Singh was with her. He had a laptop tucked under his arm. They gathered around a nearby table littered with files and reports.

"We got a break in the case," Detective Singh started.

"An anonymous tip," Detective Li confirmed.

"Like Crime Stoppers?" Well played. When Detective Singh nodded, she added, "I guess it works."

"Sometimes yes, sometimes no." He smiled. "But when it does, the public can be helpful. They're good folks out there." He opened the laptop and keyed in a password. "We've got a photo we want to show you."

She fished through her purse for her glasses, then came around the table. She stooped over his shoulder and cast her eyes on the screen. A young man stared out at her. Brown eyes and heavy eyebrows. Bushy, dark hair. High cheekbones. A hawkish nose knocked off centre. Two blue tears were tattooed to the outside corner of his left eye.

"Who is it?" she asked.

He ignored her question. "We used facial recognition technology to compare this mug shot with image in the door cam footage we acquired."

"How does that work?" She knew, but she also knew how

important it was to play along.

"It cuts down on time to identify suspects," Detective Li explained. "The mug shot, and the door cam images match the name from the anonymous tip."

Ria took a slow, deep breath. Today, more than any other day, she had to keep reminding herself to breathe. In no hurry, she took another. She opened her purse and pulled out a box of mints. She offered them to the detectives, who declined.

"Meet Jaxon Hill." Detective Singh picked a piece of lint off his shirt and then tapped his finger on the screen. "The guy's disturbed. He has quite the checkered rap sheet."

"How so?" She raised her eyebrows. Waited.

"He started young. Breaking and entering, got expelled from school. Petty stuff." Detective Singh leaned back and crossed his arms. "Then he moved on to carjacking, did a little time for extortion and was a runner in a loose knit gang."

She let out a low curse. "But isn't a runner low level business?"

Detective Singh nodded at the laptop. "Our boy's ambitious. He moved up quick to drugs and arson."

Arson? Vivid memories returned. The house she grew up in. Her mother's charred and stinking corpse. She would have paid a million dollars to see the look on the detectives' faces if they knew who they were dealing with. She stuffed two mints in her mouth to keep herself from smiling.

"He served three years and was released last summer," Detective Singh explained. "We had a team arrest him and bring him in this morning."

Sweat beaded on her upper lip, but she kept her eyes focused on the screen.

"Mr. Hill is down in the box right now." Detective Singh shrugged. "Of course, he's denying everything. But the doorcam shows he put the brick through your window and we can prove he had a connection to Jim, so it's really just a matter of time."

Yeah, she bet he was refuting it all. "Will he be formally charged today?"

When neither detective answered her, she waited again. Seconds ticked by before Detective Li shook her head slowly. "The hearing's Friday."

She nodded, disappointed, but not surprised. She forced a smile. She'd waited six weeks. Another few days wouldn't hurt. She was confident there was only one possible outcome. Then she turned and walked straight out of the police station without saying a word to anyone.

Early Friday morning, Ria set out for the Greene County Courthouse. She turned on the radio. Happy to get away from the house, she couldn't stand to hear Liam cry in his bedroom anymore. There was nothing she could do to convince him his father's death wasn't his fault. She'd given him Jim's car when he passed his driving test, and she hoped the counseling appointment she'd booked for him next week would help him manage his guilty feelings. Something. Anything.

When she arrived, she parallel parked on the main street. There were only patches of snow left on brown grass, people were still wrapped in warm clothing. Just yesterday she was on the back deck with a latte, the sky blue, the trees swaying in the wind. Springtime in New York.

Icy grass crunched underfoot as she exited the car. Ahead of her, large glass doors sparkled in the sunshine. In the security line, she placed her purse and coat in the plastic bin and walked through the metal detector. It beeped loudly. A large man with a prickly black moustache cut short over thin lips pulled her aside and scanned her with a wand.

"Empty your pockets," he ordered.

After she pulled out a coin and held it up, she went back to the conveyor belt to retrieve her belongings. Down the hall, she stopped at the desk to ask for directions. A woman, glasses on a beaded chain around her neck, sat behind it.

"Courtroom Two," she said, in a monotone voice.

Inside, Ria found a seat. The last time she'd been in a courtroom was after her mother died. The hardbacked bench she was on reminded her of a church pew. But it was so much more comfortable than the feel of the lacquered wood in her hands and the smooth leather on the backs of her legs as she'd sat for hours in the witness box, answering questions, refuting theories, denying accusations. The trial had felt like an eternity. Every second felt like an hour. Every hour felt like a year. The lawyers. Media vultures. Dr. Gibson. The scars had faded, but they'd never healed.

In the seat in front of her was a man, with a shock of white hair and a pocked and weathered face. Tufts of dark hair stuck out from his ears. Her stomach coiled. She fought the urge to tell him he needed to visit the barber to have the wild garden sprouting from his shriveled head removed.

With nothing to do but wait, she fidgeted with the buttons on her coat. The buzz in the courtroom grew as the bank of benches filled in behind her. When Jim's parents arrived, she waved them over. After they settled, her mother-in-law squeezed her knee. Ria patted her mother-in-law's hand.

A few minutes later, a beefy man with a flat nose and greasy hair tied in a ponytail sat on her other side. Too close. She wished it was Marco. She'd tried to contact him after Jim's murder on a new burner phone, but his device was disconnected. With their business concluded, she guessed he'd either changed his number or cut her off.

Two groups slipped through a side door to the left. Ria stared at the accused. Disheveled and dressed in prison garb, he huddled with his lawyer at a table. He had an ugly gash on his cheek. The way Marco had described it, she wouldn't last a night in jail, not with the overcrowding, the bunks, the stench.

The back door swung open. Dressed in black robes, the judge strolled up to her seat on the bench. She spoke briefly to the lawyers and called a recess. For fifteen minutes, there was quiet, only the occasional cough, or a whisper breaking the silence.

Someone's cell phone rang twice, before it was put on silent. Ria fished a bottle of water from her purse and took a sip.

When the judge returned, the proceedings got underway. Armed with a yellow legal pad, the Crown stood and spoke. Dark hair to her shoulders, she was articulate. Quick. Succinct. Efficient. Next, the defense. The lawyer's eyebrows were a bushy line across his forehead that bounced as he talked. Ria listened as the man in a gray suit that barely fit entered a not guilty plea to first-degree murder. It wasn't a shock. It was to be expected. When the defense returned to his table, the courtroom hushed.

"The trial will proceed next year," the judge announced.

It wasn't a revelation to her, but Ria still flinched, as if surprised. Then the judge rapped her gavel, stood from the bench, and exited the courtroom.

FORTY-ONE
Ria

One Year Later

Almost a year to the date of the hearing, Ria drove back to the courthouse. It was late April, the sun still weak and the creek was swollen. She searched for the first clusters of purple crocuses to push up through the snow. Out of the car, she drew in a breath of the spring air and smiled. It had a softness to it.

She passed through the security check and approached the open doors down the hall. Reporters with laptops scuttled back and forth. Scores of people packed the benches and dozens more stood outside, milling around signage that read *The People v. Hill*. Wary of potential violence, several armed officers stood at the back of the courtroom. Jim's firehouse buddies sat together on one side, not far from Frank and Rachel. She spotted Jim's parents, but the row they were in was already full. Why hadn't they saved her a seat? She wasn't that late.

Head held high, she marched past the family of the accused, ignoring their harsh, hissed words and parked herself in a spot in the second row. Dressed head to toe in black, she clenched her hands in her lap, praying the trial would be over quickly.

The past year she tended to the boys' needs, continued to build her business, kept her hands busy and her mind still.

While she appreciated the sympathetic looks and the copious meals dropped off at the house for the grieving widow's family, they'd all but dried up now. She was sick of keeping control of herself. Sick of suppressing her urges and bottling her true needs. She yearned for freedom she knew was waiting around the corner, the life she wanted and deserved. The bigger house. The pool. The spa bathroom, no wet towels lying on the floor. Trips to the Caribbean, trysts with Marco, a new future filled with new possibilities. Everything was ready, everything was in place. It was all so close.

"All rise," the bailiff hollered.

The judge strode through the back door. The jurors filed in next, and after the judge addressed them, the proceedings were called to order. The Prosecutor paged through the documents on the table. Then she rolled her pen between her fingers, pushed her dark hair off her face and stood to address the court.

"Members of the jury." She nodded. "We are here to determine what happened to Jim Stiles last year on the evening of Saturday, February 24. A father of two and a firefighter with the Catskill Fire Department, his body was found shortly after midnight at an abandoned strip mall. I'm confident once you've heard from the coroner, the forensic experts, and other witnesses, you'll agree this was a premeditated crime and find the defendant, Jaxon Hill, guilty of first-degree murder. The accused had motive, means and opportunity. Recently released from prison, Mr. Hill chose to return to his former lifestyle. Rather than simply manage his anger, he took matters into his own hands and callously shot Mr. Stiles three times, killing him instantly."

The defense stood next. As she dabbed her eyes with a tissue, Ria noted the man's suit was still an ugly gray, but unlike last year it was a better fit. The lawyer ran his hand across his face, glanced at the jury and cleared his throat.

"Jaxon Hill is an innocent man," he announced. "True, my client has a lengthy criminal record. True, he could've made better choices when released from prison. However, I assure you, he did not murder Mr. Stiles. He was not in the vicinity the night the victim was murdered. The weapon used in this unsolved crime has never been recovered and cannot be tied to my client. In fact, the only reason my client is in the position he's in today is because the police were quick to act on an anonymous tip, rather than conduct a proper investigation. Members of the jury, once the evidence is laid before you, I'm sure you'll draw the same conclusion."

Ria surveyed the faces of the jury. Their expressions gave nothing away. The prosecutor made a brief note on her papers, then she called Detective Singh to the stand. She went over the fine points of the evening Jim's body was found, asking questions, making remarks, like they were having a casual, everyday conversation. When the defense stepped forward to cross-examine the detective, the mood in the courtroom shifted. Ria could feel him warming to the jury, a performer ready to deliver.

"Detective Singh," the lawyer's voice rose, "Do you have any proof the gun used to shoot and kill Mr. Stiles belongs to Mr. Hill?"

"We don't."

"Of course not." He enunciated each word. "The truth is that no gun was recovered from the scene, or from my client's apartment, or the farmhouse where he was arrested by police. I'd appreciate if you answered my questions fully and honestly. Need I remind you you're under oath?" For a moment, neither spoke. The defense continued. "Were you the first to arrive at the crime scene?"

"No." Detective Singh's tone was sharp.

"Who was?"

"The attending officers."

The defense glanced at his notes and softened his voice. "Did they find my client's footsteps?"

"No."

"Because they didn't look? Did you? Did you forget?"

"No." Detective Singh's face darkened. "I didn't find *any* footprints. It was blowing snow. Even the victims weren't present."

The defense looked incredulous. He raised his arms in the air. "You don't follow investigative procedure in the winter?"

"That's not what I said," Detective Singh snapped. "It was done by the book."

The defense raised his eyebrows at the jury. "I beg to differ."

A smug smile on his face, he returned to his table. Reporters scribbled in notebooks and the court reporter typed away at a small desk to the left beneath the bench. Ria looked at her watch as the judge conferred with the prosecutor and the defense. Her stomach rumbled. Nerves? Tired? Hungry.

After the court broke for lunch, Detective Li stepped up to the stand and took a seat. Ria and everyone else in the gallery listened as the detective compared Jaxon's mug shot to the webcam footage from the street. Which one of their neighbours supplied the tape? When a lab technician was called next, she leaned forward. His unkempt brown hair flopped over one eye and there were tattoos running down one side of his neck. He didn't look old enough to shave. He explained that because Mr. Hill was apprehended at a farmhouse, his job was to process the scene for evidence of Mr. Stile's murder.

"Was he murdered at the farmhouse?" the prosecutor asked.

"No," he answered.

"What did you find there when the defendant was apprehended?"

"The tire tracks in the driveway matched the defendant's car, and I tested the fingerprints and fibers inside the kill room."

Ria's mouth fell open. A kill room? What the hell was that? The jurors looked as shocked as she felt. She made a mental note to discuss it with Marco later, then remembered that he'd cut her off and her anger surged again.

"I found six different sources of the defendant's DNA," the lab tech explained, "on soda cans, beer cans, and a metal chain."

Ria sighed with relief.

"Was Mr. Stiles' DNA present at the farmhouse?" the prosecutor asked.

"Yes." The tech nodded. "Inside a hood shoved in a corner upstairs. I believe it came from his saliva or the blood stains I tested."

"Was the defendant's DNA on the hood as well?"

He nodded again. "It was. I guess somehow the two knew each other."

"Objection," the defense shouted.

Tempers flared. The judge smacked her gavel and demanded the prosecutor and defense approach the bench. Moments later, court was dismissed for the day.

First thing the next morning, the coroner took the stand. Forensic evidence was offered, analysis was shared, wounds were discussed in detail. At first, Ria cried out and wrung her hands. Later, she turned away from the images projected on the big screen. She'd seen the real thing in the morgue. She didn't need to see them again. But when a close-up of Jim's face appeared, she inched forward, rapt with attention.

Unlike the photo Detective Singh showed her at the

morgue, this image filled the entire display. Her heart raced at the sight of the pulped, purple mess. Enmeshed with blood, there was a bullet hole and white jagged pieces of bone poking up through the skin. She contemplated how she might get her hands on it to rebuild her beloved collection. It'd be a perfect start. Beautiful. Crisp. Authentic. As she followed the red trail seeping from the dark patches of puckered skin to the point of Jim's chin, she sensed someone watching her. She blinked to refocus and redirected her gaze. Detective Li was staring from across the courtroom, eyebrows knitted. Ria eased back into her seat, slipping from her line of sight. She patted her purse to find a tissue and blew her nose loudly.

After the coroner was dismissed, the detectives returned to the stand to answer questions about a series of images of the strip mall. Late in the day Friday, Ria stifled a yawn. She dug through her purse and popped a candy in her mouth, singing songs in her head to stay awake. She couldn't wait to get home for the weekend. To be with the boys, to catch up with work, to try and call Marco. To learn everything she possibly could about a kill room.

FORTY-TWO
Ria

For the rest of the weekend, Ria busied herself. Dropping Jacob at the library, responding to clients, grocery shopping, cleaning, anything to keep her mind quiet. Time flew by quickly, and after Liam and Jacob left for school Monday morning, she drove back to the courthouse.

Dressed as the grieving widow again, she assumed the same seat and waited for the proceedings to begin. First thing, an expert witness of organized crime took the stand. He explained the dynamics of a gang, and how the leader orders the hits he expects its' members to carry out.

"In this case," the expert said, "that leader would be Dirk and the defendant, Mr. Hill, would do as he says."

When Frank was called next, Ria sat straight up. Sweat prickled her armpits, and her tongue was dry against the roof of her mouth. She gave her brother-in-law a slight nod as he peered out from the witness box. She was beyond relieved it wasn't Liam up there. While the judge had found him competent to testify and he'd been interviewed by the prosecutor and the defense, the Madame Justice agreed that providing evidence about his gambling debt in relationship to his father's death was a terrible emotional burden to impose on a grieving son. Since Frank knew all the details, the judge determined he'd take the stand instead.

After three hours of testimony, the debt was out in the

open, and the link between Jim and Dirk and Jaxon made. Ria could see the jury starting to put together the pieces. She let out a soft sigh and wiped her sweaty palms on her pants.

For the next two days, a parade of witnesses spoke and near the end of the week, the defense called Jaxon Hill to the stand. In a crisp-collared shirt and a dark suit two sizes too big, he shifted nervously on the seat. The courtroom stilled. Ria edged forward.

"Mr. Hill," his lawyer said, "did you kill Jim Stiles?"

"No." She could barely hear him.

"Did you know Jim Stiles?"

Jaxon cleared his throat. "Not personally." Ria leaned back. She could hear now.

"You've seen him, though," the defense remarked.

Jaxon nodded. "Three times. Once outside a Thai place downtown, once at the farmhouse and once on his street."

"We've heard about the farmhouse." The defense turned to the jury. "That's assault not murder." Back to Jaxon. "What were you doing on his street?"

"Looking for my sister." The defense urged him to go on. "I needed money, okay. Jaylyn wasn't home. I knew she was seeing that old guy. Mr. Stiles, I mean."

The prosecutor interrupted him. "Seeing him how exactly?"

The judge smacked her gavel. "Out of order. Wait your turn to cross-examine the witness."

Inwardly, Ria winced. It was the one detail she dreaded. Though the boys and family all knew about Jim's affair, the thought of it becoming public made her feel sick. It would hit the newspapers and social media. She could only imagine the direct messages and text threads between the in-group on the street, their frantic lacquered nails tapping at their phones. The defense continued with their questioning. After a short recess, the jury was reassembled, and the prosecutor approached the Box. Ria braced herself.

"Mr. Hill," the prosecutor said. "Please explain what you meant when you said earlier that your sister was," she glanced at her notes, "seeing that old guy, Mr. Stiles."

"They were in a relationship," Jaxon responded.

Ria's gut twisted into a tight knot. She glanced at the reporters across the aisle. They were scribbling in notebooks and typing furiously on laptops.

"How do you know?" the prosecutor persisted.

"Jaylyn told me."

"Could we have a sidebar?" the defense called out.

When the judge waved the prosecutor on, she asked, "Do you know for how long?"

"Six months." Jaxon frowned. "You know that. Jaylyn told you when you interviewed her. That's why I thought she'd be there."

The prosecutor looked straight at him. "Was she?"

"No," he mumbled.

"The relationship must have made you angry." The prosecutor stepped closer and lowered her voice. "You can't find your sister. You can't get the money you want. What did you do?"

He shrugged. "I left."

Ria recalled the footsteps in the backyard and cigarette butts she'd found on the ravine path. Had they been his? Or was it one of his gang friends sending a signal about Liam's debt?

"Mr. Hill," the Crown said firmly. "You said you needed money. Was that why you shot and killed Mr. Stiles at the strip mall? For the money?"

"No."

She raised a brow. "So, you did shoot him?"

"No," he protested. "I wasn't even there. Dirk didn't let me do pick-up."

"Why not?" she asked. "Did he use those exact words?"

The defense objected. "That's hearsay."

"I'll allow it," the judge said. "The witness may answer."

"I can't remember exactly," Jaxon finished with a sigh, "but I wasn't jumped in yet."

"Jumped in?" The prosecutor paused for effect. "What does that mean?"

Jaxon let out a low laugh. "A full associate." Then his voice rose. "But like it matters now, right? Cause I'm the one sitting here."

"You were following orders when you killed Mr. Stiles?"

"No." Jaxon smacked his palm on the wood. "I told you, I had nothing to do with it."

The prosecutor stepped back. "But you admit you know the victim. You've seen him. You've been to his house." The prosecutor glanced at the jury, then at Jaxon. "Your fingerprints are all over the farmhouse where a hood with the victim's blood and saliva were collected by a forensic team. Which proves he was in 'your house', so to speak. Did you murder him?"

The defense objected to that too, but again was overruled.

"Answer the question," the judge ordered.

"No," Jaxon said.

Ria tensed. She knew Jaxon was telling the truth. Only a few years older than Liam, she wondered what Jaxon was thinking. She forced her thoughts away. It was all for the best.

The prosecutor sighed. "Mr. Hill. We know from the evidence collected at the farmhouse you were involved in the assault of Jim Stiles. Did you assault Mr. Stiles because of his debt to Dirk or because he was sleeping with your sister?" As Jaxon's face reddened, she asked again. "Did you kill Jim Stiles because of his debt to Dirk, or because he was sleeping with your sister?"

Jaxon exploded. "I was set up! Fucking framed. They better pray I don't find out who did because I'll beat them to a pulp with my bare hands. I'll kill them."

Mayhem erupted the courtroom. Ria snuck a quick look at the jury, their faces contorted in shock, their mouths hanging open. She suppressed a grin.

"Silence." The judge smacked her gavel. "Silence."

"No questions." The prosecutor smiled and took her seat.

"We've got a verdict."

The phone call came in shortly after ten-thirty the next morning. After Ria spoke briefly to Detective Singh, she returned to the courthouse. She slid efficiently though security and reclaimed her seat in the second row. Eyes to the floor, hands in her lap, she waited.

Her head was spinning. Last night, stretched across the bed like a starfish, she'd slept. Calm. Rested. Peaceful. When she awoke, she was squashed to the right side of the mattress, as if Jim had never left. Could today finally put an end to it all?

"All rise," the bailiff called out.

The judge marched into the courtroom and sat in her chair. After the jury walked in and were seated, the judge turned to face them.

"Have you reached a verdict?" she asked.

The foreman stood. "Yes."

"Will the accused please stand?"

His face drawn and gray, Jaxon Hill rose from his seat. He held his hands together in front of him. Ria could see they were shaking.

The judge spoke again. "On the charge of murder in the

first degree?"

"We find the defendant guilty," the foreman responded.

A loud gasp filled the room. The judge rapped her gavel. "Order!" she demanded. "The defendant will remain in custody and be remanded to the West Detention Centre until his sentencing hearing."

Ria closed her eyes, let out a long breath and sat back in her seat. Relief washed over her. It was done, it was finished. She was free to get on with her life. She'd done what was needed and though she never doubted him, Marco had delivered.

With court dismissed, she walked along the hallway, past Courtroom One, the washrooms, past the open doors to the cafeteria. As she turned the corner to the front hall, she froze on the spot.

A large crowd milled around the security station. Police and firemen were throwing around equipment, barking orders, running back and forth. To the right, there was an empty white stretcher. Two paramedics were on their knees on either side of a large woman in a blue coat collapsed on the floor. A third had his hands on the woman's chest and was pumping methodically.

People cleared a path as she moved closer. Ria's pulse quickened. She stepped back to steady herself, a hand on the wall. Inhale. Exhale. The sound of dogs barking, lights flashing, whistles blowing, the buzz of human voices. So many uniforms. She hadn't seen that many since the day flames danced across the floor and engulfed her mother's house.

She composed herself as the paramedics hoisted the woman onto the stretcher. As Ria approached the front door, a young woman with eyes red and rimmed with gummy mascara stood in her path. Ria knew exactly who she was.

"Jaylyn." She forced a smile.

"My mother." She pointed a shaky finger to the woman in

the blue coat. "They think she's had a heart attack."

Ria brought her hand to her throat and used her sweetest voice. "Is it because of the trial?"

"I don't know," she sobbed. "I don't know what to do."

Ria looked at the young woman who tried to bring down her house. Long black hair a tangled mess, clothes wrinkled and disheveled, tears streaming down her face. If Jim could only see her now. What a difference a year could make. She took a step toward her and laid a hand lightly on her forearm.

"What did you expect, my dear?" Ria leaned forward and whispered in her ear. "The consequences of *a thing* are far from trivial."

Ria walked around her, heels clicking on the tile. She strode out the door and down the steps of the courthouse.

FORTY-THREE
Ria

Ria stood on the sidewalk away from the noise and the mayhem in the front hall of the courthouse. Yellow and red tulips poked up from the dark earth in the flower beds. For the first time in months, she could breathe. Before the media and the paramedics spilled out the doors to the awaiting ambulance, she crossed the parking lot.

In the car, she pulled out her phone. Still high in the sky, the sun seared her eyes. She held a hand over the screen to cut the glare and punched in Marco's number. The line was no longer in service. Where was he? She gripped the phone in her hand. A hot rage swelled up within her. After all they'd been through? Their history? The future wasn't written in stone, but after the verdict she expected he would at least reach out today.

She slammed the phone on the dashboard, cracking the screen. Adrenaline coursed through her veins. That was it? Had he not felt their connection? It wasn't over. It never would be. They'd had too much fun together. She lay her head on the steering wheel to collect her thoughts. Sadness. Anger. Not guilt. Maybe gratitude. Relief. It was all so much more complicated than that, but she didn't know how to explain it.

What she did know was that Marco had made his decision. It was clear from his actions. For the time being, she'd have to live with it. What he didn't know was that one day he'd miss her. The commonalities they shared, the sparks, the bond of kindred spirits. She was sure of it. She'd felt it in her bones. For now, she'd be patient. In time, he'd come around.

She rifled through her purse for her keys, then checked the time. Two o'clock. She considered what to throw together for dinner. It was early May, and the sky stayed light well into the evening. Maybe a family BBQ at the table on the back deck? A celebration of sorts. To thank Jim's parents who had helped through the trial. To acknowledge Frank who spoke so eloquently on the stand the week before. From the shaking of his voice, she knew it must've been difficult, but what he described to the jury had a big impact on the outcome.

A few streets down, a grocery store appeared on the right. She parked, strolled along a shaded path to the door and wandered through the aisles. Steak. Odds and ends to throw into a salad. Fresh asparagus. As she passed the bakery, her nostrils filled with the smell of cinnamon. Her mouth watered and she placed a freshly baked apple pie gently into the cart. At the last minute, she threw in a package of fresh rolls for Liam's hollow leg, and six blueberry scones for Jacob. Tucking her wallet into her purse, she lugged the bags back to the car.

Outside, it had darkened a little. Maybe they'd have to eat inside after all. She pictured the family, her family, together around the dining room table. If the boys were up to it, it'd be the perfect time to tell them about the new house she bought. Four thousand square feet, a gourmet kitchen with an island, a sunken living room, not a scuff on the floor, not a wall begging for paint.

Decades earlier, during one of her sessions with Dr. Gibson, he'd said, 'Time to grow up, get your shit together. Take responsibility.' Though it probably wasn't what he was referring to at the time, she'd taken his advice to heart. Between the money she'd stashed for years in her safety deposit box, her aunt's inheritance and the pay out from Jim's life insurance policy, she'd be living mortgage free the rest of her life. The kids may not relish the idea of moving as much as she did, but the new place was on the same street as Frank and Rachel. Surprised when she'd first told them, they'd come around quickly, and the kids would do the same. It was time to move forward. A fresh start, to put the past behind them.

Clouds rushed in as she headed home on the highway. She turned on the radio and hummed along to Top 40 songs as the traffic slowed. Heavy rain hit the windshield and pooled in potholes making a mess of the roads. As she took the turn-off, the sun broke through the sky. She lowered the window, spreading her fingers apart, feeling the warm air blow between them. When the phone rang, she put it on handsfree.

"Mom." Jacob's voice. "Was Jaxon Hill found guilty?"

"Yes, darling, he was."

"Then it's over?" There was painful hope in his voice.

"It is," she confirmed. As Jacob blew out a breath through the phone, she could picture the relief on his face.

"Are you coming home now?"

"I am." She smiled and turned onto the street. Of course, she was.

After Frank and Rachel and her in-laws left the house that evening, Ria piled the plates on the kitchen counter. When the boys began to bicker, she nudged Jacob to one side and stepped between them. They were overtired and she was exhausted too.

"Go." She pointed to the stairs. "I'll take care of this."

After Jacob and Liam disappeared to their rooms, Ria cleaned up, then went upstairs and drew a warm bath. As she soaked in the tub, she closed her eyes, grateful for the jury's decision. Every imperfection, every lie, every secret, had been hidden. Wasn't that how a family was built? Hers was.

Wrapped in a fluffy white robe, she padded downstairs and grabbed a glass of wine. In the living room, she picked up a book to read, but it failed to distract her. She turned on the television and clicked between the channels, searching for the eleven 'o'clock headlines. A news anchor with long brown hair and shiny white teeth smiled back at her.

"Good evening," she said. "Earlier today, a jury found low level gangbanger Jaxon Hill guilty of first-degree murder in the death of a man in Catskill, New York. Jim Stiles, a husband and father, was found shot to death last year. Now the trial is over, an unknown source has told us police are reinvestigating another unsolved murder on Stiles' street. A man with no connection to Stiles was shot mid-afternoon in broad daylight in his driveway almost two years ago."

For the next ten minutes, Ria lay on the couch, her eyes glued to the television. When the reporter signed off, she clicked the remote. The house was quiet, but her mind was racing. Was it true? Could Jaxon have been involved in the shooting on her street? It seemed so long ago now. Frank always questioned the similarity in the two addresses. Jim's captain had said the same thing. But from what she knew, it had to be coincidence. She thought of Demar's family and imagined what they had endured. The pain. The suffering. The grief. It'd been nothing like that for her. She raised her wine glass midair. No love lost at all.

As the coffee perked Saturday morning, Ria stood with the back doors wide open, a gentle breeze flowing through the kitchen. Last week when Frank and Rachel had come for supper to celebrate the end of the trial, they'd offered to take the boys for the weekend to show them around the neighbourhood to give her a much-needed break. She was happy to have time for herself and as they'd opened their pool early, she knew the boys would be enjoying it.

She took her cup and sat outside. The sun was already high in the sky, where white wispy clouds were scattered. Joggers, alone and in pairs, breezed by along the shaded ravine path. She scanned the flowerbeds planted along the fence, running up to the back deck. Yellow daffodils, hyacinth, pink and red gerbera, purple cornflower spreading between them. She strode down the steps and deadheaded the flowers. Dressed in a tank top and yoga pants, once black as night, now washed of colour, she laughed at the contrast.

She dithered around a bit, then back inside, she poured a second cup. At the kitchen table, she took a sip. She thought of Marco, his bright blue eyes, his full lips, his thick fingers. With the six-hour time difference between them, she assumed he was sitting somewhere in a bar enjoying happy hour with his friends.

She reached for the phone. She needed to call him. Needed to hear his voice. She tapped in his number, but like every other time she called the last week, a voice told her the number was no longer in service. It was only a matter of time before he realized he missed her. She was certain it wouldn't be much longer.

Behind her were boxes stacked high against the walls. Grateful to be alone, she considered where she should start. Thrilled to move, she dreaded packing up the house.

Loud knocking at the front door broke her from her reverie. Cup in hand, she strolled along the hall to find Detective Singh standing on the porch.

"Do you have a moment?" he said, waving.

She didn't move. He didn't wait for an answer.

"May we come in, please?" He made it sound more like a demand than a question.

Detective Li hurried from the car at the curb, jostling among the potted plants lining the brick pathway. She had a thick, yellow file tucked under her arm. When Detective Singh held a hand in front of him, Detective Li maneuvered around him and stepped inside. After she took off her shoes and placed them neatly on the mat, she looked up and smiled brightly.

"We've got a lot to talk about, Angel."

FORTY-FOUR
Ria

Ria gripped the side of the door. She thought she was going to faint. What was in that envelope? It left her unsettled. She glanced out to the street. As the screen closed, she caught a glimpse of a police car pulling up beside the detective's unmarked vehicle parked at the curb. In that instant, it was obvious this was not a routine visit.

Blood rushed to her temples. Her mind was spinning a thousand directions. Had the detectives uncovered something about her past? Who she was? How much did they know?

Unsteady on her feet, she shuffled forward. Beads of moisture rang down her forehead, stinging her eyes. She needed time to slow down, to stop so she could gather her thoughts.

How had it come to this?

In three decades, no one had dredged up her past life. Gone were the days she looked over her shoulder in public or was forced to explain herself. She'd worked hard to lose her baggage, lined everything up right, checked all the boxes. A masterful plan, flawless execution.

She'd been so careful. Until recently, at least.

Her mind was racing. Deep breath. She'd talk her way around it. She'd done it once. She could do it again.

Detective Li and Singh followed behind her along the hallway to the kitchen. A radio crackled, bouncing off the walls. The back door was wide open, beyond it the gate down to the ravine. She felt the urge to bolt. No. Mothers don't run. Widows don't run. Unless they have things to hide or were running away from something.

She stopped, planted her feet on the floor, and turned to face them. "What's going on?"

Officer Li cleared her throat, reached into the yellow envelope, and laid a clear plastic bag on the kitchen table. Bile rose in the back of her throat. Inside was her father's gun.

She swallowed hard. How did they get it? The last time she saw it was dangling off Jim's finger during their argument in the living room. And she'd put it back in a box, deep behind the jars of preserves in the root cellar. She was sure.

"Is this yours?" Detective Li asked.

"It is." She couldn't lie about it.

"Good start."

She sat down, aware of the two pairs of eyes that followed her. Silent, she gritted her teeth. Detective Li. Those eyebrows. Black and arrow thin, they reminded her of her mothers, painted on every day.

Detective Li stared back. "Telling the truth is your best move here, Angel."

Angel? That name again. And how did this gun come into it? There was no way to avoid whatever was coming next.

"Do I need a lawyer?" She kept her voice steady. Emotions couldn't play a part.

Detective Singh glanced briefly at his partner. "That's up to you. Right now, it's only a conversation."

She drew in a breath. Her heart beat hard and fast. Though she needed to calm down, she didn't see the point. They weren't arresting her, so for the time being it was best to play along. If things took a turn for the worse, she could always change her mind.

Pulling out a chair, Detective Li went on to explain. "This gun was brought to us by a concerned citizen who suggested we look for a connection between it and your husband's murder."

Ria sat rigid in the chair. Dizzy. Very dizzy. She could not wrap her head around the information. "But you know who murdered Jim. You arrested him, he was convicted, for God's sake."

"We know that Ria. And you're right. When we ran the ballistics there was no evidence to suggest this gun was used to kill Jim. It's not even the right type of weapon."

Ria exhaled. "So then you're here...why exactly?"

Detective Li and Singh exchanged another look, and a hint of a smile curled on Li's face as she went on. "We're here because on a hunch we decided to look at the gun in connection with another murder you are connected with. The murder of Demar Robinson. And what do you know—a perfect match."

Ria froze. Bile rose in her throat a second time. Shifting in the seat, she crossed and uncrossed her legs. "No, that can't be right. That gun has been down in our basement untouched for decades. I don't even know if it works. And I definitely haven't fired it. Even if it is my gun, I haven't used it to kill anyone."

Detective Li leaned forward. "Forensics found three sets of DNA on the gun. Jim's and yours." She paused. "And your son."

"What?" Ria said, giving herself a little shake. "Which one?"

The detective's eyebrows lifted. "Liam."

"That's impossible," she said confidently. How could that be? He didn't even know about the gun. Neither did Jacob.

Detective Li smiled oddly, encouraging her to continue. The heat in the room was unbearable, the air between them tense. Ria wiped the sweat from her upper lip as Detective Li took off her glasses and put them on the table.

"Every contact leaves a trace," Detective Singh informed

her.

When he flapped a hand at her, she scoffed. She knew all about DNA. She wasn't stupid. She'd figured that out a long time ago. She thought back to her childhood house and the secrets it guarded until the fire consumed it all.

"We're not concerned about Liam," Detective Singh scratched his chin. "Since we know how his prints got on the gun."

"What do you mean?" Ria's mouth was bone dry.

"Can't you guess?" Detective Li grinned. "He's the one who brought it to us."

Ria almost stopped breathing. Liam? What was he thinking? Why would he do this?

"Well, to be more accurate," Detective Singh's jaw tensed, "your neighbour Mrs. Potts brought it to us after Liam brought it to her, but she was smart enough to put it in a bag and not touch it. She doesn't think too highly of you. And apparently the boy is worried about your erratic behaviour and wanted to be sure you weren't behind his father's murder. He seemed to think you appeared pretty happy about it."

"They're all safely at the station now in case you're worried," Li added, "Both your boys and their aunt and uncle and your next-door neighbour. Telling us a whole lot of interesting information about you. And about," she looked at the file in her hand, "Angel Calarco. Who, by the way, sounds like a real piece of work."

FORTY-FIVE
Epilogue

Ria sat upright in her bunk, her cell barren. Only a sink scarred by rust and an open toilet bolted to the floor. Cracks crisscrossed the painted walls leaving winding patterns stretching up to the ceiling. She wondered how long they'd been there. Yawning, she unfolded her stiff body from the bed. The single mattress was lumpy, with filler that dug into her back.

She crossed the cell slowly numbed by the reek of ammonia and sweat. Nothing felt the same. The shouting drifting from beyond the bars, the glare of florescent lights, the putrid meals which looked like they were ladled from a sewer.

Up at six. Breakfast at seven. Work, lunch, work, dinner. Recreation. Lights out. Though Jacob would appreciate the strict routine, she detested it. It was suffocating, stifling. Lifeless. She glimpsed at herself in the mirror and turned away. Bruised face, angry red scratch marks, a clump of hair still missing. It'd grow back.

It had all happened so quickly. Her arrest, her trial. No matter how much she insisted she knew nothing about Demar's murder, the police were keen to close the case. They had her DNA on the gun, the files from the time of her mother's murder. They'd even opened an investigation into her aunt's death, previously deemed natural causes. That was probably what did it for her, just the sheer number of suspicions and coincidences.

Once they were sure she'd committed one murder, the police didn't worry they couldn't come up with a reasonable motive for Demar's murder. She was a sociopath, an uncontrollable madwoman. Dr. Gibson was only too happy to tell everyone at the trial, especially as Jim had gone to see him right before he died.

She'd barely paid attention to what was said about her. Like her lawyer had instructed, she'd kept her voice careful, quiet. No need to spook the jury, he'd said. The way they'd looked at her from the moment she took the stand, she'd known they thought she was a monster. What did it matter?

She'd seen their expressions—Frank, Rachel, her in-laws. She could tell how much they hated her. Jacob too—he wasn't at the trial and wouldn't talk to her and eventually she'd received a legal letter telling her not to try and contact him again. But she was going to see one person, finally. Today. Liam was coming to visit.

He'd been the star witness at her trial, crying about his wonderful father. How he could never have killed anyone, so it could only have been his mother. How he never wanted to turn her in, but he had to protect his little brother. That he felt so guilty. She didn't believe a word of it. In her family, lying was a blood sport. And now, finally, she was going to get some answers.

Mid-morning, a guard unlocked her door and led her along the hall. Noise escalated from the cells, calling her name, the catcalls fierce, a cacophony of promises. She closed her eyes. Part of her imagined Liam as he was at the trial, red-eyed and vulnerable; distressed at seeing his mother incarcerated. But when she opened them, there he was, flesh and blood in front of her. A smirk on his face.

"How's it going?" he asked, through the glass barrier.

She glared, a message in return. "How do you think?"

"The jumpsuit's not your colour. Better you than me, I guess."

"What?" She swallowed hard, leaned in.

"Can't you guess? Who do you think really killed Demar?" He sat back in satisfaction and mimed it for her, lifting an imaginary gun in one hand, one eye closed as he blew her away.

Every ounce of control vanished. In one quick motion, she slapped the plexiglass with her hand. Liam jerked back so fast the chair topped to the floor. He stood, his hands tightening into fists. The guard approached and repositioned it, warning her if she couldn't keep her temper in check, the visit would be her last.

Liam repositioned the chair. As he sat across from her, he patted his chest and winked. "You know what was going on with me and #TheFellas. That debt needed repaying and who do you think I could count on to help? You? Dad?? He was clueless about stuff like that, real problems. I needed to know I could take care of it myself, if it came to that. So when I found the gun, I thought I'd better practice. Just in case. Who knew I was such a good shot."

He looked at her, a sneer painted plain as day on his face. Everything unraveled, pulling apart one thread at a time. He was never his father's son. Ice in his veins, no concern for human life. He was all her. One hundred percent Angel.

She leaned toward the plexiglass. Twisty, raw. Desperate. Their eyes met. "But you set me up. Why? I'm your mother for fuck's sake."

"Why not?"

A chill crept over her skin. Liam shifted forward an inch, glanced around. She clicked her tongue, impatient.

"You made it too easy." Liam moved toward her, covering

what was left of the space between them. "Mrs. Pott's hates you, and she likes me, especially since I've taken over from Dad, shovelling her snow, running her errands. So, when I took her the gun all I did was shake a little, act all scared. The old lady lapped it up."

Liam smiled. "Same thing when I told Jacob, but I poured it on more, like, crying about it. And I told him everything." He spelled it out. "E-ver-y-thing. Your mother. Your aunt. Now he hates you, too." Then he lowered his voice. "And I'll make sure he always will."

Pressing her hands into the chair, she tried not to scream. She wanted to wipe the smug look off his face. He infuriated her. Someone once told her love doesn't stop for your child no matter how they behave. Not true.

"Good-bye, Angel," he called cheerfully as he stood up to leave, then turned and closed the gap between them to deliver one more parting message. "Rot in hell."

He walked out of the room, strong and self-assured. It was too late to stop him now. No one would believe her, anyway.

Back in her cell, she'd pulled the blanket over her head and declined to move for days. How could she have been so wrong? The signs had been clear. Taunting Jacob, skipping school, the drinking and drugs, the online gambling. The escalation. What would the future hold? Her flesh and blood. Everything she feared.

In the week since Liam's visit, the guards had suggested she see the whippet thin shrink who was older than God. For what? To resume her medication? Unburden her feelings? Share transition tips? Wouldn't be happening.

She wanted to talk to Marco. What she'd give to hear his voice right now. He could tell her how to survive ins and outs of prison culture. She replayed the entire conversation they'd had about protection, the barter system, the drug trade, picturing his clear blue eyes, the way his lips moved when he told her his secrets. She squeezed her eyes shut, willing it to go away, yet reliving it vividly and in slow motion.

"I miss you," she whispered.

She leaned over the sink, splashing cold water on her face. Despair welled up like an angry beast. She'd contained it through the trial. Numb in the witness box, memories of thirty years. Now it crept up on her when she woke up, leaving her seething through the day, or overcame her as she tossed in her bunk wondering if she'd ever sleep through the night.

Gulping in air, she sat down on the edge of her bunk. Blank white walls stared back at her. Everything unraveled, pulling apart one thread at a time. She pictured the new house, the curtains drawn, the windows gleaming, the for-sale sign on the lawn. No family BBQ's, no making spring rolls, no splashing in the pool.

She shook her anger off. It was futile. She'd have to adjust. Claiming it was a privilege, last week the guards explained under no circumstances would she be allowed to join the staff in the kitchen. She'd laughed when they'd told her. With her expertise? It was all such bullshit. She deserved better. Way better.

With two hundred and nineteen thousand hours to kill, she'd have to do something to stay busy. Maybe she could take a craft class? No knives, no glue, as a low-risk activity it must be an option. She could paint a picture of the boys or her beloved garden, bright with colour, full of blooms. That she may not ever see it again made her want to weep.

Head in her hands, she slumped on the bed. All she could think about was Marco free as a bird in Italy. A cold drink in hand, the blue sea behind him, chatting with his friends. Fresh air. She rubbed the raw patch on her scalp, her mind full of rage. It wasn't fair. She couldn't survive twenty-five years in this stinking place. Even if she did, she'd be in her late seventies before she saw the light of day.

Hatred gripped her so tightly she thought she was going to vomit. Shoving aside the panic that threated to strangle her, the solution suddenly dawned on her. The onset of glorious possibilities took shape.

The craft class.

A paintbrush. She could almost feel the smooth grain of the wood beneath her fingers and wondered how long it would take to sand to sharp point. She visualized the stark images, the precious photographs, the mess it would make. Afterall, she didn't need to hide herself anymore. There was no reason to behave perfectly, inside.

Pressing a fist to her forehead, she bent over in laughter. With no chance of getting out of here, that would have to do. Any fragment of doubt that lingered in her mind evaporated. The only way forward was to start again.

ACKNOWLEDGMENTS

Thank you to all the incredible people who helped nurture this story from the initial spark to the finished book.

Thanks to the earliest readers: Diane Bator, Bev Freedman, Donna McKenzie, Lori McMulkin, and Janet Piper for providing feedback on first messy drafts. Your unfailing encouragement means the world. To Lawrence Hill, my friend and writing mentor, whose gift for storytelling is brilliant and wise counsel invaluable. It is a privilege to work with you. To later readers: Lois Concannon, Lisa Joseph, and Barb Omland, for their keen eye for detail. Thank you, in memory, to Karen Gravitis, who always inspired me.

I'm grateful for the guidance, kindness, and insight from my editors. Adrienne Kerr for believing in this story from the get-go and steering me in the right direction. Kristen Weber, for weaving themes together with ease and grace through the developmental process. Profound thanks to the brilliant Helen Reeves who brought this story to an entire new level in the final stages, letting it soar.

I consulted a few experts while writing this novel. Cathy, Bruce, and Sean Vodden shared their horticultural and culinary knowledge. Sean, formerly a student, is now an international award-winning chef. The management staff and sous-chef chef at the RIU Antillas hotel in Aruba, who provided a kitchen tour. Will Lauder, a firefighter for the St. Catharines Fire Department, who shared the ins and outs of the fire service. Suzanne Gibson, a dear childhood friend, and her husband Keith Sutcliffe, Captain of the Hamilton Fire Department, who offered their expertise regarding everything that burns. Des Ryan, former Homicide Detective, Toronto Police Services, extended ongoing police procedure help. Sarah Edmonds, a writer and sweet childhood friend, who set me straight regarding cryptocurrency. All were generous with their time and my endless odd questions. Any mistakes are solely mine.

Thanks to my U.K. publishing team. To Hayley Paige, who sought this story out. To Faye Deeran, Daniel Eyenegho and Elise Webb, for formatting, cover design and leading the process. The entire team at Notebook Publishing has been a delight to work with.

Thank you to my wider circle of writing support including seasoned writers from Crime Writers of Canada and Sisters-in-Crime, Toronto. Also of note are the extraordinary writers in #thrillsandchills, #momswritersclub and Every Damn Day Writers, who are so welcoming during tweet chats, writing sprints, and online forums. It's a joy to work and learn together, celebrating success, discussing craft, and sharing advice.

To my readers. If you read Flat Out Lies after The Dime Box, thanks for sticking with me. If you read Flat Out Lies first, thanks for giving me a chance. Thanks also to the countless librarians who added Flat Out Lies and The Dime Box to their collections.

Finally, thanks to my family. My husband John, for who this book is dedicated. Writing would not be possible without your love and support. My daughter Jaime, who brings light and laughter to my life, and always has time to offer ideas and the right words. Our Rue, now running in dog-heaven meadow, yet who sat loyally beside me day after day as I typed. My parents, for their lessons on the value of perseverance and hard work. I am fortunate to have each one of you along on this wild ride called life.

ABOUT THE AUTHOR

Karen writes thrillers and mysteries, with a focus on twisty family saga. Her debut novel, *The Dime Box*, was selected by Amnesty International for its 2021 Book Club. The Chinese language version, retitled as *The Lost Daughters*, was published by Sharp Point Press, Taiwan, in 2023. *The Dime Box* is a story about a young woman accused of murdering her father, and embodies themes of domestic violence, justice, the search for identity, adoption, and how we, as society, define family.

Prior to writing fiction full-time, Karen worked as a teacher, Principal and Superintendent and was an executive at a digital learning organization. She earned her PhD in digital learning at the University of Toronto and splits her time between living in Toronto and Buckhorn, Ontario.

Along with thrillers and mysteries, she has flash, poems, CNF, and a short story in journals and anthologies, both in print and online. Follow her on X @kgrose2, on Facebook and Goodreads, and visit karengrose.ca.